DEEP
WATERS

DEEP
WATERS

ANN CLIFF

ROBERT HALE · LONDON

ISBN 978-0-7198-1741-0

Robert Hale Limited
Clerkenwell House
Clerkenwell Green
London EC1R 0HT

www.halebooks.com

2 4 6 8 10 9 7 5 3 1

Redcar and Cleveland Borough Council	
Askews & Holts	Aug-2015
AF	£19.99

Typeset in Janson
Printed in the UK by Berforts Information Press Ltd

For Martin and Jill, Peter and Irene,
with happy memories of Nidderdale
in the summer sun.

ONE

Nidderdale, Yorkshire, 1890

'No! I don't want to see you!' Rachel shuddered at the thought. The sounds were faint at first, growing gradually louder. Cold air moved in the shadows, going through the old house at evening.

The deliberate steps paused on every stair. Rachel knew she should have left before the light failed, locked the door and left the ghosts to their memories. Firby Hall had been notorious for its hauntings from the time of Good Queen Bess.

The sounds grew nearer and the oak door creaked open slightly, then paused. Trembling with fright, Rachel leaned on the panelled wall for support. The light was fading now and she had never been here alone in the dark before.

'Go back! Go back to where you came from!' she whispered, but she dared not shut her eyes.

A figure appeared in the doorway, the head turned towards her in surprise, as though it too might be afraid.

'You wish me to leave?' The face was in shadow, the voice was faint....

Rachel was speechless. In the silence she heard more creaking as the old timbers settled down for the night.

'You're not a ghost, are you ... here two hundred years ago?' The voice was stronger now, human, a man's voice.

Rachel slowly stood up and breathed deeply. 'What do you mean by coming in here?'

She was angry, mainly at herself for being afraid. He was only a visitor. She often showed people round the house, but never at this late hour.

'You look a little like one of the portraits on the stairs, the girl with dark hair. Not that I believe in ghosts, of course, but for a moment I thought you could be ... someone from the past.' He stepped into the room; a tall young man in riding boots, with chestnut hair.

Rachel stifled a giggle. 'So did I! There is supposed to be a ghost here, I've imagined I heard it several times and I thought that this time ...' she shuddered again. 'So how can I help you?' She smoothed her apron over the black dress. 'The Hall is only open to visitors by arrangement.'

The visitor was not to be put off. 'Isn't it beautiful? And this must be the Long Gallery. Most of the Elizabethan houses have one.' He walked over to one of the windows that ran round three sides of the room. 'I'm Roger Beckwith. I remember Firby Hall from years ago. You are the daughter of the house? You know, in this room you could have been a haunting from any age in the past.' His voice was deep and pleasant, with only a faint touch of Yorkshire. Was he laughing at her?

'Well, Mr Beckwith, I must ask you to leave. I'm – my mother is the housekeeper and the Family is expected to come home very soon. I was just checking that all's in order for them.' No doubt Her Ladyship would find some fault, Rachel added to herself. 'It will soon be dark and I have no candles here.'

'I am sorry,' Beckwith said contritely. 'I was passing and called in on impulse, since the front door was open.'

They walked down the wide staircase together and into the formal garden. Across the lane was the farmhouse where she lived and if Rachel didn't go home soon, Mother would come looking for her. Rooks cawed as they flew overhead, homing to their rookery on the edge of a wood.

They halted at the gate and Beckwith looked down at her. 'You must be Kit Garnett's daughter,' he said. 'What's your name, little ghost?'

'Rachel and I must go home, Mr Beckwith,' she said firmly. 'Did you want to make an appointment to see the house? You'll have to speak to my mother, although I'm not sure that it will be possible while Major Potts and Lady Agnes are here.'

'Doesn't matter ... I just wanted to see the old place again before it disappears. I was brought up not far from here. Well, thank you, Miss Garnett.'

'What do you mean, "disappears"?'

Beckwith turned to his horse, which was tied to the gate. 'Old houses are always being knocked down and new ones built, as fashions change.' He sounded casual. 'Seems a pity, though, there's so much history here. I suppose you know the stories, Protestants and Catholics, Cavaliers and Roundheads. Even though we're on the edge of the moors, there were some violent happenings here in the past.'

A week later, the owners of the Hall were due to come home at any minute. Firby Hall had been in uproar for weeks. Horses had been brought in from the pasture and fed up with oats, pheasants counted and the carriage cleaned and polished. Silver had been taken out of storage, Cook dragged out of retirement and an extra maid had been found. Several Shorthorn cows had been bought, to make sure there was enough milk and butter for the Family and their guests.

John the gardener was probably the best prepared; he had kept the kitchen garden going while the Potts were away. Kit the manager had sold surplus vegetables in the village and put the money back into maintenance.

The Garnetts were making the most of their last hours of freedom. The sun warm on her back, Rachel moved across a grassy slope above the Hall, basket in hand. The scent was intoxicating, a green smell of grass and the herbs they gathered. It was good to get out and into the sunshine, away from the kitchen and the barns and the hectic preparations.

'It might be the last time we get the chance...' Ruth Garnett looked up the hillside, peaceful in the afternoon light. Today they were collecting plantain leaves, dark green spikes easy to spot among the meadow grasses. Common old plantain, most folks thought, was a weed, but Mother knew better. These herbs would go into a salve for cuts and bruises, always in demand in Firby village.

'Mother! Look!' Down the valley, on the winding ribbon of the road from Masham, the Firby Hall carriage looked like a toy. 'They're here!' Quickly, the women took up their baskets and set off briskly down the slope. Sheep scattered right and left as they scrambled over a stile.

'Her Ladyship mustn't be kept waiting!'

Ruth started to walk briskly down to the field gate. Her Ladyship and the Major had been away in India for four years and the general feeling in the servants' hall was voiced by Mrs Metcalfe, the groom's wife: 'Pity they couldn't stay in India!'

Rachel sensed trouble ahead. She made a face, but out of her mother's sight. Respect for the Family, their employers, was the rule in their household.

Back at the Hall they quickly tidied their hair, put on clean aprons and slipped into place just as the carriage rolled up the drive in a spurt of gravel. Everyone knew the ritual, but they were out of practice after four years of peace.

Rachel straightened her cap and stood in the short line of servants just behind the reassuring bulk of her father, while faces were rearranged into respectful smiles. It paid to look humble, especially with the Major.

Ruth had called in their former cook and a young housemaid, both of whom lived in the village, for the duration of the visit. (How long was it going to be?) Mrs Metcalfe would also help as needed.

Firby Hall was a Nidderdale estate with a rather large old

house, standing in a sheltered valley. Rachel's father, Kit Garnett, managed the home farm, while her mother looked after the house-keeping at the Hall, as well as the farmhouse. Quite often, Rachel wished that her family had their own farm. For the last four years, they'd had the estate to themselves, but now ... anything could happen.

John the gardener ran to the horse's head while the groom jumped down and prepared to hand his employers out of the vehicle, but he was too late. Down came the Major, red-faced and puffing.

'GET OUT OF MY WAY!' He trod heavily on the groom's foot.

The hapless groom jumped to one side as Lady Agnes swept down from the door and landed on the drive with a thump. Lady Agnes was a forthright character and her voice was almost as loud as the Major's. 'Stupid man!'

Donald the groom reddened. 'Sorry, sir, m'lady.' It was not a good start.

Rachel glanced up at her father, but couldn't tell what he was thinking. He was wondering, perhaps, how long the Family would be staying and how much they would have to say about the crops, the livestock and the state of the farm. Through bad seasons as well as good, the farm was supposed to function perfectly, with not a weed out of place. The Family had high expectations and short tempers.

Guy, the son and heir, was not with them, much to everyone's relief. Perhaps he would have grown up a little in the last four years? He would have left school by now and Kit had calculated that Guy would be eighteen or nineteen.

Ruth was wondering whether there would be enough indoor staff to keep the house running properly, when Lady Agnes turned to the waiting servants.

'We will take tea in the drawing room,' she announced, steely blue eyes sweeping the line of servants.

'Welcome home, m'lady,' Ruth offered, but it was ignored.

The groom led the horse away to the stables and the gardener took their luggage into the house. A cloud passed over the sun.

Since before Rachel was born, her mother and father had worked at the Hall. Father managed the farm and kept the accounts; he also collected the rent from the tenant farms.

Her mother ran the house very well and supervised the servants when the house was in use.

Major Potts and Lady Agnes spent much time in India, but the Hall had belonged to the Potts for generations; it must be kept going and it must turn a profit, to augment the Major's army pay.

Unfortunately, army through and through as he was, the Major never made allowances for poor seasons or bad prices, which meant stormy scenes so the Garnett family dreaded the Major's visits. The rest of the staff was also nervous; Janet, a tiny maid just out of school, had never faced her employers before. With shaking hands, the girl prepared the tea tray and with a deep breath, Rachel took it into the drawing room.

Lady Agnes sat erect with her head tipped well back, looking down her nose. 'You've changed, Garnett,' she said. 'How old are you?'

Well, what did she expect in four years? Rachel had been a lass of seventeen four years ago, but now she was a young woman. 'Yes, m'lady. I'm twenty-two.'

'I shall have to decide what's to be done with you.'

Rachel felt cold. Lady Agnes had ignored her until now, but she seemed to think that she owned the Garnetts, body and soul, to be disposed of as she saw fit.

To be fair, the subject of what was to be done with Rachel had sometimes been discussed by her family as she grew up. Teaching little ones in a village school would be ideal, but there wasn't enough money to pay for her training. The college for women in Ripon had been training teachers for thirty years and the idea of learning there was attractive.

'Working with us suits you,' Mother had decided. 'And you'll be wed before long, I'm sure.'

'The Major will maybe expect you to stay at the Hall and work here as you are now,' Kit Garnett had said thoughtfully. Rachel had helped out in their home and at the Hall since leaving school. 'Until you get married, that is, and settle down.'

Now the Major looked up from pouring whisky from a hip flask into his cup of tea.

'Tell Garnett to report to me in the morning,' he barked.

'Yes, sir. Will that be all, my Lady?' Rachel turned for the door.

'It will not. Come here, girl.' Lady Agnes looked her over as though she were a sheep at a sale. 'You can read and write, I suppose? Write down a list of what you can do. Bring it to me after breakfast tomorrow. It is time I took an interest in the staff.'

The Major snorted, just before Rachel closed the door. 'Waste of time, Agnes. Village women get married and that's that.'

The old farmhouse seemed a haven of security, now that the Hall was occupied once more. After supper, Kit Garnett lit the oil lamp and went through his accounts, preparing his report. Ruth spread out her herbs to dry in the stillroom and Rachel took out a piece of paper and a pencil. It wouldn't take long to make a list of her skills, but what did Lady Agnes have in mind?

Her father shook his head. 'It's so long since they were here, nobody knows what to expect. Donald says the Major's not in the best of tempers.' Donald the groom had driven them home from the railway station in Masham. 'He thinks they won't stay long. Not much luggage, they'll be off back to London soon.'

'I hope so,' Rachel murmured. Perhaps Lady Agnes's interest in her would not last long.

Rachel took up her pencil to make a list of her virtues. To start with, she could read and write very well ... but would that be seen as giving her ideas above her station? Kit Garnett had passed on to his only child a love of reading, as well as an interest in science.

Secondly, Rachel's head was full of plants and their uses. She had been taught by her mother how to prepare herb teas, salves and lotions, but this was old-fashioned stuff for cottagers. Those who could afford it called in the doctor, these days.

Should she add her farm skills to the list? It was Rachel's job to milk the Hall house cows and to make butter and sometimes, soft cheese in the summer. She helped her father with the sheep at busy times, such as lambing and shearing, and fed the pigs. The animals at the Grange had a good life; Rachel and her father saw to that.

She could cook and clean, like all the village women. If she'd been a lad, how different things would be....

A knock at the door made them jump. Jim Angram, bachelor of the parish, loomed on the doorstep. 'Come out for a walk, lass, it's a grand night.'

With a nod of consent from her father, Rachel slipped out and they wandered through the orchard and across the road, to where the river flowed quietly down the valley.

'Keep out of sight of the house,' Rachel warned. 'Major's back.'

Jim laughed. 'Everybody knows Major's back. I've come to see if you've survived! Thank goodness my dad's not a tenant of his. Things are hard enough, without him stamping and shouting.'

'Shush!' Rachel looked round nervously, but there was no one else in the green lane. 'Lady Agnes says she doesn't know what to do with me.'

'Tell her you're going to marry me,' the lad said carelessly. 'That should keep her quiet. We know it'll happen one day.'

'One day! It's years away! Jim, you know that your dad's not going to give up the farm just to let you take over, not until he's ready. I think we should forget about it ... for now, at any rate.'

Rachel didn't want to upset him, but Jim was a casual suitor. She liked him, but there was no real bond between them. Maybe this was how most country girls found a husband, but there was no excitement in it.

Serene in the half light, Jim slid an arm round her waist. 'You're my girl, you know it.'

A nice lad, Jim, but not the love of her life. 'Jim, you might find another lass, you know, one that you can't live without. Wait and see.' Jim shook his head.

The evening light was lovely; the sheltered valley gave back the warmth of the day. The last of the sunset faded behind the moor as Rachel turned back to the house. *I'm not sure that I want to wait about for years, for the chance to be a small farmer's wife.... But how can I tell him that?* Impulsively she turned to him.

'Should you like to go to Australia, Jim? We could start a new life, see the rest of the world ...'

An owl flew by on silent wings as the dusk deepened over the familiar landscape. The silence lengthened.

'Nay, we'll not do that,' Jim said, decisive for once. They walked back to the farmhouse in silence. Rachel opened the door to let him in, but he gave her a brief peck on the cheek and turned away. 'Night, love. Good luck with the Major.'

With a sigh, Rachel closed the door on the glimmering land-scape and went into the kitchen, which felt stuffy. She and Jim were like an old married couple, with nothing new to say. Where was the romance?

Ruth Garnett noticed her daughter's sigh. 'What ails you, Rachel? Think on, there's many a lass would be thrilled to be walking out with Jim. He's a big strong lad, nice-looking too, with his fair hair and blue eyes. Count your blessings, lass, and try to be cheerful.'

Rachel sat at the table and took up her pencil once more. Not only had she to list her accomplishments, she now had to count her blessings as well. Of course Jim was a blessing, with a nice little farm to come – eventually; a little higher on the social scale than the Garnetts, though not so well educated.

By the time she went to bed, Rachel had mentally added a few more lines to her list of desirable accomplishments: *I can put up with folks telling me what's good for me, I do as I'm told, I think my own thoughts.*

The next morning dawned with mist, rain falling from the dark sky. Kit went round the sheep while Rachel milked the cows and fed the calves. Her mother had gone over to the Hall to supervise the big breakfast that the Major always demanded. She would keep

15

a close eye on things for the first few days.

Bracing himself, Kit went to see the Major at nine o'clock. Rachel was crossing the yard with scraps for the hens when a horseman rode in. He swung down from a big bay horse, drenched with rain but smiling happily.

'Rachel Garnett, good morning! Does it always rain like this up here? It's wonderful! It's a fine morning down in Pateley.' It was the man she'd mistaken for a ghost in the old house.

Rachel glared at him. 'Of course not. But what's good about it? We've had enough rain this month, there's oats to harvest yet.' Was the lad mad? She could see as he took off the big hat that Beckwith went on smiling.

'A high rainfall is just what we want, you see. We've been looking for a place like this. Water is very important, young lady, and you have plenty of it.'

What did he mean? Was he serious? Rachel suddenly remembered her manners. 'Have you come to see Father? He's with the owner at present, I can tell him you're here if you like. Come under the barn, out of the rain.' Her father could deal with this confident young man who talked in riddles. Up here in the hills of Nidderdale, visitors were usually on some sort of business.

Kit Garnett emerged from the Hall looking flustered, and no wonder, he'd been with the Major. Rachel introduced him to the visitor and went about her business, but before she drove the geese across the yard she lingered, trying to hear what the man said. The geese, let out from their night pen, were happy to pause on their way down to the pond.

'Wonderful location … impervious geology … is the owner likely to see me today?'

Father was looking grimmer than ever, it was time to go. Rachel waved her long stick and the geese obediently turned and went through the gate in single file, sedately walking through the orchard. The rain didn't affect them, but Rachel felt a trickle of water down her neck and shivered.

As they passed the ivy-covered walls of the Hall, Rachel felt eyes upon her. From an upstairs window, Lady Agnes was watching the slow procession to the water. The Lady, it seemed, had decided to take an interest in farming. Well, she could help to pluck the geese at Christmas if she wanted to get her hands dirty, but that wasn't likely. It was always Rachel's job and the butchers in Masham depended on her for their Christmas geese.

The morning wore on, the rain still fell. Rachel was busy in the farmhouse kitchen, making a stew for dinner when her father came in. His mind was running on what the Major had told him.

'We've got to make more profit,' he said gloomily. 'How, I don't know ... I thought he'd be happy with last year's results, but he wants more. He can't very well put up the rents for the tenants, so he comes back to me. More profit. We'll have to carry more stock.'

'Never mind, Father, have a cup of tea,' Rachel murmured. 'And take your wet coat off, you'll catch a cold. Now, who is that visitor? He talked differently to us and he didn't make sense. Seemed to think it was wonderful to get wet!'

'Don't worry about him, lass. Major'll deal with young Roger Beckwith, of that I'm sure.' A brief smile crossed Kit's brown face.

Through the open kitchen door, Rachel heard a commotion in the yard. Peering out, she saw the Major stamping through the wet, roaring. The young man was striding towards his horse, but not fast enough for the Major, who pushed him roughly.

'OUT! Get out of here and don't come back! Never heard such rubbish in my life!'

The Major continued to fume, but he was ignored, which probably made it worse. Deliberately Roger Beckwith tightened the girth, untied his horse and mounted. He was still smiling and he waved to Rachel as he went out of the yard, leaving the Major standing in a puddle of water, flailing his arms in a very different salute.

'You didn't know young Roger? I remembered him, once he said who he was. He's Dr Beckwith's son, they used to come up dale on holidays when he was a lad. He went to be an engineer, must be out of his training by now.' Kit shut the kitchen door

17

firmly, blotting out the sight of the Major in the yard. 'Forget about him, lass, it was nothing. We've more to worry about than Roger.'

Rachel forgot about the visitor immediately, because her mother came to fetch her.

'Her Ladyship wants to see you, look sharp and brush your hair, now.'

By the time Rachel tiptoed through the rain to the Hall, the Major had disappeared. Lady Agnes was in the library, sitting at a desk.

'Ah, the goose girl,' she said briskly. 'I believe you have been helping at home since you left school. Your father tells me that you are available to work and I propose to supervise you myself.' This sounded far more businesslike than the remote being of yesterday. Then the sting in the tail: 'Your father is the farm manager, of course, but he would be inclined to be too lenient with you as his own child.'

Not so I've noticed, she thought ruefully. Rachel's heart sank; this sounded as though they expected to stay at the Hall.

'Wha-what would you like me to do, m'lady?'

'The geese took my fancy, this morning. Tell me about them, goose girl.'

This was easier than talking about herself, but wasn't the Goose Girl in a fairy story?

'Well, we buy goslings from a poultry farm and pen them till they feather, then turn them out on grass down by the beck. They eat grass, and a bit of grain. We sell a few at Michaelmas, ready dressed, and the rest at Christmas. I lock them in a hut at night, or the fox'll get them.'

Lady Agnes wanted more. Her cold eyes were piercing as she turned them on her goose girl. How much did each gosling cost, how much grain did they eat, what was the end price for the dressed bird?

'It does vary, especially the grain in a bad harvest...' As it happened, Rachel knew how much profit there was in keeping geese.

She and her father had done calculations once. 'Plucking and dressing's the worst job and it takes time....'

'That's what you are paid for. I think we should breed the birds ourselves, and keep more of them.'

'Yes, m'lady. But you can only breed geese in spring.'

'And it's September ... well, I shall have to think of something else. But be sure that you find some goose eggs, next spring.'

TWO

RACHEL MANAGED TO avoid Lady Agnes for the next few days, as Her Ladyship paid a round of duty visits to her dear friends and relations. In the four years the Potts had been away, the friends had been seldom in touch and she wanted to remind them of her continued existence.

Donald Metcalfe, the groom and handyman, trundled out the dog cart in the afternoons, praying that it wouldn't rain because that would mean wet gear and her Ladyship angry. It was good to get out round the countryside again, though Donald knew he had the best job at the Hall. His wife told him so, on every possible occasion.

Willow Grange was the destination on a mild and sunny day towards the end of the week, the residence of Lady Agnes's cousin Sybil Walton and her husband Rupert, a retired judge. Donald sometimes pondered the fact that the gentry always 'resided' in a country seat or a town house, whereas ordinary folk just 'lived' in a cottage or a farmhouse. This was a bigger estate than Major Potts's and like his, the land was mainly in the valley, sheltered from the cold north winds.

The Major excused himself from the visit on the grounds that he was too busy cleaning his guns. He disliked duty visits. Donald was relieved; the Major sometimes liked to take the reins and drive faster than was safe, to frighten his wife as well as to get the visit over quickly. The last thing a groom wanted was a horse with grazed knees and broken harness.

Lady Agnes decided to enjoy the afternoon. As they rolled through the stone gateway of Willow Grange, it was obvious that improvements had been made since her last visit some years ago. Rupert must be spending his retirement bothering the gardeners.

The stately trees lining the drive had been cut back in places to reveal statues and mysterious grottoes. There were fleeting, picturesque glimpses of the moors beyond the estate. Lady Agnes smiled to herself; surely no one would keep a hermit in a grotto, these days? Little winding paths led away into a shrubbery. The Grange was on a south-facing slope and this, together with a walled kitchen garden much bigger than the Potts', meant that they could put on a better show than was possible at Firby Hall.

As the house came into sight, Lady Agnes saw another new feature: a little waterfall cascading over rocks, through ferns and into a pool lined with water lilies. It was presided over by a stone nymph with a smug expression. Smooth lawns rolled down to a ha-ha, beyond which fluffy, clean sheep grazed. It was all too much. Why could the Hall not look more civilized, more in fashion?

Everyone had statues, except the Potts. She would speak to Garnett, tell him that the Hall grounds were out of date, medieval in fact, and must be landscaped. The Hall was two hundred years behind the times. It had no space around it, the formal garden was tiny and the farmyard was far too close. The only thing she could boast about was its age.

'My dear Agnes, I know what you would like. Come with me, we will take a walk.' Sybil Walton and her cousin were standing on the terrace at Willow Grange, looking out across the sunlit fields.

Lady Agnes smiled. 'I see you haven't changed, Sybil. You always preferred the fresh air to the drawing room.' No doubt she was to be shown Rupert's improvements.

A smooth gravel path led through the gardens to a gate into the park, a gate that opened easily without a sound and Sybil sighed. There was so much to do at home and so few servants. They really must try to be more efficient ... it seemed that she was to be spared a tour of the garden.

Under the shade of oak trees was a group of black cattle, cows and calves, resting, chewing the cud thoughtfully.

'Now,' said Sybil proudly, 'do you know what these are?' One of the cows stood up, stretched and walked towards them and Sybil scratched its head between the horns. 'This is Rupert's pride and joy,' Sybil added. 'We have started a dairy, you know. Our dairy-maid makes cheese, as well as butter and cream. Of course, you won't be able to do anything like this.'

'Why not?' Lady Agnes enquired crossly. She looked over the back of the little cow at her cousin. 'We have cows, and milk and cream.' She would tell Rachel Garnett to make cheese. That would give the girl something to do and it might be possible to sell it, to make the farm more profitable.

'Well, it's rather different for you, away in India so much of the time. We do like to supervise, to make sure everything is done properly....' Of course they did. The whole place looked thoroughly supervised.

'How small they are! This cow is much smaller than our house cows. What breed are they, Sybil?'

'These are Dexter-Kerry, from a poor part of Ireland, you know. The Duchess of Devonshire breeds them, they are quite fashionable now. Being in India, you won't have seen anything of farming for a long time. Rupert believes that they have a good future.'

Lady Agnes nodded wisely; she knew nothing about cattle and was rather afraid of them. The little black cows looked less fearsome than the ones they had at home.

'They were originally a poor man's cow, of course, but they look well in the park and they produce wonderful milk for cheese. And then, the meat is excellent, so we plan to increase the herd.'

The visitor's brain began to race. This might be just the thing for Firby Hall and that great girl Rachel could work a few more hours. 'But surely these cows are too small to make much profit?

Or do I sound vulgar?'

Sybil smiled and managed to look just like the nymph in the grotto. 'But they are so economical! Rupert says they eat anything, all the weeds, and of course more animals of this size can be kept on the acreage. And they look so sweet, do they not? All my friends are entranced by them!' The old girl was more animated than Agnes had seen her.

On the way home, Lady Agnes was thoughtful.

'Have you heard of Dexter-Kerry cattle, Metcalfe?' she asked the groom.

'Aye, m'lady. That's what's in park yonder, they're tough little beggars, folks say.' He waved the whip in the direction of the Grange behind them. 'All gentry seem to be keeping them these days – it's a fashion, like.'

First things first, Lady Agnes decided as they arrived back at the Hall. As a contrast with Willow Grange, it looked very old and plain. Garnett kept the place tidy, but there was nothing to boast about. The goose girl must be organized, she thought.

Beside the front door stood a trap with a stylish horse in the shafts.

'It's Mr Richards, the solicitor and accountant, m'lady,' Donald told her in reply to the raised eyebrows.

Lady Agnes could hear her husband's raised voice from the hall; there was trouble ahead. The library door opened and a man ducked out, nodded to her briefly and scurried down the hall to his vehicle. It seemed best to go upstairs, take off her hat and coat and wash her hands, gaining time before going down again.

'I'm off back to India!' the Major announced as soon as his wife appeared. He had obviously settled down and seemed rather pleased with the idea. 'The only solution. You will have to stay here and organize the farm, make some money.'

'Would you like to tell me who that man is, and what has happened?' Lady Agnes glanced at the ornate gold clock on the mantelpiece and poured two small glasses of sherry.

Major Potts shook his heavy head. 'Our finances are dire,

Agnes. It's the shares again, I'm afraid, as well as Guy. That boy is a liability to us, he will have to mend his ways. Richards has paid some of Guy's debts out of the main Hall account, he did it before we came home. Can't you stop him gambling? Get him to come home, live quietly in the country for a while.'

'But – India? Surely we can borrow some money...' Agnes looked down at her diamond rings, put on for the visit to Sybil. She'd always said they were insurance for a rainy day.

'I can't stay on half pay, might have to go back to the army, to promotion if possible. We've no money to speak of, Richards says. He suggested I sell the Hall, but I won't do that. Never sell the Hall, y'know. At least, I don't think so. Not unless the price was right.'

Sipping her sherry thoughtfully, Agnes surveyed her own options. Of course he should not sell the Hall; she wanted to improve it. On the bright side, she would have a free hand without the Major. But how much could she achieve with no money? She sighed.

It was quite a challenge, but at least her husband would be far away. On the other hand, what should she do with Guy? Their adopted son and heir was now nineteen, with no sign of maturity. He should probably join the army, but a commission would be expensive and he might be tempted to gamble more often.

If Guy could be persuaded to come home to Firby instead of lurking in the London house, they could perhaps interest him in the running of the estate. He could be an asset instead of a problem. They would appeal to his better nature and get him away from his gambling friends.

'No, m'lady, it's too late to hatch any more geese out this year. They've stopped laying.' Rachel felt nervous; it wouldn't do to lecture Lady Agnes. 'We can keep more of this year's flock for breeding next year, but then there'll be less to sell. The butcher depends on us for Christmas geese.'

Rachel was standing in front of the desk in the library, trying not to fidget. Her list of accomplishments had been received in silence, and after the geese, Lady Agnes started to ask about the milking cows.

'Yes, m'lady, I can show you the dairy.' Why would the woman want to see her dairy? It was spotless; she couldn't find fault with it, Rachel thought as she led the way down the stairs and over the farmyard. Dairies had to be spotless at all times, or the milk would go bad.

'Tell me all about it,' Lady Agnes commanded.

How much did she already know? 'Our cows are Shorthorns, they're out grazing until I bring them in for milking about four o'clock.' They went into the cool, lime-washed room where the milk was handled. A large shallow pan of milk stood on a stone slab and Rachel explained that this was a setting pan. 'Cream comes to the top of the milk and then I skim it off, cream for the House and to make butter.'

Lady Agnes peered at the pan. 'What do you do with the rest of the milk, after the cream has been skimmed off?'

Rachel said patiently, 'The skimmed milk goes to feed the calves and pigs. But I can make cheese with it, not the best cheese of course, it's a bit hard. M'lady.'

Lady Agnes actually smiled. 'So you know how to make cheese. You need not bore me with the details, but I would like you to make a batch of cheese tomorrow, with whole milk, no cream taken off. Bring it to the kitchen for our dinner tomorrow night.'

Rachel tried not to panic; she was asking the impossible. 'Well, m'lady, it won't be ready by then. Proper cheese is put in a press and turned and bandaged … it's pressed for a few days, and then, you wouldn't want to eat it too fresh. It's kept for a few months and turned every day, and …' But her employer had lost interest.

'Tell me how much cheese costs to produce and how much a grocer will pay for it. Ask Garnett to work it out.' Lady Agnes swept from the dairy.

Kit Garnett looked unusually serious as he took his place at the supper table, a week after Roger Beckwith's visit. Rachel thought he must be worrying about one of the calves. 'I think the red calf is better now, Father. She can have a full ration of milk tomorrow—'

'Good, good,' Kit said absently and his hands gripped the sides of the table. 'I'm afraid there's more to worry about than Bluebell's calf. I probably should have told you before, but I never thought it would come to this.'

'What's wrong, love?' his wife asked quietly.

'They are going to build a reservoir up here, water for Leeds. I'm not sure just where, they are still working it out, but some of our land might – we might be under the water.'

Ruth Garnett laughed. 'They were talking about water when my father was a boy and it never came to anything. My pa always said we shouldn't lose any sleep over it and he's still there, farming his land … which reminds me, Rachel, you should bake a few scones and take them over to him tomorrow.'

'Leeds and Bradford are even bigger than they were when your father was a lad and more desperate for water. We have the rain up here in the hills, we can't deny it and the valleys are deep, just asking to be flooded.' Kit Garnett shook his head.

'But they can't just take land, can they? The Major would never agree …' Rachel realized that this was why Roger Beckwith had been here. Saying goodbye to the Hall, because it would disappear under the water.

Kit raised his eyes to his daughter's face. 'At first the Major would have none of it, you heard him shouting at Beckwith. But then he had second thoughts. The money, you see. He'd be paid for the land and if the Hall's flooded, he'll get a new house. I must say I'm fair bowled over by this. I thought the Major would fight to keep the Hall, but it seems he needs the money – he almost said as much. And even if he doesn't agree, in some cases they can still take the land.'

Ruth Garnett looked pale. 'And we, we'll get – nothing. It all belongs to the Major, but if there's no land, there will be no work for us.'

'That Beckwith man must be heartless! He was so cheerful.' Rachel blinked tears from her eyes. 'Why must they wreck our lives for nothing? Surely there is plenty of water in other places in the West Riding.'

Her father sighed. 'Leeds and Bradford are huge, dirty industrial towns, love. They've grown very fast and they're short of water for people to drink, and then they need pure water for the woollen mills. They say there's outbreaks of typhoid fever there, because the water is so bad.'

'But we're so far away!'

They had all seen debates about water in the newspapers. Bradford had a few small reservoirs already in the West Riding.

'Bradford wanted to come up here, but Leeds beat them to it,' Kit told them. 'Roger works for Leeds Corporation, he can tell you all about how they dam up a valley and let the river fill it … they need a place where the bottom can be sealed to stop it leaking and they'll build a great big embankment.'

They tried to eat the evening meal, but none of them had any appetite. Rachel jumped up to collect the supper plates and she answered a knock at the door, expecting to see Jim. But a tall straight figure loomed in the evening light. Ben the sheepdog was watching him carefully.

Rachel left him at the door.

'It's Mr Beckwith,' she said between clenched teeth. 'The man we don't want to see.'

Her father went out to talk to the visitor.

'What about the village?' Ruth wanted to know. 'Is the whole of Firby village to be lost? Oh, Rachel, I don't know where we'd go if we were turned out. Life would never be the same again.'

Rachel had thought of another problem. 'All the crops are grown in the valleys, that's the best land and it's sheltered. If the valleys are flooded we'll only have the moors. Folks could only run a few sheep, there'd be nobody left. I wonder whether the Leeds folk have thought of what misery they will cause.' She glared at the door, on the other side of which Kit was talking to the enemy.

'Does that Beckwith man have any idea?'

Kit came in again and spoke to his wife. 'Roger says he has to spend some time here, he's making a survey – wants to board with us. He says Leeds will pay good expenses. What do you say, lass?'

'No!' Rachel burst out, but her father quelled her with a look.

'The money would be right handy, we'll have to start to look for another place, if it happens,' Ruth said slowly. 'What kind of a lad is he? He won't be too rough, if he's an engineer, I suppose.'

'A decent enough lad, if he wasn't bringing bad news,' Kit admitted. 'I told him the other day that we sometimes take in guests, walkers and such. Most of the farms do the same, so if you don't want him he'll look elsewhere. He says he'd understand.'

'It's dark now, he won't want to go looking for a bed at this time of night. Tell him to come in,' Rachel's mother said heavily. 'We'll take him for a day or two and see how we get on and whether he wants to stay. We might not be good enough, we're only farming folk.'

'Helping the enemy!' Rachel muttered when her father had gone out again to stable the man's horse. 'Why did he leave it so late to go looking for lodgings? It's very careless to turn up here at dead of night and expect us to take pity on him. I hate him! He's going to ruin our lives.'

A subdued Roger Beckwith came into the kitchen and was given a plate of stew, which he received gratefully. 'Thank you, Mrs Garnett. I'm sorry to come here at such short notice and so late in the day. I was held up by an accident on the road, a trap overturned and I had to stop and help the driver.'

'Don't worry, Mr Beckwith, there's plenty of stew left. We didn't feel hungry, after the news we just heard. You! You are going to take away our living and drown the village in a reservoir. We're in a doomed valley.' Rachel could not hide her bitterness.

The engineer had the grace to look guilty. 'I am sorry, Miss Garnett, I sympathize with how you feel. It's the sad part of my job, seeing people affected by the decisions of landowners. But I suppose it's inevitable, a part of progress.'

'It shouldn't be inevitable, not here. We're in a lovely valley, with good land, there are hundreds of people living and working round Firby. All of us will be thrown out, just to please Leeds Corporation. Why can't you take your engineering up to the moors – where it would only frighten a few sheep?' Rachel looked at her father, but he only shook his head.

'Rachel, will you put sheets on the spare room bed for our guest?' Ruth Garnett spoke more sharply than usual. Her daughter had broken the rules. The Garnetts never quarrelled and they were never rude to guests; this man had already disrupted their lives.

Running upstairs, Rachel found clean sheets in the linen cupboard. She was tempted to look for lumpy objects to put under the mattress to keep the man awake, but thought better of it. She dusted the dressing table and checked the wardrobe, then put out a bowl and jug on the wash stand.

Going downstairs with a frown still on her face, Rachel encountered Roger Beckwith's wry grin. 'Did you put a hedgehog in my bed? I wouldn't blame you if you did.'

Rachel laughed and the atmosphere lightened a little. 'I did think of it, but it wouldn't be fair to the hedgehog. I'll leave a jug of hot water at your door in the morning.'

THREE

IT WAS TIME to harvest the oats. Golden September days with a hint of mist in the mornings were welcome, after the heat of summer. As soon as the weather cleared, Kit greased the binder, yoked up the horses and went off to cut the crop himself. Two labourers followed, picking up the sheaves and leaning them together in groups of six so that the breeze could flow through them. Soon the field was covered in stooks of golden grain and Rachel was surprised how many there were. 'It's a heavy crop this year,' she told her mother.

Ruth Garnett smiled wryly. 'As long as the weather holds,' she said.

The oats had to stand drying in the field, traditionally until they had heard the church bells three times – three Sundays. Three continuous weeks of fine weather in September was a rare event in Nidderdale.

It was Rachel's job to take the mid-morning 'drinkings' to the workers, who were always ready for a break. Rachel's Fat Rascals were rich scones, dripping with butter and full of currants.

'I reckon you make best butter in dale, lass,' said Bert. He was an older man who worked his own holding and came to the Hall farm in busy times.

Rachel smiled, proud of her butter. 'Tell that to Lady Agnes!'

A light breeze gently lifted the ears of corn. Rachel shaded her eyes against the sun and looked down the long sloping field to the little wood at the far side. It was a beautiful place, soil cultivated for hundreds of years. The farms here had good land on the lower slopes, rising to moorland above the valley of the river Nidd and its tributaries.

It was tragic to Rachel that all this could be lost, drowned under a dam, so that only the poorer soils of the moorland would be above the water. Surely something could be done, someone with power could intervene?

Back at the farmhouse, Ruth Garnett wrapped up more scones in a cloth and put them in the basket with a jar of blackberry jam. 'Ask your grandfather if he'd like to eat his Sunday dinner with us,' she reminded Rachel. 'It's a grand day for a walk, I'd love to come myself but there's washing to do.' They had to take advantage of fine days.

Nathan Brown was mending a fence when Rachel arrived at his farm. He downed tools and came to meet her, taking the basket from her.

'Two miles with this heavy basket! You do well, lass. I'm right pleased to see you.'

His grey eyes twinkled in his leathery face. Her mother's dad was not a typical grandfather; he didn't lean on a stick but stood straight and tall, carrying his years lightly. He bent down easily to pat the collie Ben, who always shadowed Rachel wherever she went unless he was working with sheep.

They walked up the farm track to the house together and Rachel admired Nathan's herd of Beef Shorthorn cows, grazing the sweet upland turf. They talked about the cows and their success at local shows, most recently at Pateley Show, the last of the season.

'My old Agatha beat 'em all, Rachel!' he told her proudly. 'Best in Show, against all the other breeds. You can't beat a Shorthorn.' After all his forty years of showing, Nathan Brown still got a thrill out of the competition.

As soon as she could, Rachel brought up the subject that was on her mind. 'Have you heard that the folks from Leeds are here again, Grandfather? Looking for land to take for a reservoir. Father's worried.'

She put the scones on the kitchen table and looked round. As usual, the place was clean and tidy.

Nathan turned to face her. 'I don't believe a word of it,' he said deliberately. 'Bradford and Leeds, they've both been talking about it since I was a lad. Of course, they need water. Leeds is a mucky hole and Bradford's not much better, and they need to wash the wool. But mark my words, lass, in the end they'll go down dale. We're too far away, to my mind. It would cost too much to send water from here to there. In '68, that's a while ago now, they carried on about it and then built a dam near Huddersfield, thank goodness.'

They walked outside and stood on the farm track. 'I can't stay, Grandfather, we're busy ... well ... I hope you're right about the dam. Anyway, Mother says will you come for dinner on Sunday? You can talk about it then ...' Rachel stopped, looking over the ridge of moor behind the house where a horseman was making his way down the slope. 'You've got another visitor, I see.'

The man rode up to them and dismounted, a wide smile on his face. Rachel retreated; she had seen that smile before.

'Mr Brown?' He held out his hand. 'Roger Beckwith, I would like to talk to you if I may.' He nodded pleasantly to Rachel. 'Good day, Miss Garnett.'

'Don't talk to him!' Rachel was aware that she sounded shrill and lowered her voice with an effort. 'He's from Leeds!' Ben looked alarmed, but didn't bark.

'Well, you can't help bad luck,' Nathan said calmly. He looked keenly at the young man. 'I know you, lad, you're Doc Beckwith's son.'

They shook hands and Beckwith looked pleased to be remembered. 'Best days of my school holidays, coming up here, Mr Brown. I didn't think you'd remember.'

'I don't forget a face,' said Nathan complacently. 'I remember you with red hair as a lad, brighter red than it is now. We used to catch minnows in the beck yonder, before you went down in the world and went to Leeds. What brings you this way, Roger?' He looked enquiringly at Rachel, as though he thought she was the attraction.

Roger's horse nuzzled him affectionately; it obviously had no idea how bad he was.

'This man is working for the people in Leeds who want to take our land. They want to flood the valley and we've got to stop them!' Rachel glared at the man, but her grandfather only smiled. 'And he even seems to think it's a good idea!'

'I've seen it all before and it came to nowt,' he told the young man patiently. 'They come up here and survey land and take rock samples and measure rainfall, but they can't move Nidderdale any nearer to Leeds.'

'They have plans for viaducts and tunnels, Mr Brown,' Roger said mildly. He seemed in no hurry to convert Nathan Brown. 'I'm with Leeds Corporation, here to carry out a survey. A tunnel might be part of the plan, to get the pipeline down to Leeds.'

'Tunnel through Pennines? That would cost a pretty penny.' Nathan took out his pipe and lit it. 'You should know, you're the engineer.'

Rachel took a deep breath and walked away, looking over the sunlit moors with their moving cloud shadows. A couple of grouse flew up from the heather beside her feet. If only Grandfather were right. He was so secure in his own world, playing the organ at church on Sundays and thinking well of all men. But Grandfather's world would be torn apart, if Roger and his masters got their way.

'Goodbye, Grandfather,' she said as she turned abruptly for home. 'We've a lot to do today. See you on Sunday.'

'Don't you worry, lass,' Nathan said with his usual gentleness. 'It will all be the same in a hundred years ... now lad, what is it you want to tell me?'

Whatever Roger said to Nathan, it didn't take long. Rachel was only halfway home with her empty basket when he overtook her and dismounted to walk beside her. Head up, Rachel tried to ignore him as she swung along, wishing he would go away.

'Good job I'm a country boy, a city lad wouldn't keep up with you…. Your grandfather's a fine old gentleman, isn't he?' Roger had fallen into step beside her, with the horse following on behind. 'Not many men are still farming at his age, and he's making a good job of it too. The farm is very neat.' Ben sniffed at Roger and was rewarded with a pat.

'Why can't you leave us in peace? Grandfather will probably die if you take his neat little farm away, our valley will be gone and our lives with it. If you're a country boy, you should understand. Where is your conscience, Roger?'

Scowling, Rachel tried to breathe more slowly. Nathan Brown had survived droughts, floods and the death of his wife, had seen stock and wool prices rise and fall. He was tough, but in the end he would be very vulnerable when it came to the land. 'He's too old to take another farm and start again.'

Roger said gently, 'Do you think I like this job? I was sent here to talk to the local folks because I used to know them, my father was the Pateley doctor. But I feel for you all, I understand that losing land is never easy.'

'Why did you agree to it?' Rachel was furious. How could he keep smiling? 'Why don't you report back to say the place is unsuitable for a reservoir? How can you let us all down, just for money?' She quickened her pace.

'It's progress, Rachel. Progress has a price. We're changing, society is changing and manufacturing is now almost more important than farming, although you may find this hard to believe. In some places, farming is in recession. People are leaving the land and the towns are getting bigger.'

'Well, we don't want to leave the land!' Rachel flashed.

'And remember, there will be compensation for lost land. It could be the right time for Mr Brown to retire, to live in comfort, with something to pass on to his grandchildren.' Roger was looking solemn for a change.

That was the last straw. 'If you think I'm waiting to inherit from Grandfather, you are ... despicable! Go away, I don't want to talk to you.' Rachel suddenly remembered that this man was going to be their house guest, but it was too late now to be polite.

'Of course I didn't mean to imply that you're waiting for an inheritance! I'm sorry you're so ... hostile, lass. Your dog seems to like me.' Roger grinned.

'It just shows what poor taste he has,' Rachel snapped, but then she smiled at the ridiculous conversation. Ben wagged his tail and looked from one to the other.

'I do understand your concern,' Roger said slowly, but he stuck to his place at her side. 'One of the reasons I accepted the job was to try to ensure a fair deal for the small farmers up here. The estate owners have influence as a rule, they can have more of their own way and negotiate their own terms.' He paused. 'I'm hoping that the larger landowners will negotiate a good deal for everyone in the dale.'

'Can they avoid losing land to a reservoir?' Rachel asked eagerly. Maybe the Major could save them.... 'If they all agree to fight it?'

'I must admit they can, sometimes. Big projects like this require an Act of Parliament and some men can ... influence the vote.' He looked at Rachel carefully. 'But an intelligent girl like you will understand that there's no holding back progress. We have to accept it, make the best of it and move on, wherever our lives take us.'

They went into the farmyard; Roger said he had more calls to make and went off again. With a very bad grace, Rachel went into the house to prepare supper for the enemy. Should she put a handful of salt in his soup? That would be a waste of good food ... she wanted to make him suffer. He was far too happy for a man bringing bad news.

The family were gathered at the supper table when Roger came downstairs, his freshly brushed chestnut hair gleaming in the lamplight. He looked round with a smile at the glowing fire and the food on the table.

'How pleasant this is! It's a cold evening out there. I do appreciate your kindness in allowing me to stay here,' he said quietly. 'This house is so homely, it's a great change for me.'

'Do you have a family of your own?' Ruth asked him. 'Please sit here…. You must often be away from home.'

The lad sat at the table and Rachel noticed he had changed his clothes. 'Only a sister in York, that's all that's left of my family. In Leeds, I board with a policeman's widow and she looks after me very well, but I do travel a great deal.'

Rachel silently passed round plates of soup, unadulterated by her bad impulses. Why did he have to come and spoil their lives? How long would he stay? They couldn't even talk freely with a boarder in the house.

'I remember your dad,' Kit said reflectively. 'A very good doctor, he was. Reach to and help yourself to bread, lad. You're welcome here, even though you may be bringing bad news.'

The talk turned to the oat crop and the chance of rain, Roger asking several questions about the farm. Of course, he tried to be pleasant, he was bound to – somebody was paying him to sell the idea of losing your home to a dam. He should have realized that he didn't need to waste his charm on the Garnetts.

Rachel found herself scowling as he talked easily to her parents. They discussed his newly acquired horse, Charlie, and what was the available feed for him. Roger had waited to ask, before giving the horse hay. She had to admit that the lad's manners were excellent, but he must know that the Garnetts themselves had no land. They were dependent on the Major for their living and their future was in his hands.

When Roger went out to see to his horse after the meal, Rachel turned to her mother. 'How long do we have to put up with him and feed his stupid horse?' She started to clear the dishes from the table.

Ruth Garnett said soothingly, 'He's a very pleasant young man,

Rachel. It's no hardship and remember, he's a paying guest. The money will be useful, we need some new curtains...' She stopped suddenly. 'Once we find out where we'll live, of course.'

'New curtains would be a waste if this house is to be under the waves, Mother,' Rachel said bitterly as she poured hot water for washing up.

When Roger came back, she hoped he would go to his room, but Kit invited him to sit by the fire.

'Now, lad, I expect you've had enough of reservoirs for the day,' he said kindly. 'But could you just tell us how things are looking? We've heard a lot of different stories over the past few years. Will our valley get flooded, or not? Might they go somewhere else? We don't blame you, of course, but it would help us to know the situation.'

Roger looked into the fire for a moment before he answered. 'I'm only a junior engineer, Mr Garnett. I'm not sure what will happen. It might depend on what the big landowners want to do, as I said to you, Rachel,' he said, looking over and including her in the conversation. 'If ... if Major Potts, Judge Walton and maybe the owner of Cranby Park all get together to oppose it, they might be heard.' He chuckled. 'I think you saw the Major's first reaction, he threw me out! But sometimes, when people look at the money side, they change their minds. And this is an excellent site.'

'I suppose you are here to make sure they give up their land,' Rachel said crossly. 'That must be what they pay you to do.'

'I'm here to get the full picture and as you may imagine, I feel for the smaller landowners,' Roger said quietly. 'The senior engineer is a city man, very experienced in engineering, but Walter Bromley doesn't know much about farming and country communities. But he will take notice of powerful men, he knows they can arrange for a bill to be rejected in Parliament. He's been in Wharfedale recently, he comes here tomorrow. And ... I might as well admit it, I am hoping he's found another suitable valley, nearer to Leeds and Bradford, but I doubt it. '

Kit nodded, then changed the subject. 'We have several books here you might like to read, borrow any that you fancy. We tend to read in the dark evenings.'

The next morning, Ruth returned from her housekeeping duties looking sombre. She came into the dairy where Rachel was turning the wooden churn to make butter.

'When you've done there, lass, you'd better get over to the Hall. Mr Guy has come home from his tour of Europe and they want his room making ready. Your father and I are going to Masham market, I hope we'll sell some butter ... how much is there for sale?' Lady Agnes was certainly pushing her staff to make money for the farm.

Another unwelcome guest. With a sinking heart, Rachel looked at her mother. 'When will he be here?' She knew better than to say anything about Guy. They both knew that he'd been a spoiled child who pulled the wings off butterflies; Rachel had done her best to avoid him when she was a child.

'He's here already.' Ruth smiled grimly. 'I did suggest that perhaps we could hire another indoor servant, with three in the Family and any of Guy's friends who may come to stay, but Her Ladyship put her foot down. No more staff, the wages are too expensive already. Even though we've more cows to milk when the Potts are here.'

Kit and Ruth set off in the trap for Masham with a big basket of butter and Rachel was left to finish the chores. As she was crossing the yard, she ran into Roger Beckwith, who was just riding out for the day after a good breakfast.

'I believe you said that a tour of the Hall could be arranged? My colleague Mr Bromley would like to see the place, could you ask if it will be possible this afternoon?'

'My mother's not here ...' Rachel began, but then realized that she sounded childish. She stood up very straight. 'We will ask Lady Agnes and let you know tonight, but I doubt whether it will be possible.' She turned and left him.

Rachel hadn't expected to see Her Ladyship and thought of waiting until her mother came home, but the lady was floating down the stairs as the maid went up with her arms full of sheets and pillow cases. She stood aside, hoping to be ignored but Lady Agnes stopped and peered at her.

'I hope you have cleaned Mr Guy's room properly?' she said crossly. 'He is most particular.'

'Yes, m'lady. Er ... may I ask you something?' Good idea to ask when she was in a bad mood. 'Two gentlemen would like to tour the historic part of the house, but I said that it was usually closed to the public when the Family is in residence.'

Her Ladyship looked interested. 'As it happens, I was going to talk to your mother about this. We should be charging a fee for visitors and encourage them to come to view the house. You can show them the rooms we don't use. I will arrange for ropes to head them away from our rooms.'

'So – you want me to show them round, m'lady?' Rachel's voice was flat.

The woman looked at her keenly. 'I suppose you know something of the history? You've taken people round before? Then do so, and ask your father to suggest a suitable fee. The house must pay its way.' She paused for a moment. 'You need not inform me of when the visits are to occur, but you must keep a strict record of all monies taken.'

Rachel sighed and went on up the stairs. She had shown visitors the Elizabethan part of the Hall for years, sticking to a route that kept them away from the Family's rooms. But the two men from Leeds were different. How could they pretend to be interested in something they were about to destroy?

At the top of the wide staircase, Rachel met her next problem. A heavy youth stood there, looking out of the windows into the park. He was pale, with regular features marred by a sulky, sneering expression. Turning suddenly, he grabbed her round the waist and she dropped the sheets. 'Did I startle you? That's a pity, you might have wet your knickers.'

Rachel tried to twist out of his grasp. 'Leave me alone!'

Guy sniggered. 'Ah, it's young Garnett! My, how you've grown! I can have some fun with you!'

FOUR

AFTERWARDS, RACHEL COULDN'T remember how she had found the courage to stand up to Guy Potts. She couldn't run away every time she met him, so something had to be done and she was the only person who could do it. She glared into the sneering face.

'Mr Guy, please leave me alone, or I will report you to your mother.' He laughed and moved nearer, and to emphasize the point, she stamped heavily on his foot. Guy howled and hopped about, swearing.

'What's the matter with you? Country girls are supposed to enjoy a bit of fun ... especially the pretty ones. I can get you sent off, you know ... if you don't co-operate.'

Rachel moved quickly out of his way, wondering why he was so uncouth. Guy was coming towards her again and Rachel tripped him so that he fell heavily.

Major Potts had heard the commotion and came storming out of the library in his usual temper. 'What the hell is going on here? There's no peace in this house. Garnett, keep away from my son or I will have you dismissed. Guy, come with me. You are not to fraternize with the maids.'

The youth scowled and followed the Major into the library, banging the door after them. Rachel scuttled along the corridor, threw the sheets into a cupboard and left the house as fast as she could. Her mother would have to make up the bed. She was very willing to leave the young master severely alone. The encounter had been a shock, but Rachel smiled as she remembered the thud with which he had hit the floor.

'Perhaps he won't stay long, it's too quiet for him here,' her mother said when she heard about the problem.

The next day, Roger came into the farmyard with a man who rode badly and was obviously not enjoying the experience.

'This is my colleague, Mr Bromley,' he announced. Rachel opened the stable door and the men led the horses in. 'May we visit the house? Did you get permission? Can we go now?' His cheerful face looked even happier beside that of the older man, who was solemn.

Mr Bromley's pale city face turned towards Rachel for scrutiny. 'Hmm. I had expected to be shown the house by someone who is knowledgeable concerning the history of the area, rather than by a maid. Some historic mansions have trained guides.'

Roger hid a smile. 'Miss Garnett is the Assistant Housekeeper and knows the history of this house very well, Mr Bromley,' he said gravely.

'I will find out whether the Housekeeper is available,' the maid said frostily and in her best English. But Ruth Garnett was making jam and she only laughed. 'You know quite as much as I do, lass, and you've done the tour plenty of times. Don't forget to take their money before you go round the house, give them a ticket to make it look official – and don't put the money in your apron pocket! There's a box in the hall, Lady Agnes is keen to see it in use.'

'This way, please,' Rachel said crisply to the waiting men, leading the way to the massive front door of the old part of the Hall. She decided not to apologize for the lack of a proper guide. 'You will understand that the Family is in residence, in their part of the house. We will visit the Elizabethan rooms only.' She took them straight to the cash box. 'This is where tickets are issued.' The visitors looked surprised, but paid up, although Bromley wondered aloud whether he would get value for money. Roger just laughed and winked at Rachel.

As Roger and Bromley gazed about them, Rachel stood in silence for a moment. The stone-flagged floor was worn by centuries of feet; the large stone fireplace had four arches. Larger than human scale, it was an impressive sight, built to impress by the original Tudor landowner.

'This was the main dining hall,' she told them and Roger admired the long oak table, flanked by benches and set with old pewter plates and dishes. 'The Family used to entertain the Guns for lunch here during pheasant shoots,' she added. Paying visitors were entitled to know as much as she knew and Bromley was after value for money. She would see that he got it, even to the point of boredom. 'Please feel free to ask questions if you wish.'

Once she got over Bromley's pale disapproval, Rachel took the men confidently through the early history of the site, which had belonged to one of the great abbeys until the dissolution of the monasteries. 'In the sixteenth century during the reign of Henry VIII, as you will know,' she added. 'At that time it came into the hands of a Yorkshire Member of Parliament. He built the Hall from about 1547 and his family lived in it for 200 years.'

'No, neither Major Potts nor Lady Agnes is descended from the original owners. The Major's grandfather bought the estate about seventy years ago,' Rachel explained. 'The present Family spend much of their time in India.'

As they went through the house, Roger remarked on the beautiful proportions of the rooms. 'I love this place,' he said. 'Look at the mullioned windows and the lead in the panes!'

Bromley was less enthusiastic. 'Knock it down and you could build two houses with all this stone, a hall and a good farmhouse. You could re-use the panelling ... the rooms are too high, hard to keep warm. It could be scaled down.' Rachel shuddered and Roger grinned at her.

They went up the stairs and paced the Long Gallery, where they spent some time looking at the portraits. There was Sir John, the MP and his wife, and his descendants down the centuries. Roger stopped in front of an eighteenth century portrait. 'That man ... he looks so much like Nathan Brown, don't you think, Rachel?'

Rachel looked up at the painting with affection; they had often said that he looked like Grandfather. 'I believe that the Browns were descended from the builder of the Hall. They have held their own farm for many generations,' she said primly.

Roger told Bromley, 'Miss Garnett is Nathan Brown's grand-daughter. Can you see the likeness to this bonny young woman on the wall?' He walked across to a painting of a dark-haired Victorian miss in a dress of white lace.

Bromley looked up at the portrait, then down his nose at Rachel. 'It would be an illegitimate branch, I suppose. These things are common on country estates. Maids get themselves into trouble.'

Ignoring him, Rachel continued the tour. 'There is a tradition at Firby Hall of a ghost, a man with a long cloak …' she told them as they passed through a gloomy passage. Bromley looked behind him nervously into the shadows. 'His footsteps are sometimes heard on the stairs.'

'You should charge extra for the ghost,' Roger suggested.

In the library, they admired rows of ancient, leather-bound books, secure behind locked cabinet doors. 'I'm not allowed to open the doors to show you the books,' she said. 'Some of them date from the sixteenth century, so they're rather fragile.' One or two were manuscripts from even earlier.

'Couldn't you just open one door, to let us see them properly?' Bromley looked interested for the first time.

Rachel knew the keys to the book cases were kept in the desk drawer, because she had to dust the volumes from time to time. Historians with a special interest in old books were sometimes allowed to handle them, but not engineers from the City of Leeds. 'Sorry, Mr Bromley, it's not allowed.'

'They'll be worth a pretty penny,' he remarked, with his nose up against the glass. 'They won't go down with the ship. A lot of value in those old books.'

There was a movement at the far side of the room. Guy Potts jumped up from where he had been sitting in the window recess and glared at Bromley. 'How much are they worth?'

'I couldn't say, you'd have to get them valued,' Bromley told him. Guy left the room, muttering about peasants invading his house. Rachel decided that she would tell the Potts in future when tourists were expected, in the hope that Guy would not be disturbed.

Continuing the tour, they passed through vast bedrooms with heavy four-poster beds and tapestries on the walls. They looked into the attics, where there were servants' rooms and a nursery, long disused. It was true that the house was cold and parts of it were dark, but the sense of history here was strong. The rooms occupied by the Major and his wife were more comfortable additions, built on early in the nineteenth century.

Eventually, Rachel turned to the visitors and said what was on her mind. 'Please tell me – do you think that the reservoir will be built? You spoke of knocking the Hall down....'

Bromley said firmly, 'I'm sure of it. And a good thing, too. This place is obsolete, a big gloomy place with rooms that nobody lives in. Waste of money to keep it going.' He laughed. 'They should sell up, especially those musty old books, they alone'll be worth a fortune. My father's a bookseller, so I know.'

Nothing more was said and the visitors soon went back to the stables to collect their horses. Rachel was left with a cold shadow on her heart, the feeling that the life she knew was about to come to an end.

A few weeks went by and Roger continued his work in the area. There seemed to be no sign of the boarder departing. On the evenings when Jim called to see Rachel, Roger chatted to him easily.

One night as he was leaving, Rachel went with Jim to the stable for his horse and he gave her a kiss. 'Don't get too friendly with yon engineer,' he warned her. 'You're my girl!'

'Don't be silly, Jim, he's the enemy.' Rachel glared at him. 'He's going to take our homes and our jobs, we can never forget that.'

One day in October, the Major called in his farm manager for a conference and when he came back, Kit was grim.

'Make a cup of tea, lass,' he said to Rachel and the Garnetts sat at the kitchen table to hear the worst.

Kit spoke very quietly. 'They've agreed to sell the estate, they need the money. The Major knows we can't make much more money from the farm, however much he rages. Farming's in a sort of depression, has been for years. He'd rather not sell of course, so ...' Kit didn't finish, but they knew what he meant. So obviously, he would be even more bad-tempered, if that were possible.

'But – what about the others? Nobody wants to leave Firby, or lose their land.' Rachel thought about Roger's remark that if the estate owners got together, they might be able to stop the project.

'Some of the smaller landholders have agreed, after the price went up a bit. So,' and he sighed heavily, 'this is the end of Firby Hall. We'll have to find another place.'

Ruth Garnett was pale. 'How much land will the farm lose? They might still need a manager for what's left.'

'There will only be the moor, sheep run, and then above that, peat bogs and the heather. Maybe they'll have to farm grouse!' He was trying to lighten the mood, but nobody laughed.

'There'll be work for a shepherd maybe, but not enough for a manager and family.' Kit sighed. 'Some of the estate farms will survive, but anybody can collect farm rents and listen to the tenants' complaints.' For years, Kit had been in effect the estate manager, but the Potts thought of him as a farm foreman and paid him accordingly.

'It wouldn't surprise me,' Ruth said slowly, 'if the Potts sold the rest as well and left the district. They have a house in London.'

'They spend so little time here that they wouldn't miss the place ... not like we will. If we're really living in Doomed Valley, maybe we should think of leaving now.' Rachel looked at her father. 'Shall we look at the *Herald* 'Wanted' page, to see whether anyone needs an experienced farm manager?'

'We've been here for twenty-five years, your mother and me,' Kit told her. 'It won't be easy to leave.'

That evening, Kit and Ruth went up to see Ruth's father, Nathan, to talk over the disaster. They wanted to see how he was coping with the probability of losing his land.

'You'll have to give Roger his supper,' Rachel was told. 'He's late tonight.'

Little had been said about the reservoir when Roger was in the house. Kit Garnett had felt that the young engineer was doing a difficult job and would need a rest from it in the evenings, so the talk round the supper table had been of other things.

Without the manager and his wife, the house was quiet and Rachel found little to say. Roger ate his mutton in silence for a while and then looked across at Rachel, who had no appetite for supper.

'What's wrong, lass?'

'The Major has agreed to sell the estate ... so I suppose the reservoir will be bound to go ahead. You'll be pleased, Roger, it's what you want. But I won't bore you with it now.'

Roger's blue eyes widened. 'Has he now? You poor girl, you must feel devastated. Sometimes, I wish I had another job. This project is affecting decent people.'

'So, I remember you said that if people worked together, maybe they could stop the project. Surely you could find another valley, one with no good land and nobody living in it?' Rachel got up to put the kettle on the range and busied herself with stoking up the fire.

There was silence for a while; Roger finished his meal and pushed his plate away. 'I still think it's not too late, if only people knew. Bromley is telling them all it's a foregone conclusion, but I think differently. If farmers and landowners could realize that no one wants a reservoir here, then ... perhaps Leeds would look else-where. Even the Major might change his mind.'

Rachel sat down opposite him. 'But they don't know, do they? There's the village, of course, some of those houses belong to the Major. But most folks live in scattered farms all over the valley and the moor. Some of those farmers may be worrying about it right now, thinking they have no choice. There's no way to reach them ... except ...' She looked into the fire. 'They all read the paper, I suppose?'

'Yes, everybody reads the *Herald*.' Roger smiled. 'You could write a letter to the editor, Rachel. That might raise a bit of dust, you know! I'd better say no more, I'm supposed to be promoting the project. I'll go and groom Charlie.' At the door, he looked back with a smile that was somehow comforting. Roger Beckwith was not quite so hateful as she'd thought.

Rachel Garnett, writing a letter to the paper? Was it likely? Perhaps, if she concealed the fact that she was a young woman, a person of no importance. She would have to sound confident. The style was easy, she'd been reading the paper since she was small and noticing the different ways in which opinions were put down in print. Some people got quite heated about subjects like the town drains.

When the dishes were done, Rachel sat down with a pencil and tried to compose a suitable letter to the Ripon *Herald*. Her heart sank; it was too hard. But then for a fleeting moment, she thought of her ancestors on the walls of the Long Gallery, people who probably did have some power in their time. How would they have gone about this? Their blood was in her veins, she should at least make an effort to save Firby Hall, if only for the ghosts.

It would be better to state the facts clearly and simply, she thought, rather than to tell people what to think.

To the Editor:

Dear Sir,

Will they flood our valley?

Your readers may be aware (that was a good start) *that it is proposed to build a reservoir in the Firby area ... that Leeds Corporation is looking for water and maybe Bradford too ...*

Rachel bit the end of her pencil. This was more difficult than she thought.

Roger came back, said goodnight and went to his room. The grandfather clock in the corner ticked loudly in the unusual silence as Rachel struggled with the letter. After a few false starts, she decided to keep it short.

'This would mean that the mixed farms of our area would disappear. We grow crops on the valley land, oats for the horses, turnips and good hay for the winter. Our cattle graze the sides of the valley, while the sheep live on the moorland above. Imagine the valley filled with water! There will be no good land left, no village, no historic houses. A way of life will have gone. If this goes on, our dales will be left to the sheep. Will the people of Firby fight this, before it is too late?
R. G. ....'

Rachel made the signature illegible.

She added a note at the bottom of the page. 'I would like this letter to be signed 'Concerned.'

It was possible to imagine that in the future, the greedy industrial cities could take the whole Nidd valley, with a string of dams across it. What a thought!

Rachel too went to bed before Kit and Ruth returned. She decided not to tell them about the letter, but to post it in the village the next day. Just before sleep, she realized that she might not be such a helpless female after all.

Alexander Finlay sat at his big mahogany desk in the *Herald* office, looking out of the window. Summer was ending and autumn leaves were drifting across the Ripon market place below. As the new *Herald* editor, he was expected to give the old newspaper a new look and to 'Investigate the affairs of the day,' he'd been told by the owners, elderly gents who tended to speak in headlines. The list of people attending weddings and funerals was no longer enough to fascinate the readers, some of whom were drifting like the autumn leaves away from the *Herald* to other papers.

A junior brought in the day's mail and Alex sifted through it. Letters to the editor often needed much editing, especially the ones that ran to five pages of bad spelling. Good old 'Disgruntled, Blossomgate' was taking another swipe at the potholes in the roads. Guessing the identity of these letter writers was a local sport, sometimes with bets taken, but the editor was sworn to secrecy.

A neatly written letter of only a single sheet caught his eye.

WILL THEY FLOOD OUR VALLEY? That was eye catching, it could have been written by a senior reporter. Alex read the letter and whistled. Here was an 'affair' that needed the paper's attention. Why had he not known about it before?

Summoned to the editor's office, his assistant, Rodney Dacre, shook his head.

'But they've been talking about reservoirs up there for as long as I can remember,' he protested. 'How can we know whether this time it might actually happen?' His expression implied that it was old news, from dead files.

'Can't it be revisited? A backward look, if nothing else?' Finlay sat back in his chair. 'It would do no harm to mention the possibility. Man, if they flooded a whole valley with people living in it, the effect on the community would be drastic. Some country people never move from the village where they were born … it would ruin their lives! What a story it would make!'

Rodney picked up the letter. 'You should be a novelist,' he said sourly, scanning the page quickly. 'Nothing definite, no contracts signed,' he grunted. 'Just some old codger getting into a panic, if you ask me.' He looked up at the boss. 'Maybe we should support progress, argue for the reservoir as a good thing.'

'Find out,' said Alex tersely. 'I've only been here a few months, I need to know all about it.' He ran his hands through his curly brown hair and took off his spectacles. 'Have you any idea who R. G. might be? You'd better dig out any information you can in the files, Rod, and try to whip up some enthusiasm! And I ...' He looked out of the window again; the sun was turning the autumn leaves to gold. 'I will take a ride out to Firby tomorrow.'

Rodney shrugged and turned to go back to his desk. 'Wild goose chase,' he muttered. 'Football season's starting soon, I've got to interview the Ripon captain. And then there's that cow with triplets out at Studley.'

Alex was still thinking about the reservoir. 'What if the church goes under...?' He remembered old tales of church bells ringing under the water, on the site of drowned cities. 'Do you think they would move the graves in the churchyard?'

Rodney grunted again and Alex wondered why Yorkshire people were so dour. Was it the cold climate, or indigestion? The food here did tend to be rich.

FIVE

ALEX FINLAY HIRED a horse from the stable at The Unicorn Hotel in Ripon for his journey to Firby and set out in the late morning. He planned to gather enough information for an editorial column, to be published at the same time as the letter from 'Concerned'. The day was cool but fine; it was good to ride out of town and turn the horse's head towards the west and the high ground of the grouse moors above Ripon.

He had been in the editor's seat at the *Herald* for two months and was beginning to appreciate this corner of the world. The decision to work on a country newspaper was deliberate; Alex had been brought up in the country and hated working in big cities. When he eventually married, he wanted to live in beautiful countryside.

From Ripon he rode through the pretty village of West Tanfield to Masham, where he paused to ask the way.

Rodney had suggested sourly before his editor left Ripon that the villagers might be living in squalor and be only too happy to be housed elsewhere.

'Some of those picturesque old cottages are in ruins, landlords won't spend any money. It's been going on for years, since farm prices went down. How would you like to live with a leaking roof and mould everywhere? There's no money on the land and no future for the villages. Sensible folks are moving to the towns.'

'Yes, there is a recession, but surely only for corn? I thought that the demand for dairy produce and beef was going up, and Firby's a – a grassland area. Maybe you should write a report on local economics, Rodney.'

'Too depressing,' was Rodney's verdict.

It must be the indigestion, Alex thought as he cleared his desk.

Sunshine bathed the little village in a golden afternoon light as Alex clopped down the main street of Firby. The houses were of a light grey stone, well built and with neat gardens and orchards. The Fox and Hounds had a swinging sign advertising home-brewed ale.

Rodney couldn't have been to Firby. There was an atmosphere of modest prosperity; these people wouldn't be desperate to leave their homes.

Where were the villagers? There was nobody standing at a cottage door, nobody driving cows in for milking. The street was so quiet it seemed deserted ... surely the place hadn't been evacuated already? But then an unholy racket erupted as small children poured out of their schoolroom for the afternoon break.

Led by the noise, Alex rode up to the school. It was built into the side of a south-facing slope, in pleasant grounds set with large trees. Dismounting, he asked a small boy where to find the head-teacher and was directed to where a middle-aged man was coming out into the sunshine.

'There he is, that gaffer, Mr Jackson.'

The teacher welcomed Alex to the village with a warm hand-shake. 'Alex Finlay from the newspaper? You'll not have been here before, we don't make much news in Firby. Tie up your horse and come inside, where we can hear ourselves think.' He led the way into the building, which was small but neat and clean. 'We have ten minutes before the children come back.'

Alex took out a notebook. 'Thank you, Mr Jackson. I'm interested in the proposal to build a reservoir here. What will it mean to the village?'

The head motioned him to sit down and took his own chair behind a desk, his pleasant face serious. 'It will destroy the village, and our community. The water, I believe, will reach yon birch tree.' He pointed to where the window looked out on the back of the school, where the land rose steeply to a ridge. 'Of course, we hope they will go elsewhere. There are other valleys farther up the dale, lonely places more suited to flooding. Here, there is too much to lose.'

'Can anything be done? I'm willing to publish information about the proposal, if that will help.' Already, Alex felt himself siding with the people who didn't want the reservoir, didn't want to see this sunny, sheltered valley submerged in dark water. But perhaps as a good journalist, he should look at both sides of the story. 'Is there anyone in favour of the scheme?'

Jackson shrugged. 'Leeds and Bradford Corporations both, it seems. I feel that if one doesn't take us, the other will, desperate for water as they are. You see, Mr Finlay, we have three main estates here and the landowners will call the tune, I'm afraid. The rest of the valley is owned by small farmers with no influence at all ... and from what I can gather, the landowners are not against it, they will be happy to sell their land. Possibly because they have land elsewhere and would like to get their hands on some cash. None of the estate owners lives here permanently.'

Alex wrote furiously as Mr Jackson told him all he knew about the proposed size of the reservoir and the type and number of farms in the valley, as well as the population of the village. This was more than he had hoped.

'If you're interested in history, there is a small but beautiful Elizabethan manor house here, owned by a Major Potts, one of the landowners I mentioned. It's sometimes open to the public; I intend to take the children there for a visit and get them to write about it, before ... it disappears.'

'I will certainly visit the house, but not today, I have to get back to Ripon before dark.'

Jackson jumped up. 'I should have offered you some refreshment after your journey. Will you take a cup of tea?' But it was time to start lessons again; the bell clanged and a beautiful young woman herded the children back into the classroom. Alex saw that they were all taught in one big room, but in two classes, one to each teacher.

'Thank you, I'll take a drink of water,' Alex said, and drank with appreciation. 'The water here is excellent, so pure compared with town water!'

Jackson smiled gently. 'So is the air, and our food is fresh, but I think many of us will have to move to live in the town.' So that was it; he had accepted the inevitable. 'I've told Miss Ward, my assistant, to look for another position. Violet Ward is a good teacher.' The beautiful girl looked up and smiled; Alex caught a glimpse of lovely blue eyes in a heart-shaped face.

Riding down into Ripon as the sun set behind him, Alex saw the smoke from many fires lying over the little city like a blanket, with the cathedral towers visible above the haze.

Ripon could be smoky on evenings such as this, but he knew the industrial West Riding was much worse. He remembered a visit to Leeds. The smoke haze from tall chimneys had blocked out the sun and the handsome buildings in the city centre were black with soot. If the folks of Firby left their valley, he was sure it would not be of their own free will.

Kit's heart sank when he saw Guy Potts and his friend striding over the farmyard on a grey afternoon, just as he was going out to check the sheep.

'Garnett!' the youth bellowed, in a good imitation of the Major. 'We want to shoot pheasant, now it's October.'

'Well, Mr Guy, what does your father say?' Kit knew it wouldn't be approved. There were not many pheasants about and the Major was expected to put on a shoot for his neighbours during the season.

Guy pouted. 'He said we should shoot rabbits ... but he's gone off for the day to see old Rupert, he won't know.'

Kit looked them over; Guy was tending to put on weight in spite of his youth and had bags under his eyes. A walk would no doubt do them good. 'Rabbits, yes. Pheasants, no. I'll give you single-barrelled shotguns, one shot at a time. You haven't been here at the Hall enough to have much experience.'

'Freddy's a good shot, lots of experience.' Guy indicated his friend. Freddy, a tall, thin lad, looked uncomfortable.

Kit rather unwillingly took them to the gun room, gave them guns and safety warnings and told them not to go into any fields that held livestock. He gave them three cartridges each and two hours only, after which the guns had to be back and they had to be cleaned. Trust Guy to try this on behind his father's back.

He decided to keep an eye on them. Kit called the collie Ben and walked away, but on a route where he could keep them under observation.

Clouds hung low over the moors above them as the young guns set out to shoot rabbits.

'I knew the old misery wouldn't let us go after pheasants, but it was worth a try,' Guy muttered.

'I thought that early morning was the best time for rabbits, or maybe at dusk,' Freddy volunteered. 'But I don't know much about shooting, as you well know.'

'Who's going to get up early?' Guy scoffed. 'I'm not. This is such a boring place, there's nothing to get up for. I only come here when I have to.'

'It was about time we came here, you've been to my home for most school holidays for years,' Freddy pointed out. 'Just because my pa used to know your father and your folks were in India.'

'But you're near London, it's much more interesting. None of these boring green fields and cold moors. Here, there's no theatres, no girls and no gaming. I hate this place, I tell you. Be glad when it's sold ... did you know they're going to flood the estate to make a reservoir? I can't wait for the day when I can get my hands on some of the money. Otherwise, debts will catch up and they'll push me into taking a job ... they mentioned law, how boring! Money's the thing, I need lots of it.' He licked his lips.

'Don't start moaning about your debts again, you've only got yourself to blame.' Freddy glared at Guy. 'It's time you faced reality, you know. We're not children now.'

They trudged across a field, holding the guns awkwardly. 'You're as bad as my mother. It was my bad luck in the first place that got me adopted by the Potts. I should've had better parents – who wouldn't pick my friends for me.' Guy glared back. 'Oh well, we're stuck with each other again.'

'Not for long, we're not,' Freddy told him. 'My folks have written, they want me back in London as soon as I can catch a train, to see about getting into the army. I'm off as soon as I can get a ride to Masham. I'm looking forward to it, I'm sick of waiting.'

'You didn't tell me!' Guy swung round to face him. 'How can you look forward to being ordered about in the army? I wouldn't do it, although Pa wants me to.'

'I don't tell you anything when you're in such a bad temper. Is that gun loaded? Don't point it at me. I know enough about guns to be very careful with them.'

'Spoken like a good army officer! You'll go far, Dawson,' Guy scoffed.

They climbed over a stile and went diagonally across a slope to the edge of a small wood, where Guy stopped. 'Just make a note of where we are, Freddy. I could easily get lost in this damned place, especially if the fog rolls in.' He put his foot in a rabbit hole and swore.

'At least we know there's a rabbit here,' Freddy said, grinning.

They walked at the edge of the wood, Freddy keeping well behind Guy. Nothing stirred. The light was poor, but when at last he saw a movement between the trees, Guy fired. There was a yelp and then silence.

'That wasn't a rabbit!' Freddy started towards the sound.

'Leave it alone, probably only a wild cat. We'll try a bit further on.' Guy reloaded and strode off, but Freddy walked towards where he thought the sound had come from.

A collie dog lay at the foot of a tree, whimpering. Freddy knelt down and patted the soft head. 'What's wrong, old boy?' Then he saw the problem; the dog's left front leg was wounded and bleeding.

'Guy! Come here! You've shot a dog!' Freddy shouted, but Guy ignored him. The animal was not a heavy type of sheepdog, but it might be rather too big for one person to carry. 'Guy! We've got to get this dog back to the farm!'

'Probably only a stray. Shall I shoot it?' Guy offered when at last he came back.

Freddy lost his temper. 'You will not, you rat! This dog belongs to the Garnetts, I've seen it in the farmyard. We must get it home.'

'Everything here belongs to the Potts,' Guy said coldly. 'So it's my dog and I will do as I please. I'm the sole heir, remember.'

'Go to hell, Guy, I'm taking him home.' Freddy's anger gave him strength and he scooped up the dog in his arms and set off back to the farm. Guy picked up Freddy's gun and walked off, cursing.

Kit had been hovering not far from the boys, which was why Ben the sheepdog was in the wood. He saw what had happened and together, he and Freddy carried the dog into a stable and laid him on the straw.

'I blame myself, I should never have given you guns,' Kit said grimly. 'It's broken … I think we can save the leg, but we must stop the bleeding … where's Ruth? We need some of her salve.'

Freddy was almost crying as he patted the dog and Ben licked his hand. 'Are you able to set his leg?' he asked.

'I hope so, lad. I did have a calf once with a broken leg and we managed to save it. Go and fetch my wife, will you?'

Freddy stayed with the dog as Ruth gently cleaned the leg and Kit made a splint from a piece of wood.

'I'll get the farrier to look at him tomorrow,' Kit said. He looked into the darkening farmyard when the job was done. 'I suppose Guy's gone home? I should like to see the guns safely back.'

'I'll go and find out,' Freddy offered. 'Hell, Mr Garnett, he could have shot you! What an idiot!'

Rachel was milking the cows; when she saw Ben she could hardly hold back tears.

'Never let Guy have a gun again!' she said fiercely to Kit. 'He will kill somebody one day. And he won't care.'

'Unfortunately, I can't tell Guy what to do,' Kit reminded her.

Freddy found the Hall in darkness and neither Guy nor the guns were there. As he crossed the yard to the stable again, Roger Beckwith rode in.

'It's very foggy now,' he said, blowing on his hands to warm them as he went into the stable. 'Goodness, what's happened to old Ben here?'

'Shot by the young master,' said Kit briefly.

'Who is now missing,' Freddy added as he came into the lamplight. 'He's not at home, Mr Garnett. Maybe he stayed out to get some rabbits as dusk came on. He said it would be easy to get lost …'

'We'd better look for him. Will you come, Mr Dawson?'

'Of course, and it's Freddy. He went off along the edge of the wood. Have you a lantern I might borrow?'

'I'll come too,' Roger offered. He put his horse into its box and rubbed it down quickly.

Rachel came in from the dairy and went straight over to Ben again. She said nothing, but knelt down and patted him.

'We'd better find him before the Major comes home,' Kit told them, but Ruth said there was no hurry because the Potts were out to dinner and would be coming home late.

'I don't envy Donald, driving them home through this fog,' she added.

Rachel gave the dog a drink of water and went into the house to prepare the supper. Poor Ben would be out of action for a while. It was good of Roger to offer to help with the search for that idiot Guy, who obviously couldn't even find his way around the home farm. Roger was proving to be much more sympathetic than she'd supposed. Or was he just trying to soften them up, so he could feel less guilty?

When the fire was blown into life and the pan of vegetables on the hob, Rachel turned to the *Herald* which lay unopened on the table. There on the letters page was her own letter, published just as she'd sent it in, at the top of the page. Underneath it was a note saying: *See also the editorial on page 2.*

In his own column, the editor made it clear that he had visited Firby and found it hard to believe that such a pleasant village could be lost, taken by the water. He said that he hoped the community would get together to fight the Leeds Corporation and any other body that wanted to destroy their homes. He touched on the fact that the valley land was far more productive than the moorland above; good land would be lost to food production, in a part of Yorkshire with a great deal of poor land.

The editor even mentioned the three estates affected: Major Potts's Firby Hall, Willow Grange owned by Judge Rupert Walton and Granville Sutton's Cranby Chase. Perhaps, he suggested, these owners might take the lead in an effort to reverse the decision.

It was good to know that her letter had stirred things up, but Rachel was afraid of being discovered as 'Concerned'. She had scribbled a signature on the letter and hoped that this Mr Finlay couldn't read it

That night, nobody else had time to read the *Herald.* At about eight, Kit and Roger came in wearily, having failed to find the missing heir.

'Serves him right if he stays out all night,' muttered Roger. They brought Freddy with them and Ruth offered him supper, which brought a grin to his pale face.

'Yes, please, Mrs Garnett.'

Ruth went across to the Hall to make up the fires for the Potts' return, but Guy was not there. She left a lamp in a window, in case it would help him to find his way home. The Major and Lady Agnes would probably not look for Guy that night, assuming that he was in bed.

Freddy looked across the table at Kit as he finished his meal.

'There's one place he might be, Mr Garnett. He could have gone to the Fox and Hounds – that would be like him. He goes there when his folks are not watching.'

Kit groaned. 'I've had enough for one day, lad. But I am worried about those guns.'

Eventually it was decided that Roger and Freddy would walk down to the inn, which was not far away, and bring Guy home with the firearms. Freddy was right. Guy was there, leaning over the bar to stare at the barmaid's bosom. The company at the inn, especially the barmaid, was relieved to see Guy hauled off home by two sober young men.

'Take him away, we've had enough of him,' they groaned, and not in jest.

'And the guns?' Freddy asked him grittily. 'We are responsible for those guns.'

'How should I know? Wasn't going to drag them up here, was I? Go and find them yourself, if you're so worried. I left them leaning against a tree. Can't be sure where.'

The next morning, PC Bradley came into the farmyard as Kit was going in for breakfast.

'I heard a report that young Mr Potts sold two guns in the pub last night, for cash … lad might be in the right, but I thought you should know, Kit.' He paused. 'I don't like to bother the Major.'

Later in the day, Kit went into the village and soon found out from the landlord of the Fox and Hounds that the guns had been sold to two Dale brothers, sensible lads. He called at their farm and retrieved the guns, apologizing for the deception.

'They were not his to sell,' he explained.

'What about our money?' he was asked.

'Potts has denied selling them, so it may take me a while to get it back for you. I'll do my best,' Kit told them.

'By, I wouldn't fancy your job,' one of the men said quietly. 'Major would be bad enough, but that young Guy seems to cause nothing but trouble.'

Kit rarely talked about his employers, but he had had enough.

'Just before he sold the guns, he shot one of my dogs.' Seeing their shocked expressions he added, 'He'll recover, but it will take time – his leg's broken. And he's our best sheepdog.'

Rachel was clearing the breakfast dishes as Roger came downstairs in his riding clothes.

'I have to go back to Leeds in a few days, to draw up plans,' he said, without his usual smile.

This was the day that she'd looked forward to at first, so why did her heart sink a little?

'Will you ... be coming back?' Rachel poured hot water into the sink.

Then Roger did smile. 'I was going to ask your mother whether I can leave my things here, in my trunk. I will need to come back, there's much to see to ... where to put up huts for the workmen, how to get the raw materials to the site, that sort of thing.' He paused. 'I've so enjoyed staying here, Rachel, and getting to know you all.'

'We have got used to your company, even though you're the enemy,' Rachel told him. 'What will you do with your horse?'

'Mr Brown has offered to look after Charlie, while I'm away.' He looked down at Rachel. 'I'm afraid the idea of going back to Leeds is not appealing.'

Rachel looked up into the clear blue eyes. 'Perhaps you'd be happier working in the country? You don't seem like a city lad to me.'

'I'm a Pateley lad, remember? But jobs for engineers are city-based. Maybe one day, I'll give it up and become a gamekeeper.'

'If you do that you'll be even more unpopular than you are now,' Rachel told him kindly, and watched him wince. 'Gamekeepers are like policemen. They can't afford to have friends.'

SIX

'Have you seen the *Herald*?' Kit asked at breakfast the following day. 'Folks at Ripon have noticed we're in trouble up here.' Rachel felt herself blushing and hoped that it wouldn't be noticed.

Ruth opened the newspaper and read the letter under bold headlines. 'I wonder who wrote this? Mr Jackson, maybe.' She looked up at a knock on the door and Nathan Brown came in, damp from the drizzling rain. 'Good day, Father, what brings you here this early?'

'You've seen the paper ... I've been talking to John Jackson up at the school.' Nathan accepted a cup of tea from Rachel. 'Thanks, lass. It's a bad time of year in one way, shorter days – but we think we should call a meeting. Get everybody together, to see what can be done.'

Kit took another slice of toast and buttered it thickly. 'Do you think the people that really matter are going to come to a village meeting? If Judge Rupert, the Major and Mr Sutton all used their weight, we might have a chance. If they all opposed the scheme, then Leeds could have to look somewhere else. But for the rest of us to mutter and grumble to each other – what good will that be?'

Nathan smiled serenely, as usual. 'That letter to the paper, and what the editor says, has got everybody talking. The worst thing we can do is to keep quiet.' He looked round. 'It's a pity young Beckwith isn't here. He's working for Leeds, of course. Firby is the nearest and the easiest site for them, but they're not counting the cost to the folks who live here.'

Ruth sighed. 'I think Roger sees now how it is for us and if he can do anything to help us, he will. But he's young, and his boss Mr Bromley doesn't care at all how many people lose their homes and their work.'

'Well, John Jackson's calling a meeting for next Thursday night. He's putting notices all over the village and sending one to the *Herald*.' Nathan finished his tea and stood up. 'He wants to provide tea and scones on the night, so maybe you could help with that? Rachel's scones are the best in the parish. Now, can I have a look at that dog, Kit? It was a bad job, that shooting. Young fella should be horsewhipped.'

'Ben's much better, Grandfather,' Rachel assured him. Kit finished his toast and the men went out to the stables.

As soon as the dishes were washed, Rachel slipped upstairs. She made the beds quickly and then sat down to plan another letter to the *Herald*, to emphasize the need for as many people as possible to come to the meeting. Her first letter had started something that was already gaining momentum. Perhaps she could just touch on the subject of power....

The leaders in our little community must have the power to persuade ... if they all agree that the reservoir should be built elsewhere.

She wrote out the letter in a fair hand, signed it 'Concerned', scribbled R. Garnett at the bottom and put it in an envelope, ready for posting.

'There's a visitor to show round this afternoon, a Miss Sutton,' Ruth said as they ate the midday meal. 'The Major and Her Ladyship have gone out for the day and she said we might show the visitor round.' Ruth smiled. 'The more visitors we get, the happier Lady Agnes will be. But I'll have to hide the money box, I think Guy has had his fingers in it.'

'Rachel can show her round, I won't need her until milking time.' Kit looked at his daughter.

'You'll need a clean apron, lass, and brush your hair,' her mother said.

The owners of the *Herald* newspaper were quite impressed with their new editor; he had found a fine new subject of controversy and circulation would no doubt increase. Alex himself decided that another visit to Firby was called for and this time, he would have a look at the doomed Elizabethan manor. Demolition of an old house, of centuries of history, was a scandal in the making. It would be good to find out who the letter writer might be; the second letter from 'Concerned' was as good as the first. It would be even better to get an interview with the owner of the house, Major Potts. He must be one of the landowners who could influence the decision.

The distant sound of gunfire startled Alex as he rode out of Masham on his way to Firby, but he remembered that these moors were famous for grouse and no doubt there was a shoot in progress.

'Keep your head down, girl,' he said to Mary the mare, the same quiet horse he'd hired on the last visit. One day he would buy himself a horse, but then he would need a stable.

A watery sun broke through the clouds as Alex rode through the village to find Firby Hall. A little apart from the village, it stood not far from the road. Alex reined in and sat on his horse, looking at the mullion windows with their leaded panes, the long chimneys and the beautiful proportions of the building. The roof tiles were covered in moss and the house sat in the landscape naturally, surrounded by a small formal garden. From what he had seen, there were very few such houses in this area; it was a rare jewel on the edge of the moors.

He could see that a more recent wing had been added and that it had a separate entrance and stables. This must be where the Potts lived, but it was unobtrusive and was not obvious from the road.

A horse and trap was being tied up at the gate by a young woman, dressed for the country in stout boots.

'Are you visiting the Hall? You should tie your horse over there,' she instructed in a clear, upper class voice. 'My mare may bite, you see.'

Alex meekly did as he was told.

In a few minutes the Hall door opened.

'Good afternoon, I'm Rachel Garnett and I will take you on a tour of the house.' She wore a black dress and a white apron like a housekeeper, but Alex thought she looked rather young. 'You must be Miss Sutton? Lady Agnes told us to expect you.' She turned to Alex. 'You wish to join us, sir?'

'Thank you,' Alex murmured. 'I'm passing through Firby and hoped to be able to visit the house.' He would not give his name yet.

Rachel asked how much time they had.

'I have an hour only,' Miss Sutton announced. 'I am expected on the moor, to pick up the Guns at two o'clock. One of the keepers is ill.' It rather looked as though Miss Sutton belonged to the landowner's family, the Suttons of Cranby Chase. 'I've never seen the inside of the old part of house and soon, it may be too late.' She had dimples when she smiled and seemed less fearsome. 'We are all in two minds about this reservoir business, but it seems wicked to destroy such a beautiful building.'

As she conducted the visitors through the old house, Rachel was wondering whether she should mention 'this reservoir business' to Miss Susan Sutton, the daughter of the man with influence. It was a pity that the other visitor had turned up.

Both visitors asked so many questions that progress was slow; they were obviously impressed with the history of Firby Hall. They peered into the priest hole and into a cellar that looked like a dungeon, as well as lingering in the main bedrooms with their heavy oak furniture. The man seemed to be very well informed about the history of the area and he made Miss Sutton laugh once or twice.

They were in the Long Gallery when Miss Sutton announced that she must leave. The man lingered, looking at the portraits while the two women walked down the wide staircase to the front door. Now was her chance, Rachel decided, and turned to face the visitor.

'Excuse me, Miss Sutton, for speaking to you. But do you not think that this is the wrong place for a reservoir? There are several valleys higher on the moors, places where nobody lives ... if all the people with influence were to use it, Firby might escape.' She looked eagerly into the pretty face, hoping for a reaction.

'I do see what you mean,' Susan Sutton said thoughtfully. 'My father is the one to speak to, of course. Perhaps the Major should speak to him.' She lowered her voice as they walked down the path to where her horse stood waiting, resting one leg. 'Who is that man that came round with us? He's quite – pleasant, isn't he? There are so few educated men up here.'

Rachel hid a smile and said that she didn't know who the man was, but would find out. Miss Sutton said she would call again one day, to complete the tour.

'Perhaps you could bring Mr Sutton with you?' Rachel asked boldly. 'He might like to see the house.' And she might get the chance to whisper in his ear, although that was rather unlikely. Important men didn't usually speak to young lasses in white aprons except to order them about.

Back in the Long Gallery, the visitor was leaning on a window sill, looking out into the autumn garden. 'It seems so sad that this house may be lost to a reservoir,' he said thoughtfully. 'I wonder what the ghosts feel about it.'

It was nearly time to fetch the cows for milking, which was usually Rachel's job, but it was important that as many people as possible should know what was going on.

'Most of us here are very worried about it, although I can't speak for the ghosts.' Rachel smiled. 'If you're staying in the area, sir, you should come to the public meeting. It's at the school, on Thursday night. How – how did you hear about the reservoir?'

'From the Ripon *Herald*, of course. I am the editor, as a matter of fact – Alex Finlay. I'm trying to find out as much as I can about the scheme.' He drew a paper out of his pocket, while Rachel stood very still. 'Two very good letters from "Concerned" have been published, you may have read them. I wonder whether you could decipher this signature for me? It would be good to meet the writer, he must live locally.'

Should she admit it? If the editor thought a man had written the letters, he might not be very happy to find out it was only a girl. Many men believed that women had no brains, in spite of very good evidence that they had. She took a deep breath and decided to be honest.

'I – I wrote those letters,' she stammered. 'Nobody knows it was me, please don't tell anyone …'

The editor looked down at her. 'You wrote them? My word, I assumed it was a man. You write very well. So what's your name, Miss Concerned? Where do you fit into the story?'

The eyes behind his glasses were kind; he seemed to be genuinely interested in Firby and its problems. This was a powerful friend, Rachel thought, but he could make a dangerous enemy if he was against you. The editor would decide what was published in the *Herald* and even what people should think about it.

Rachel explained that she was the assistant to her mother at the Hall, that her father was the farm manager. It affected them personally because they would lose their jobs and their home if the valley were flooded. 'But it's not just for us that I'm concerned,' she told him. 'The whole community, the little village and the good farms, will all be lost. Why can't they choose a lonely valley with nobody in it?'

'That is an important point. Well, I'm surprised that the letters didn't come from the school teacher, or an older farmer. But why shouldn't a young woman write good, sensible English? Women are taking an interest in general affairs, these days.' He looked at his watch. 'I'd like to get back to Ripon before dark. Now, Miss Rachel, will you send me a report of the village meeting? I will pay you for any reports you can send me. "From our correspondent" will cover your tracks, if you prefer.'

Shaking a little, Rachel agreed. She would have to tell Kit and Ruth eventually ... but she didn't want the rest of the village to know.

'But how – do I do it? I haven't reported on anything before. It sounds a bit like spying. People might be annoyed if they knew their words were being recorded.'

The editor laughed. 'If you record facts, nobody can complain. Facts usually speak for themselves. Opinions can be important, of course, if you get them from people who matter.' He looked down at Rachel. 'I haven't been at the *Herald* for very long ... and to tell you the truth, Rachel, it's been a boring paper. Now we have the chance to liven it up a little!'

'Where do I start, Mr Finlay? It's exciting, but I feel out of my depth ... oh, that's the wrong thing to say about this subject!'

Alex Finlay laughed. 'Thank you, you've given me a headline: OUT OF THEIR DEPTH: THE PEOPLE WHO FIGHT A RESERVOIR.' The editor wrote it down. 'Where to start? It's simple, really. Take a notebook ... and observe people and listen carefully. Don't try to record unless you understand.' He rubbed his chin thoughtfully. 'You can't write down everything, but try to get the main points. That's harder than you think, with people who wrap everything up in too many words!' He smiled. 'Fortunately, they often repeat themselves.'

'Thank you,' said Rachel faintly. Could she manage it?

'And quote the actual words people use if you can, but be sure you get them right.' The editor beamed at her. 'There, that's a correspondent's first lesson. It's a job that you learn by doing it and of course, I can smooth out any errors of grammar. I need to know the facts, and also, I would like an idea of the atmosphere of the meeting.'

'Thank you ... I'll do my best, Mr Finlay.'

They walked down the stairs.

'Is Major Potts available? I was afraid not.' The editor ran a hand through his hair. 'Perhaps you can tell me where the Suttons live? I should try to get an interview with Mr Granville Sutton one day.'

Rachel wondered whether perhaps Mr Finlay was hoping to see Miss Sutton again. She was tempted to tell him it was mutual, but her boldness wouldn't carry her that far, so she gave him directions to Cranby Chase. 'It's nearer to Ripon than we are, but quite a lot of their land will be flooded.'

The editor lingered on the landing to write the address in his notebook, while Rachel went down to open the door. Guy Potts appeared from the manor stables, a whip in his hand. When he saw Rachel he dropped the whip, rushed up to her and embraced her tightly.

'Now I've got you, and there's nothing you can do about it,' he jeered. 'Nobody here but you and me, so you'll have to be nice to me.' His fingers dug into her sharply.

Rachel concentrated on trying to get away from the man's grip.

'What I have in mind is a roll in one of those big beds, I've always fancied—' He broke off as the editor came down the stairs, but he didn't let go of Rachel.

'What are you doing?' Finlay asked coldly.

'Mind your own business. Who are you anyway, trespassing in my house? She likes a cuddle, these women are always pestering me.' Guy's face was flushed. 'Go away, before I take the whip to you!'

'Please help me,' Rachel gasped. Guy had an arm round her throat and she could hardly breathe.

Alex Finlay bent and picked up the whip in a swift movement.

'Let the girl go, or I will use this on you.' He spoke quietly, but it was clear he meant what he said. Sullenly, Guy walked away from Rachel and up to Alex. He punched the editor hard on the arm, making Alex drop the whip. He grabbed his whip and disappeared.

'That,' Rachel said to Alex, who was rubbing his arm, 'is Mr Guy Potts, the Major's son.'

'He has a medieval notion of his position, I gather. Has he hurt you, Rachel? The man's a menace, he can't be allowed to behave like that. I've never seen anything like it.'

'I have a few scratches, that's all, thank you. I try to keep out of his way. This is the second time he's interrupted a tour of the house. Please come with me, Mr Finlay, my mother will like to meet you.' Rachel led the way across from the Hall to the farm house.

Ruth Garnett had a remedy for everything, including painful shock. She welcomed Alex to the farmhouse kitchen and pre-scribed a cup of sweet tea.

'I am ashamed to think that the son of the Family treated you in this way.' Ruth's lips were compressed; she was angrier than Rachel remembered seeing her.

'I'm grateful to you, Mr Finlay. Guy is dangerous, I must be careful to keep away from him.' Rachel poured the tea into three cups. 'And I worry for our maid, Janet, she will be in danger too from that man.' The poor little maid had no confidence to begin with.

'Cook looks after Janet, she's mainly in the kitchen. But you're a better guide than me,' her mother told her. 'You can remember more of the history and you have a way with words.'

Finlay looked at Rachel and she nodded. He said to Ruth, 'She has indeed, so I've asked Rachel to send me an account of the village meeting and anything else of interest. Rachel can post her stories to me and I will send her a cheque.'

'You mean – Rachel's story will be in the paper? I suppose you'll have to correct it a lot,' Ruth said doubtfully.

Alex laughed and then winced. 'That's what editors are for, Mrs Garnett, they edit stories to make them fit. But we do need a cor-respondent in Firby. I haven't the time to ride up here very often, much as I would like to.'

'It would be a wonder if you ever came back, after today.' Ruth shook her head. 'Someone should teach that lad a lesson. He can't go round punching strangers.'

Rachel walked out with Finlay to his horse and she felt that she owed him something, after the way he had stood up to Guy.

'Miss Susan Sutton,' she began diffidently, 'when I walked down the stairs with her, asked me who you were.' She paused, then said, 'She said there aren't many intelligent men in this area.' It seemed strange to be talking to an editor like this.

'Really?' He smiled. 'I hope she included me in their number. I do hope to visit them soon and, you know, talk to them about the human cost of this project. Perhaps we can persuade Mr Sutton to fight against the dam.'

He mounted his horse and as he left Rachel said, 'It is very good to know that you are on our side, Mr Finlay.'

That night, Kit Garnett heard about Guy's behaviour during supper.

'We can't let him go on molesting poor Rachel, quite apart from upsetting a tour of the house,' Ruth said.

Kit was quiet until he'd heard the whole story. 'I will speak to the Major, he's the only person who can do anything about it. I hope he will send Guy away – the youth obviously wants to go to London. He hates living here.' He smiled grimly. 'I'm glad he's not my son. I feel sorry for the Major and Lady Agnes.'

The next day, the Major went with Kit to inspect a group of fat cattle.

'I want you to see them,' Kit explained, glad to have found his employer in a quiet frame of mind. 'If you like, we could sell them as required to the Masham butcher and ask him to send some of our beef to the Hall as part of your regular order.'

They were sleek Shorthorns, grazing quietly, a pleasant and soothing scene in the autumn sunshine. It was a good time to bring up a difficult subject.

The Major admired the cattle and agreed to the plan. On the way back through the pasture, Kit said quietly, 'I would like to talk to you about Mr Guy, sir. I am worried about him.'

The Major looked at Kit for a long moment as though he would like to dismiss him on the spot. 'Not your business, Garnett, you are insubordinate,' he barked.

Kit looked straight in front of him and said nothing.

The Major sighed. 'Selling the estate is my main concern and I do it against my will. Guy is young and has much to learn, but his future is not here. He will be an infantry army officer.'

Heaven help the poor bloody infantry, thought Kit, who never swore.

SEVEN

T HERE WAS A buzz of conversation in the room, but no heads turned as the *Herald*'s special correspondent took her seat on the night of the village meeting. Rachel wondered whether anyone would notice a farm girl taking notes, but for now the notebook was hidden under her warm shawl.

Paraffin lamps cast a mellow glow at intervals down the room. It looked like the start of a village concert, with school desks cleared away, a platform at one end of the room and at the other, the fire stacked high with logs. Sitting between Kit and Ruth, Rachel tried to count the number of people there. That would show the level of concern and should be reported.

Her scones had been delivered to the kitchen but were totally eclipsed by a row of deep yellow sponge cakes with their filling of cream. The real depth of feeling in Firby, Rachel knew, was represented by those magnificent sponges. The women who made them had felt that this was an important occasion and they had brought out their best. Should the cakes be mentioned in the report? Perhaps not, but they were truly a sign of the atmosphere in the village.

Ruth had respectfully told Lady Agnes about the meeting, but Her Ladyship had curled her lip. She never attended village events unless she was the star, the opener of the fête. Lady Agnes had nothing to say about the reservoir, for or against.

The Major had been away in the army for so long that he

hardly remembered anyone in Firby, or cared about them. He did seem to care about the estate, though, according to Kit; he had talked about planting more trees just before planning to sell.

It was good to see that the Major's friend Judge Rupert was there, leaning on a stick. He was one of the "people with influence" and he'd been a lawyer. Surely that meant he could see what was fair and right?

Jim Angram leaned over Rachel. 'See you tomorrow night, then?' He put a casual hand on her shoulder and looked curiously at the notebook and pencil on her knee. Rachel felt more than ever like a spy, but then she reflected that Jim never knew what she was thinking.

'You look well, Jim.' Ruth smiled and the lad nodded and went to stand at the back of the room with some of the other young farmers. By this time the room was full almost to bursting point and there were no seats left. Rachel made a note.

Mr Jackson, the head-teacher, stood on a platform with Grandfather Nathan, who looked handsome in an elderly way, his white hair neatly cut. In his Sunday suit, Nathan could easily be mistaken for a person with influence. His refined features wore their usual serene expression.

Mr Jackson called for silence in his strong teaching voice and an expectant hush fell on the room. He outlined the reason for the meeting and then said that a well-run meeting needed an agenda. He asked people who wished to speak to put up their hands and wait their turn.

'Our agenda falls into three parts,' Mr Jackson said. 'Firstly, we should hear from people who object to the proposal to build a reservoir here. Then, we must allow those who support the scheme to have their say. Lastly, we need to consider what can or should be done.' That, thought Rachel, gave her the main headings for the report.

There was a short silence; no one wanted to be the first to speak. Nathan Brown looked round the room and said in his quiet voice, 'I will begin, although the ideas of the young folks are more important than mine. All my life, there has been talk of a reservoir here, but I never thought it would happen.'

Older people in the audience murmured their agreement.

'Some of you will know that other valleys have been flooded, other little villages lost. I made it my business to go over to one and talk to the folks who'd been displaced.' He paused and the silence in the room was profound. 'Those folks lost their land, they lost their way of life. They were never the same again, and for some it was hard times. I reckon that some lives were cut short even. Surely it would be better to flood a valley up on moors and only displace a few ewes?'

Following his lead, several farmers spoke. Jesse Angram, Jim's father, said he couldn't understand why Firby had been chosen. 'They'd better tell us where the water will lie,' he said truculently. 'I don't know whether my farm will be lost, or whether we'll just be sitting on the edge of a great big lake. Either way, nothing will ever be as it was.'

The landlord of the Fox and Hounds agreed; he knew the depth of feeling in the village, at least among the men who drank beer. He was one of those who depended on the Major's decision. Rachel managed to record the main points of the argument.

Of course, no woman would raise her hand, although some were there with their menfolk. If a woman wanted to make a point, convention decreed that she had to persuade a man to speak for her. And yet women were half of the population and just as important as men, Rachel believed.

Several more men spoke, the blacksmith and the village joiner and undertaker among them. Then Mr Jackson called for item two of the agenda: what were the arguments in favour of the scheme? Villagers looked doubtful – were there any?

The vicar rose to his feet and cleared his throat. 'We must realize that this is God's will for Firby,' he said, his voice rolling round the room. The Reverend Jeremiah Jones had plenty of practice in pronouncing doom every Sunday; rarely did he mention love and forgiveness. Now, he looked round at his parishioners. 'It has pleased God to take away our village, we will even lose our church. We must search our hearts to know what we have done to deserve this … and repent our sins.'

Rachel stopped writing. It was too much.

From the back of the room another voice spoke. 'I'm a Methodist,' a young man said, 'and we believe the Lord helps those as help themselves.' Several brave people clapped and the gloom lifted.

Judge Rupert stood up, leaning on his stick. 'I believe,' he said in his upper-class accent, 'in progress. We must accept progress for our great county of Yorkshire. We are leading the world in manufacture and the West Riding needs the water. It is selfish of us to want to preserve our little village and few acres, if it stands in the way of progress. Manufacture is more important than farming, in England now.'

Rachel's heart sank; the man of influence was going to support the other side.

Kit said in her ear, 'He must own a factory in Leeds.'

Judge Rupert had not quite finished and Rachel saw that Mrs Walton was beside him, jogging his elbow. 'My wife's against all this, of course,' he added as an afterthought. 'She is devoted to her little farm.' He sat down heavily. Sybil Walton half-rose in her seat and Rachel hoped she would say something, but she subsided.

Nathan Brown looked round the room. 'Mr Sutton, what are your views? You stand to lose a considerable amount of land, if the scheme is approved.'

Rachel peered over her shoulder. Mr Granville Sutton, now rising to his feet, was a large man with a short white beard. Unlike most people in the room, he looked quite cheerful. 'To tell the truth, I'm undecided, that's why I didn't get into the argument. Of course, my residence is out of the danger zone, but as you say I will lose hundreds of acres of good land.' He smiled. 'If my home were to be flooded I would certainly fight against it, so in all fairness, I do sympathize with the people of Firby.' His pink face did look quite sympathetic.

A small farmer who was known to be in debt spoke next, saying that there was a lot to be said for selling the land. 'There's no brass in farming for us small men, that's a fact,' he said. 'Plenty of muck, but no brass.' Two others agreed with him.

Mr Jackson suggested that it was time to consider what could or should be done, after which they could all enjoy a cup of tea. Several women went into the kitchen to put out the cups and saucers.

Opinions on what should be done were divided. Petitions to the Lord Mayor of Leeds were voted down, but there was a general feeling that action was needed. 'Otherwise, we will feel we should have done more, when the water's lapping at our doors,' someone said.

Kit Garnett put up his hand to speak for the first time that evening. 'From what I have been able to find out, it is possible that another site could be used. But we are not going to be heard, are we? We are too small. We need the men of influence to talk on our behalf, to Members of Parliament and the leaders of Leeds Corporation. If the three major landowners were to oppose this scheme, we might have a chance to save Firby.' He paused and the only sound was the clink of cups and saucers at the back of the room. 'Two of those men of influence are here tonight.'

Mr Jackson put it to the vote, and a large majority of those present voted to ask the landowners to do as Kit suggested. Mr Brown and Mr Jackson were nominated to talk to the landowners, on behalf of the rest and to ask them to take action immediately.

Judge Rupert looked sourly round the room, but his wife smiled as though she relished a fight. She had raised her hand to vote for Kit's suggestion.

'Just before you close the meeting,' Mr Sutton said, heaving himself to his feet, 'I suggest that you arrange a second meeting, in two weeks' time. If by that time nothing can be done, well, that's an end to it. We will presume that the vicar is right and we deserve a reservoir.'

To many people, he was signing the death warrant for Firby,

judging by the mutter that ran round the room.

'That's clever,' Kit muttered. 'Not much can be done in two weeks. He must be all for the dam.'

It was a subdued group that queued at the tea urn and bit into the scones and cake. The atmosphere, Rachel noted with her pencil, was not very hopeful. One landowner was for reservoirs and progress, one was undecided and the third, Major Potts, had not bothered to attend the meeting. Was there any chance at all that the villagers would or could persuade the men of influence?

Violet, the new assistant teacher, was handing round a plate of scones and attracting attention from the young farmers.

'That young teacher won't last very long,' Ruth commented to Rachel. 'She's too pretty to stay single!'

Grandfather Nathan came over to Rachel. 'I saw you were writing things down, lass. You'll be sending a report to the *Herald*, no doubt,' he joked.

Rachel decided she might as well admit it. 'As a matter of fact, I am.... I met the editor the other day and he asked me to send him information.'

Nathan's smile widened. 'Well done, young Rachel. As I remember, you were good at writing when you were here at school. If there's anything you missed, I might be able to help.'

'Thank you, Grandfather. You've never told me I couldn't do something because I'm a girl! But don't tell anybody – Mother and Father know, but nobody else.'

Rachel was chatting to her grandfather when she saw Violet go up to Jim Angram with her plate. It was a moment missed by everybody else, but afterwards she remembered it. Jim refused the food, but he looked down at her intently, gazing into those large blue eyes. They talked for a while, then Violet gently detached herself and went back to the kitchen. Jim watched her all the way.

Kit and Ruth signalled to Rachel that it was time to go home and she joined them at the door, where Richard Sayer, the landlord of the Fox and Hounds, was waiting for a word with Kit.

'But not about the reservoir ... I'm fair worn out with worry,' he told Kit. 'It's that lad of Potts, he's a right handful. Bad behaviour whenever he comes in, drinks too much and borrows money. He'll get us a bad name, the lads won't put up with him much longer, and then they'll get the blame. Gentry never do.'

'What usually happens when a lad behaves badly?" Kit asked gently. Rachel wondered whether he had been threatening Richard's daughter, who worked with him. Guy Potts was dangerous.

'This is an orderly village and I run a quiet pub. If any of the farm boys step out of line, the rest of them put him in his place.' The landlord grinned. 'Cold water soon sobers 'em up. But none of us dare touch Guy Potts. For one thing, his pa owns some of the farms and one or two houses in the village that go with the Firby Hall estate. Guy's been hinting that if he says the word, the Major will throw us off. I suppose you know that he owns the Fox and Hounds as well.' He paused. 'And, I hate to say it, but the young lad's the heir and will own the whole estate one day. It wouldn't do to cross him. He makes that point himself.'

So practically everyone had their hands tied. 'I'll think about it,' Kit told him. 'It's not easy telling the Major anything, between you and me.'

The room was nearly empty, but two younger men hung back and now they joined Sayer. 'If you're talking about Potts, what about our money? We bought a gun apiece from him, he said they were his to sell. And then Mr Garnett here took 'em back, but we haven't seen our money yet.'

'Nor likely to,' said the other man gloomily. 'I'd love to throw him in the pond, but I daren't.'

The Dale brothers, Tom and Alfred, were a few years older than Rachel.

Kit nodded to them. 'I felt bad about it, but I had to put them back, or we'd all have been in trouble, lads. He'd say they'd been stolen and that would mean jail for the pair of you. I'll try to get your money for you.'

'I blame his bringing up,' Sayer said as he turned to go. 'Sent to boarding school, his folks always abroad, no home life. No wonder he's not human.'

'Plenty of bairns with army parents are the same, but most of them turn out well,' Ruth said quietly.

It was difficult to get out of that room. Mr Jackson stood at the door, thanking people for coming to the meeting. To Kit he said, 'There's a dead tree at the back of the school, it looks dangerous. Can you tell me who could cut it down? I would be thankful to see it gone, cut up into firewood one Saturday when the children are not at school.'

Kit thought for a moment. 'Jesse Angram would be capable, he's felled a lot of trees and young Jim could help him. I think he'd do it if you gave him some of the wood.'

In a subdued frame of mind, the Garnetts walked home in silence. Stars twinkled in one of the first frosts of the season. High and remote, a half-moon hung in the sky and far over the shadowy fields, Rachel heard a fox bark. The farm could be gone within a few years; here where they walked would be deep, cold water under the moon.

To Rachel's surprise, the lamp was lit in the kitchen when they got home and a bright fire was burning. Roger Beckwith was back, sitting by the fire with the collie Ben by his side. Ben's head lay across Roger's feet. It was a homely scene and once more Rachel realized what they would lose when the waters came.

Roger stood up politely as they came in, the lamplight shining on his hair.

'I came back unexpectedly, sorry I couldn't let you know.' The young engineer seemed to have lost his city pallor and his face had a healthy, open air look. He was much more one of them than at first. He smiled at Rachel and suddenly, she felt weak. She sat down quickly, but the overwhelming giddiness persisted.

Kit and Ruth went off to put away their coats. Roger looked steadily at Rachel, still with that smile and she gazed back at him.

'Rachel, you look beautiful tonight,' he said softly. 'It's so good to be back in Firby.'

'Roger ...' She stopped and could say no more. What was happening? For weeks Roger had been staying at the farm. She remembered that when he arrived she'd hated him, but now she was used to his presence. Why was it suddenly affecting her so much?

Kit came back into the kitchen, rubbing his hands. 'You'll need an extra blanket tonight, lad,' he said to Roger.

The dog went over to Kit and held up his bandaged leg, making them all laugh. Things in the kitchen seemed normal, but for Rachel, everything had changed. Roger had looked at her with love.

'I kept the fire going for you, since it's such a cold night,' Roger said apologetically. 'I hope you don't mind.'

Of course they didn't mind; Kit told him he was like one of the family. Often, when they were all at home and had a visitor, Roger went quietly off to read in bed. He never seemed to be in the way and they enjoyed his company.

'You're the best boarder we've ever had,' Kit told him.

Somehow, Rachel got to her feet and made them all a cup of tea. 'Tired, love?' her mother asked. 'It's been a long day.'

By tomorrow, she would feel normal again. This feeling was just tiredness after all, due to the concentration needed to take notes at the meeting. Roger wanted to know what had happened at the meeting and Kit told him. He offered to talk to Nathan and Mr Jackson again, and to try to get Mr Bromley to consider the other site.

Rachel went to bed in a strange frame of mind. When she looked in the dressing table mirror, the face that looked back was pale and strained, but the eyes were bright. Roger was back; it was surprising how happy that made her.

Roger sometimes went to Pateley on Sundays, to see old friends. One was Mrs Watson, a widow who had been a friend of his mother. 'You're a grand lad,' she often told him, after he had chopped firewood for her and done other little jobs in the house and garden. 'You deserve a good wife.'

'I can only hope, Mrs Watson,' he said. What could he offer a young woman? He had no farm and no property ... he was well-educated and had a good job, but that might not be enough for a country girl.

On the Saturday after his return, he found that his horse was slightly lame. Kit examined the leg and hoof and thought that with rest, it should recover. That meant no Sunday ride to Pateley. Roger went for a brisk walk in the morning and sat down to write letters in the early afternoon.

On Sunday afternoon, the Garnett family went to visit Nathan Brown for a cup of tea. As always, they had to be home for the evening milking and feeding routine, but it was a fine day and Ruth said a ride out in the trap would do her good. Rachel went with them.

'Jim may come over for tea, but we'll be home by then,' she said.

Roger had nearly finished his letters when he had a visitor. A knock at the door was followed by the entry of Jim Angram, washed and changed for Sunday afternoon.

'Where's Rachel? Gone to see Grandpa, has she?' Jim was not put out, but sat at the table as usual. 'They'll be home for milking, that's for sure.'

Jim entertained Roger with stories of clever sheepdogs they had owned. Then he said, 'Do you mind talking about the dam? I'd like to know that our farm won't be flooded, whatever happens,' he said.

'We can look at the plans,' Roger offered. 'It's not the end of the story, of course, but if Firby is to be the site, the lines have been drawn.' He unrolled a big map of the area. 'Now, where exactly is your farm?'

They bent over the map and followed the contours of the scheme, as planned by Bromley and Roger for Leeds Corporation. The Angrams' farm was just above the line; they would only lose a few acres.

'That's good, I was hoping it would be there for me to take over when Pa retires.'

'That won't be for some years?' Roger asked.

'Nay, I'm in no hurry,' Jim grinned. 'I like things the way they are.'

Roger hesitated, then looked across at the lad. 'And – you're going to marry Rachel, I gather?'

'Of course I am,' said Jim carelessly. 'She's a right good worker, the lass is.'

So however casual he was, Jim claimed ownership of Rachel. Roger's heart sank; there was no chance for him. Over the past few weeks he had fallen in love with somebody else's girl.

Jim was looking at him carefully. 'I've an idea that you might fancy Rachel,' he said slowly. 'Well, I'm warning you off, Roger Beckwith. She's my lass and I want you to remember that. Can't be helped, you spend time with her when you're boarding here. But don't you go putting ideas in her head. She's only a woman, after all and women's heads can be … turned, by a nice-looking young man.'

'Jim, I give you my word that I will not turn Rachel's head.' They shook hands.

EIGHT

THE OCTOBER SUN shone through the window and the warm smell of baking bread filled the kitchen. Rachel put more wood on the fire to keep the oven temperature constant and then tried to concentrate on making a batch of scones, but Roger's presence was distracting. She knew that he would soon be gone from their lives, back to his work in the city. Why should this make her feel desolate?

Rolling out the scone mixture, Rachel worked automatically. Her future was with Jim Angram; the farm he would eventually own was just above the valley and the doom of flood water. She was lucky to have such a safe future planned for her. It was wicked to wish otherwise, to feel the attraction of another man.

'Have you seen the Fewston reservoir, over near Otley? That was filled about fifteen years ago, water for Leeds.' Roger sat at the kitchen table with a sheaf of drawings. 'Before that, they built Swinsty.' He paused. 'If you've seen them, you'll know what a big job this is. Bromley and I have drawn up plans for Firby, while I was in Leeds. I thought you might like to see them. This is only a first stage, of course.'

So it would go ahead – this was the beginning of the end. Rachel didn't want to look at the map.

'You're too young to remember,' Kit told him. 'Two good watermills were demolished when Fewston was built – and they used the stone to build a wall round the dam.'

Rachel tried to imagine Firby's little valley with all the stone houses in ruins, men carting away the stone … it was like a nightmare. Alex Finlay was expecting another report soon for the *Herald*. 'Our correspondent' should perhaps describe how the lovely old buildings of Firby village would be knocked down and the stones, carefully dressed by stone masons long gone, would be used to build the embankment that would halt the flow of the river and cause the water to rise. *Herald* readers needed to be confronted – especially the men of influence. Rachel knew that the Major read the *Herald* … but it was probably too late.

Her father echoed Rachel's thoughts. 'I suppose we have to face it, lad. Everything is going to change – we'll have to find somewhere to live, as well as work to do.'

'You might get a job as supervisor, they will need skilled men as well as labourers,' Roger said. He seemed more subdued than usual. 'They will need new roads above the water line and a little railway to cart stone from the quarry. The embankment will be built right across the width of the valley, to dam the river flow and hold in the water. It's a huge job, will take years. They will build huts for the workers up here, and workshops.' He indicated a spot on the map.

Kit bent over the table, interested in the practical details, but Rachel had heard enough for her next report. Putting the scones in the oven, she went across the yard to the dairy. At this time of year there was less milk to be handled, but Kit had bought three newly calved cows so that there would be enough milk, cream and butter for the whole household.

Skimming cream from the top of the large, shallow setting pans took concentration and Rachel tried to shut out thoughts of the future from her mind. A large shadow fell across the doorway and she looked up to see Lady Agnes bearing down on her with purpose. Her Ladyship never did anything by halves.

'Garnett, or Rachel, I suppose I must call you,' she boomed. 'It's too confusing to have three servants with the same name. Now, girl, the Major and I would like some cheese. I have asked for cheese before, but to no avail. I suppose you can make cheese?'

'Er ... not very well, m'lady. I've not had much experience, we have mostly made butter to sell.' Rachel stood dutifully beside the cream pans.

'Why not cheese to sell? It keeps longer than butter, I think. Surely it's not too difficult to make cheese.' Lady Agnes looked round the dairy critically. 'And you have plenty of room here.'

Rachel stood up straight. 'Lady Agnes, cheese-making takes a lot of time. I can make cream cheese of course, but for hard cheese you need a cheese press and other things. It takes all day to make and months for hard cheese to ripen.' She remembered Grandmother Brown's delicious Wensleydale cheese. If only she were still alive and could help now!

'Well, get Garnett to make a cheese press!' the woman said impatiently.

It was hard to find the courage to speak to Lady Agnes. 'It's nearly winter, m'lady, and cheese are usually made in spring and summer. For several reasons—'

Rachel broke off as she saw two young men ride into the yard. They both dismounted, strode over to the dairy and looked inside. Rachel knew them, they were neighbours, the brothers Tom and Alfred Dale.

'Good day, Rachel, where's your father? We want to talk to him about Guy Potts.' Tom looked serious.

'I'll fetch him, just wait here,' Rachel said, trying to edge them away from the dairy, but it was too late.

'What about Mr Potts? I think you need to speak to me, not to Garnett.' Lady Agnes came out into the yard and looked down her long nose at the young farmers, who were not tenants of the Potts and therefore not known to her. 'I am his mother,' she announced.

The brothers looked confused for a moment, but then Alfred spoke. 'Well, m'lady, we didn't know you were there. We don't want to cause trouble, we were just going to ask Kit Garnett ...'

'For his advice,' finished Tom. 'It's a matter of brass, we wouldn't want to trouble you with it.'

'I insist you tell me immediately, if it has to do with my son.'

Alfred took a deep breath and his broad, outdoor face went red. 'Well, ma'am, your son sold us a gun apiece. Both same, single-barrelled shotguns they were, as he said belonged to him. He wanted some cash, so we paid him five pounds each. That's a lot of brass for small farmers. But then we heard Kit Garnett was looking for two guns, same description, gone missing – he'd spent time looking for them in Bluebell Wood. I thought I should tell him what we bought.'

'So we handed them back, and Mr Garnett took 'em, see,' Tom added. 'And we really need to get our money back, but we can't get it.'

'There has obviously been a misunderstanding,' Lady Agnes said loftily. At that moment Guy Potts slouched into the yard in riding clothes, whip in hand. He started when he saw the Dale brothers.

'What are you doing here? You are trespassing.' He looked at his mother. 'Have they been pestering you?'

'Do you owe these men money?' Lady Agnes glared at her son.

'Of course not. I don't know what you're talking about. Now excuse me, Mama, I must go, I have an appointment in Masham.' He strode towards the stables, but as he passed the men, Guy brought down the whip on Alfred's shoulders. 'Be off with you, before I call the constable!'

Alfred put up his fists and turned to go after Guy, but his brother restrained him. 'Nay, lad, you'll only get us into bother,' he said calmly. 'Lady Agnes will want to see fair play, she'll get brass for us, now she's heard about it.' He looked hopefully towards the lady.

'You expect me to believe you, when my son knows nothing of what you say?' Her Ladyship spoke coldly.

Alfred rubbed his shoulders. 'Surely you can see what sort of a man he is? He's dangerous.'

There was a clatter as Guy rode furiously out of the yard; Donald the groom had obviously got the horse ready for him. The

Dales' horses moved restlessly and the brothers turned to go. Lady Agnes swept away without a word, to Rachel's relief. Would she ever face the truth about her son?

The Hall Shorthorn cows were eating hay just over the fence and the Dales crossed the yard to look at them.

'Kit's got a good eye for a beast,' Tom said generously. He looked at Rachel. 'What will you folks do when they build the dam? There's not so many places for a family like yours.'

Rachel shook her head.

'Did you see that piece in the *Herald* about our meeting?' Alfred asked. 'It were right good.'

'Aye,' said his brother. 'That might ginger things up a bit!'

Rachel promised to speak to her father about the guns and went back to her cream. It was good to think that perhaps her reports in the *Herald* might 'ginger things up' after all.

Lady Agnes was annoyed by the Dale brothers and their lack of respect for their betters, but a cold doubt began to creep in as she went back to the Hall. Guy had behaved badly, taking his whip to that man. What if he had sold the guns? Perhaps he needed some discipline, she thought.

'Charles, I think you should try to have some influence with Guy,' she told the Major, who was reading the account of the Firby meeting in the newspaper. 'We have spent very little time with him, after all. Do you realize we have been in India for most of Guy's life? I feel that he may be a little too – headstrong. He was rude to me the other day and today, he took his whip to a young farmer. I saw it.'

Major Potts yawned. 'Boys will be boys. He doesn't have any occupation, that's his trouble. Guy should be in the army, the sooner the better and whether he likes it or not. I have an idea he's drinking too much.' He waved his hand at the *Herald*. 'Have you seen this column about the new dam? The peasants are hoping I will vote against it. They seem to think it can be stopped.'

'And will you? Charles, I would much rather stay here than see our home taken for a reservoir.' Lady Agnes picked up the paper.

'Of course we have to sell, Agnes, I thought you realized that,' the Major barked impatiently. 'What with our shares and Guy's debts there's no choice. This project is providential, gets us out of trouble. Guy owes a lot of money, and I'm not sure we know the whole story.'

'Yes,' said Guy's mother quietly. 'He is a liability. Can I not persuade you to keep the estate, Charles? Sell the London house and send Guy into the army.'

'It's not as simple as that.'

'All the time we lived in India, you talked about coming back to Firby, holding pheasant shoots, planting trees … you were going to make it the best estate in Yorkshire. Charles, you would not be happy without your land.'

Lady Agnes was still brooding about the sale of the estate the next day, when her cousin Sybil paid a visit. Of course Firby Hall was shabby compared with the Waltons' gracious abode, but it had one advantage: its great age and long history. To show these off, it was necessary to take visitors up to the Long Gallery and impress them with portraits and panelling.

Fortunately when Sybil arrived it was raining, so a stroll in the grounds was not possible. Sybil was wearing a walking skirt that cleared the ground, of a practical dark green, flaring from a tiny waist. Her smart hat was topped with a bow and beside her, Agnes felt rather dowdy in her grey afternoon dress. The Long Gallery might compensate for her lack of fashion.

Sybil's reaction soothed Agnes' spirits. 'It's years since I saw this room, isn't it divine? We have nothing like this at the Grange….' She studied the portraits for a while and then said, 'I have a particular reason for this visit, Agnes. What do you think of the reservoir project?' She looked up at the taller woman earnestly. 'Do you want to lose this lovely old house and all the estate? I thought when you came back from India this time, you might settle down – if the Major agreed. We talked about breeding Dexter cattle, did we not?'

Agnes thought for a moment; she must watch her words. 'I

would love to stay here and I have several plans for the farm. But I fear that the reservoir is a fait accompli, my dear. It is bound to happen. Charles is ... resigned to selling the property.'

They sat in one of the deep window seats and Sybil arranged her skirt carefully around her. 'Well, Rupert and I were at the village meeting, you know. It does seem that if the landowners, that is to say Rupert, Charles and Granville Sutton, were to oppose the scheme, then the Leeds Corporation might look elsewhere.' She laughed. 'And I rather think it is up to us, weak women though we are, to help them to change their minds.'

'What does Rupert think? Surely, he would be devastated to lose Willow Grange, especially after all your improvements.' Agnes felt a spark of interest; it could be a good fight.

'Oh, Rupert stood up and spoke of progress, trying to put a good face on things. He didn't want to be seen to be coerced into selling. Since then he seems to have realized just what it would mean to lose the land. And where would we go? He is so proud of our landscaping and improvements, but all that work would be lost ... Leeds Corporation are not going to pay any more for landscaped grounds or well-kept farms.'

'What about Granville Sutton? We haven't seen him since we came home.'

'At the meeting, Sutton said he was undecided ... if Rupert does agree to oppose it, I will ask him to speak to Sutton.'

'A special Act of Parliament would be needed, I believe,' said Agnes thoughtfully. 'My brother Peregrine sits in the Lords, of course ... and he loves a good fight. He's well known for it.'

'Do you think Lord Danby would use his influence?' Sybil asked eagerly.

'I will write to him. Meanwhile, you and I should talk to our husbands, I think. Let's go down to the drawing room and drink tea.' Agnes led the way to the stairs.

While Agnes was entertaining her visitor, the Major was giving some thought to organizing a pheasant shoot. With no gamekeeper on the estate, the number of pheasants was small, but it would be a pleasant day out with the neighbours.

Instead of riding round the estate, he decided to walk. It would give him a better idea of where to place the guns; it was years since he'd walked these fields and copses.

The day was mild, with the nostalgic smells of autumn rising from the damp woods. Carrying a shotgun in case of rabbits, the Major walked the once familiar paths. For days he had been trying to put the loss of the estate to the back of his mind, but now it came back with great force. He did not want to lose his home. Damn that boy and his gambling! Without Guy's debts, he would have put up a fight to keep the land.

Major Potts had realized with some surprise that he was calmer, better in health and temper, since coming home to Firby. The last few months in Madras had been hectic and he had no wish to go back to the regiment, especially in the heat of southern India. When the estate was sold, he supposed they could live in London.

Pheasants rose with a whirr of wings at his approach. The Major opened a gate into the wood and noted that the fence was repaired and the gate swung easily. Garnett was a good foreman, no doubt, a useful man to carry out improvements. But it was too late now to make plans for the farm's future.

He walked through the trees and came to a cottage at the far side, where a retired farm worker lived, Daniel Wood. As the Major approached, Daniel looked over his garden fence.

'Good day, Major! We've not seen you for many a year. Will ye step in for a cup of tea?'

'Why not?' The gun was unloaded and the Major went into the cottage, where Daniel had lived alone since his wife died.

It was surprising how pleasant it was to sit by a cottage fire, to drink black tea and talk about the old days with one of the peasants.

'There's not so many take up farming, these days. There's cottages empty in the village. The young ones, they don't want to stay here, they're off to the town,' Daniel said wistfully when asked about his children. 'I expect your young gentleman will be the same?'

'Just the same,' the Major said grimly.

Daniel had plenty of time to think, he told the Major, and he thought that breeding pheasants would be a good idea. 'If you was to hire a keeper, now, sir, his wages could be paid if you let out the shooting,' he suggested. 'Folks pay good money these days for a shoot and think on, Firby Hall's big enough for a fair-sized syndicate. You could turn a profit.'

The Major laughed. 'I suppose you have the keeper's job in mind for yourself?'

'Nay, I'm ower old for chasing poachers, it's a young man's job, Major. Up half the night in the season, watching for villains. And then if you shoot a few foxes, the hunt's on to you, but you got to control foxes. I could rear a few pheasants round here for ye though, if I had a bit of grain.' Daniel scratched his head. 'Give me summat to do, like.'

'There's not much point,' his landlord said shortly. 'The estate will go when the reservoir is built.'

'Nay, it's not all ower yet.' Daniel's eyes were bright as he looked across the hearth at his visitor. 'Excuse my plain speaking, Major, but I've known you since you were a lad. Now, if you read yon *Herald* newspaper, it says that you can fight those Leeds folks. You and the old Judge and Mr Sutton.'

'You think I should?'

'Aye, that I do,' said the old man earnestly. 'How could you ever find as good a place as this to spend your days, Major? You couldn't and that's a fact.' He paused and in the silence, a robin piped outside the window, a reminder of the coming winter. 'I'll say no more, but we all depend on you to save Firby Hall.'

In a thoughtful mood, the Major walked back to the Hall by a different route. Old Daniel had made him wonder whether even at this late hour, it could be possible to save the estate. Why should Guy be allowed to wreck the lives of so many people, because of his debts? 'How could you ever find a place as good as this to spend your days...' Daniel was right.

Looking across the farm land, crops and pasture, the Major remembered the plans he'd made in India. It would have been good to try some of the new scientific farming methods and the improved breeds of cattle and sheep. He was surprised to see a figure stumbling towards him as he got closer to home.

Guy was walking badly and clearly annoyed. 'Where've you been? Ma sent me to look for you, she thought you must have fallen over or something,' he said crossly. 'I hate walking through wet grass.'

'You should do more walking, you're out of condition.' The Major avoided looking at the youth. Nobody should speak like that to a parent. The coming generation had no manners at all.

'Lord, Pa, I'm not a horse!'

They walked in silence for a while and then Guy said, 'How long before you sell up, Pa? I desperately need to get my hands on some money – but if I can say when the debts will be paid—'

Resisting the urge to shout, the Major felt his face go red. 'What would you say if I told you we will not sell the estate?' He spoke to annoy his son, but the words held some comfort. What if...?

Guy looked ready to explode. 'You can't say that! I need the money and in any case, I don't want to inherit this hole, I'm going to live in London!' He glared at his father. 'Your life's nearly over, it doesn't matter to you if the place is sold. It's selfish to hang on to your money when I need it. Don't you understand I need the money now?'

It was like the calm before going into action. Major Potts felt that he could at last see clearly what needed to be done. Guy had pushed him too far.

It was up to his parents to save this young man from himself, to preserve the way of life they had and to keep the valley safe for the so-called peasants. For the first time, he wondered fleetingly what the Garnett family would do if the estate were to be sold. He had taken them for granted, but they were all good servants.

'I have made up my mind,' he said quietly. 'You will go into the army and if necessary, I will sell off one of the farms to buy you a commission. But not to pay debts. We will not sell the estate in my lifetime!'

Guy flounced away cursing, and the Major was left to reflect that he would need to convince his fellow landowners of the need to save the valley. But the decision gave him profound relief. Agnes, bless her, had suggested they sell the London house and she also had plans to make the farm pay. With army methods of organization, he was sure he would succeed.

NINE

KIT GARNETT WAS given precise instructions about the forth-coming pheasant shoot. The Major was brisk, but in a good humour as he talked to his surrogate gamekeeper. Kit wondered privately what had happened to make the Major less irritable.

'I hope you can find a few pheasants, Garnett. My father's keeper used to sprinkle oats on the edge of Bluebell Wood to encourage them ... in the good old days. I suppose there will be beaters available? I think we will need beaters.' He sighed. 'It won't be anything like a tiger shoot. A tiger shoot is most exciting, I can tell you. We hunt from elephants.'

Thank goodness our only problem is pheasants, Kit said to himself. 'Life in Firby must be very different after living in India, Major. Yes, sir, I can find beaters....'

Young farm workers were often pleased to earn a shilling or two and have a change of scene, if they could get away from their work for a few hours to drive the pheasants nearer to the guns.

In the farmhouse kitchen, there was a family conference as Ruth made her plans for the lunch. Lady Agnes had decided the menu: leek soup, roast venison and apple pie. The six or eight guests were to take lunch in the main hall of the old manor house; there would be more if they brought their wives. The beaters would be given their meal separately, in a small room off the hall, where they could enjoy themselves without the constraint of being with their superiors.

Knocking, Jim Angram came into the kitchen that morning. 'I've come to ask a favour, Mr Garnett,' he said. 'On Saturday, Mr Jackson wants us to knock down that old tree at the school, but as you know the big saw needs two men. My father's hurt his back, so I wondered if you'd help me. It shouldn't take long.'

Kit agreed, because as he said later, he thought the job needed a man with experience. Jim was very steady for a young lad, but he was only twenty-three.

'There's a shoot here this Saturday, but I can help you the week after,' he promised. 'Would you like to come as a beater on the shoot, Jim?'

'Aye, Mr Garnett, I'd like that.' Rachel handed Jim a cup of tea. 'Have you seen the *Herald* this week? It makes you think, you know.' Jim sat at the table and took a scone. 'All about moving folks out of Firby, knocking down the houses and school and that ... is it worth felling the tree, or doing owt else, if all's to be flooded?' He paused for a bite. 'But all the same, the chap who wrote it says that there's a slight chance they could build it up on the moors, the dam I mean. He must know summat. Beckwith says that our farm won't be flooded, we're higher up than you are here.'

Rachel turned away to hide her confusion. Perhaps she should have told Jim that she was the 'correspondent', but it seemed so unusual for a farm lass. She loved writing for the *Herald*, posting off her story every week and it was good to be paid for the work. But if folks knew about it, they might think she was getting above herself. Firby folk didn't like that.

Jim didn't seem to notice Rachel's blush, or Ruth's quiet smile. 'My ma asked me to say we're killing pig tomorrow; if you'd like some black pudding you could come and help.' The two families usually helped each other at such times and shared the meat.

Rachel looked at her mother, knowing that the pheasant shoot was going to cause extra work.

'I'll be working things out with Cook tomorrow, and Janet can clean the big dining room. You go to help Jim, love,' Ruth said.

'Well, Jim, if Mother can spare me I'll be glad to come. You know I'm the best sausage maker in the dale!' That at least was a suitable skill for Rachel Garnett.

'You're right good at it, lass,' Jim said lightly. 'That's why I'm courting you, isn't it?'

Was that a good reason to marry a girl – because she was a good sausage maker?

It wasn't very romantic – and neither was an invitation to a pig killing. It would have been good to be invited to a day out at Pateley Show, but Jim hadn't mentioned it. Afterwards, Rachel had found out that Jim had gone to the show with neighbours. Is this how Cinderella might have felt?

The farm men took a cartload of big logs to the house that week. 'These pheasant shoots make a sight of work,' one of them said to Kit.

'Aye, we'll just have to go a bit faster, then,' Kit replied in the time-honoured way of foremen, and they both laughed. 'We're all in it together and we want the Hall to look good to the visitors. First time for years that we've had a shoot, so we mustn't grumble.'

On the morning of the shoot, Janet the housemaid lit a huge fire in the old dining room, to make it ready for the luncheon. For some of the Guns this was the highlight of the day, good food and drink and the talk at the table. It was sometimes an important forum for local politics. It was a long time since there had been such a gathering at Firby Hall, which made it that much more interesting.

Kit assembled his group of beaters and told them where to stand and what to do when they were given a signal; most of them had done it before. Some of the lads wore light-coloured clothing, not wanting to risk being peppered with shotgun pellets.

'One shoot I was on, the gaffer gave us white jackets,' Kit was told by an older man who had come to Firby from another dale.

'You'll just have to trust the men with the guns,' he was told. 'It's not a big shoot, we should be safe enough and the guests all have years of experience.'

The Major was out early. 'My son is coming with us,' he said rather grimly. 'But he's still in bed.'

Kit got the feeling that the son and heir was in the Major's black books. He hoped that this would lead to some discipline; surely his parents must know by now that Guy was causing too much trouble.

The visitors did not bring grooms, but drove themselves. Donald Metcalfe met them, parked the traps in a row and stabled the horses. Some of them had brought gun dogs of various breeds.

Judge Walton had brought his wife, who came to watch the shoot and visit her cousin Agnes. Mr Sutton rolled up in a stylish gig driven by his daughter, who looked as though she would like to race the vehicle. Mr Sutton was obviously very proud of his valuable Labrador retriever; it sat just behind him, quietly waiting for orders and ignoring the other dogs, as it was supposed to do. Kit hoped that Guy wouldn't manage to shoot it.

In fact, Guy was the chief danger to the success of the shoot and Kit intended to keep as close an eye on him as he could. The youth was careless with a gun and what was worse, callous. He had never asked how the collie Ben was recovering, or apologized for shooting him. Never before had Kit had to deal with a problem like this. It seemed to have no solution.

The men stood about in the drive for a while, discussing the merits of their guns and admiring the dogs. Serving coffee in the entrance hall to the ladies, Rachel was noticed by Miss Sutton.

'I promised to bring my father here, to remind him of the importance of your historic house,' she said to Lady Agnes. 'And I would like this young woman to show him round if possible, after the shoot. She explains the history very well.'

Rachel smiled dutifully. 'Thank you, Miss Sutton.' Would there be a chance to speak to him about the reservoir – and would he take any notice if she did?

'Well, Susan, if you can persuade him that the reservoir should not be built here, that will be a good thing,' Lady Sybil boomed.

As Rachel collected the cups, she heard Mrs Walton tell

her cousin Agnes that she had been working hard to convince Rupert to fight against the dam project. She said quietly, 'He was impressed by the articles in the *Herald*. He'll be talking about it to Charles today.'

Rachel nearly dropped her tray as her heart gave a leap. Mr Finlay had been right when he talked about the power of the press. Would people believe her stories though, if they knew who had written them? 'Our Correspondent' sounded like an important person – a man, of course. The editor had known what he was doing.

Then Mrs Walton added, 'But Rupert knows a lot of legal men, of course, and he says that no one can save Firby from the water.' Rachel's heart took a downward dive.

The shooting party moved off, Guy catching up at the last minute.

'Be careful with the gun, Mr Guy,' Kit told him sternly and the young heir scowled.

Kit followed the group, watching out for trouble. He wasn't expected to shadow his employer as some keepers did; the Major liked to load the gun for himself. Major Potts was a good shot and had won shooting competitions in his youth.

A few pheasants flew over, flushed out by the beaters walking in a line; the guns popped and the dogs retrieved. By lunch time, Kit was beginning to relax. He knew that the luncheon would last for about two hours in all, since it was a social occasion. Then he planned to take the group to the other side of the estate, where the birds hadn't yet been disturbed.

The old dining hall looked inviting, transformed by the huge log fire. The silver cutlery, cleaned by Rachel, sparkled on the polished oak refectory table. For hundreds of years this room had seen feasting, as well as meetings and probably one or two conspiracies.

Kit took the gentlemen Guns in to luncheon and then went to sit in the back room with the beaters. 'So far, so good,' he said to Rachel.

At one end of the long table, Judge Rupert sat deep in conversation with Major Potts and Granville Sutton, the three men of influence together. Guy Potts sat with them, his face black with temper. As the roast was eaten, one or two of the other men glanced at them from time to time. Eventually Mr Murray, a local solicitor leaned over the table with a smile. 'Are you gentlemen going to save our valley, or not? That's what we'd all like to know!'

A young farmer laughed at this. 'Murray will be looking for a fee, if you're going to fight the dam,' he warned. 'It could be a long battle, too. That venison was very good, Major!'

Rachel was carrying plates out to the kitchen and dared not wait for the reply; when she came back to the dining room with dessert, others were giving their opinion on the project. But it seemed that Mr Sutton was not now in favour of a second village meeting about the reservoir.

'Waste of time, now, the way things are,' he said. That was not encouraging ... did he mean they had all given up?

Rachel was proud of her mother's housekeeping that day and even Her Ladyship was satisfied. Everything went well, the guests enjoyed their meal and the cook was commended by all the guests.

After the meal was over and the guests had moved outside again, Kit realized that Guy had been drinking. It was usual to offer the guests wine with the meal, but keen sportsmen usually drank little, for fear of spoiling their aim. There had been several partly empty decanters of wine on the table and he must have finished them off.

The shooting party drove their vehicles to the other side of the estate, where Daniel Wood was waiting to take charge of the horses, 'delighted to be doing summat,' as he put it. He would probably be given tips by the Guns. Kit drove the Major, Guy and a couple of beaters. It was hard to ignore Guy's suppressed fury; what had annoyed him? His scowl had deepened and he was fidgety.

Keeping close to Guy and the Major, Kit watched as the event unfolded. Guy was flushed and unsteady when he got down from

101

the vehicle, probably not safe with a gun, but the Major ignored him. The young man hung back a little, muttering to himself as the party moved off and Kit decided to walk beside him.

'Miserable old codger ... the old man won't help me. And you're as bad. You know Garnett, when I inherit, the first thing I'll do is turn you off, along with your miserable family! Then I'll sell the place and live in London.' He glanced at Kit, daring him to retaliate, trying to force a quarrel.

You didn't argue with the Family. Kit said reasonably, 'We'll all be gone long before you inherit, Mr Guy. The reservoir will cover this land.'

Guy spluttered and said thickly, 'No it won't! My father and the other two old geezers, Walton and Sutton, they've all got together and they're going to work with my uncle Peregrine, Lord Danby as well ... they're going to tell Leeds Corporation to go to hell. They have it all worked out, to keep their mi-miserable acres ...'

'Well, that's good news!' Kit said, and meant it. 'Nobody wants a reservoir here, Mr Guy.'

'It's terrible, he's got to sell! I need the money now,' Guy stuttered. They stood behind a group of men who had come to a halt.

The beaters advanced. Several pheasants flew overhead and Guy threw up his gun to his shoulder, but instead of aiming for a bird, he brought the barrel lower. With a frenzied look on his face he was aiming straight at the Major, who had his head turned away.

As Guy fired, Kit deflected the gun downwards with his stick and the pellets went harmlessly into the ground. Weak with relief he said to the youth, 'What on earth do you think you're doing? You could have killed him!' The other men were watching where the birds fell and sending their dogs in.

His face twisted with fury, Guy turned the gun on Kit. The trigger clicked.

'Only one barrel, son,' Kit said as calmly as he could and speaking quietly, so as not to draw attention to the incident. The fact that he'd given Guy a single-barrelled gun had probably saved his life.

Kit took a deep breath and went up to Guy. 'Now give that gun to me, you're not fit to carry it.' He realized his hands were shaking. 'You nearly shot your father and you tried to kill me. You're too drunk to know what you're doing.' The man was mad, a potential killer. But had he known what he was doing ... and fired in cold blood?

Guy swore, but he saw another man watching so he handed over the gun. Kit put it in the Firby Hall trap and the youth lurched off, disappearing into the wood.

'Well done, Garnett,' a voice said beside him. Granville Sutton had seen the whole thing; the others had been a little ahead, looking skyward at the birds. 'Do you think it was intentional?' he asked in a low voice. 'Can't wait for his inheritance?' The pink face looked anxious. 'I couldn't believe my eyes!'

'I hope not, Mr Sutton. It doesn't bear thinking of.'

'He's the worse for drink, of course. A bad business ... I suppose I should have a word with the Major.' Mr Sutton stroked his beard. 'You certainly acted quickly, he owes his life to you.'

Miss Sutton had spent the afternoon with the Guns and walked the fields in her stout boots, but she was still keen to show her father the old house before they went home. Rachel took a candlestick with her, explaining that she didn't want to be caught in the dark.

'Is there a ghost?' Susan asked. 'I would love to see one! Now, Father, you must agree that this house is unique. There are very few Elizabethan manor houses in our part of the world. What a pity it would be, if it were to be lost!'

Rachel led them up the wide staircase into the Long Gallery and as she expected, Mr Sutton was impressed. 'I haven't been here since I was a boy, although I've visited the Potts in their wing of the house, the last time they were at home,' he told Rachel. 'I'd forgotten all about it until Susan said she'd been here.' He walked forward to inspect the fireplace and Rachel looked at his daughter.

'You may remember the last time I was here,' Miss Sutton said quietly. 'The gentleman who visited that day has since been to the Chase, to get my father's opinion about the reservoir project. He's the editor of the *Herald*, as you may have found out by now.' She smiled. 'He got on well with my father and he's coming to dinner with us next week.'

'Yes, miss, he gave me his name after you had gone.' Rachel wondered whether this was the start of a romance.

Mr Sutton wanted to know the history of the house, but Rachel cut it short; dusk was falling and the long room was already full of shadows.

'Now, Papa, do you agree that you should work with the Major and Judge Rupert to fight against the reservoir? It's not just the old house and all the history, although that is irreplaceable. It's the effect on a whole village and the good valley land that will be lost. Some of our best land will be under the water. We can't let that happen!'

Rachel sighed with relief; his daughter was doing what she had steeled herself to do. Mr Sutton looked down at the women from his great height.

'What do you know?' he said suddenly to Rachel. 'The young engineer is living here at the farm, I hear. He has probably told you how the scheme is going.'

'Yes, sir, he has,' Rachel said. She took a deep breath. 'Mr Beckwith believes that if you, the Major and Sir Rupert will all agree to use your influence, it's possible the dam could be built higher on the moor, rather than on good agricultural land.' She paused, but he was smiling at her. 'I do so hope you will agree.'

In the following silence, Rachel thought she heard quiet footsteps on the stairs; the ghost of Firby Hall might be on their side. The room seemed a little colder.

'You can tell your father that we do agree, as of today, although Judge Rupert believes it's a lost cause.' Sutton turned to go down the stairs, but then looked back at Rachel.

'Garnett is a very competent and reliable man. He averted a tragedy this afternoon. He deserves to know that there is a slight chance of saving the valley.'

'No doubt it will take time, Papa?' his daughter asked, probably wondering what tragedy had been averted.

'It will, but I for one am prepared to spend time. It's not just the land, is it, Miss Garnett? It's the people, the village, their whole way of life. Finlay made me see the truth of it.'

Miss Sutton smiled as they left. 'Thank you, Miss Garnett. You are a very capable housekeeper.'

When the Garnetts gathered for supper in the farmhouse kitchen, there was plenty to report. The shoot had been successful; there would be some pheasants for the butcher in Masham. A brace had been reserved for the Major and Lady Agnes, but Ruth knew she would need to hang them in the pantry for at least a week before they were mature enough for the Major's taste.

Kit had decided to say as little as possible about Guy's behaviour, apart from warning his family to keep well clear of him. But Rachel reported what Mr Sutton had said and asked, 'What was the tragedy you averted, Father? It sounds very dramatic.'

'Did you notice Guy drinking at lunch time?' Kit asked.

Rachel nodded. 'He drank what was left of the wine after the guests had gone outside again. I wished I'd taken it away before he got his hands on it. I couldn't stop him, of course.'

'He should never have been allowed back on the shoot. The idiot nearly shot the Major,' Kit said briefly. 'Sutton saw what happened and said he would speak to his father.'

'He was in a terrible temper, all through the lunch.' Rachel looked at Kit. 'He was listening to his father, Judge Walton and Mr Sutton ... I wondered at the time what they said to upset him, but it must have been about the reservoir. Mr Sutton told me to let you know, they all agreed to fight the reservoir project.'

Kit said happily. 'The Major as well ... he's changed his mind. But Guy is desperate for him to sell. That's all he can think of.' His smile faded. 'I have never before met a human being with no conscience, no thought for others.'

Rachel agreed. 'I believe that Guy is insane.'

TEN

JIM ANGRAM LIKED chopping down trees. He enjoyed the hard physical work of sawing and the sharp smell of newly-cut wood. There was a hint of danger in tackling objects so much bigger than yourself and a sense of satisfaction in cutting them down. Normally he worked with his father, a cautious man, but Jim was sure he could manage quite well, going on past experience. Kit would be necessary only because the big saw needed two men.

He collected Kit Garnett on the following Saturday morning, his trap full of saws and axes, ropes and log splitters. Rachel waved to Jim from the wash house, not realizing that this day would change the course of their lives. Ben the collie was on guard as usual, sitting outside the door.

This was a new beginning, the first day of Rachel's new cheese-making project, to produce the hard cheese Lady Agnes was so keen to get her teeth into. Now that the fear of flooding had receded a little, the lady was bent upon increasing the farm produce, for sale as well as for home consumption. If possible, she wanted Christmas cheese to sell in Masham in December, which was not very far away.

To make cheese you had to keep the milk warm, impossible in the cold dairy at this time of the year. The dairy was designed to keep milk and butter cool. Rachel had set up her utensils in the wash house, choosing Saturday because the laundry was finished for the week. A bright fire was burning, over which she was heating the pan of milk.

Ruth Garnett had said she would look in at the cheese later, but she encouraged Rachel to work by herself. 'You won't always have me at your elbow, better get used to thinking for yourself,' she said.

It was pleasant work at this time of the year and Rachel sang as she worked, an old folk song she had learned at school. It was true that she needed to think independently. The *Herald* editor had shown her that she could do it; it was too easy to work with her parents and let them make the decisions. Farmers' daughters usually did this, until they married and their husbands took over the responsibility. Jim would naturally tell her what to do, once they were married. She sighed. Did he always know best?

Soon after Kit and Jim had clopped out of sight, Ben gave a warning bark, followed by a growl. He still walked with a limp, but Ruth's comfrey ointment had helped him to heal quickly. As soon as he could, he had gone back to shadowing Rachel, although rounding up sheep was still beyond him.

Rachel looked up quickly to find that Guy had appeared beside her in the wash house. 'Where's Garnett gone?' he wanted to know. 'Has he got permission to go off like that?'

Rachel felt like telling him to mind his own business, but decided against it. She felt very alone, with nobody in the yard except herself; it would be better not to annoy the youth. 'They've gone to chop down a dangerous tree at the school,' she said quietly. 'He did tell the Major about it.'

'I am supposed to help my father manage the estate and I need to know what the servants are doing,' Guy announced. 'He should have told me.' This was bad news; if the Major had decided to involve Guy in the estate, life would be difficult for all of them. He turned to look at Rachel with bloodshot eyes. 'And what are you doing, hot little Rachel? Perhaps you should tell me what you are up to.' He put an arm round her waist. 'My, you do feel hot! Just the way I like my women!'

Rachel moved away from him. 'I am making cheese, the milk is getting warm and I am adding rennet to set the curd,' she said firmly. 'Please leave, Mr Guy.' Deliberately, she took the pan off the fire and added rennet to the milk. The fire scorched her face.

'How long will it take to set the curd?' Guy asked, peering at the milk as though he were interested in the process. He closed the door.

'It varies … about twenty minutes, I suppose,' she told him. 'Up to half an hour.'

The man grinned. 'Quite long enough for what I have in mind. I've been planning it for a long time. It won't interrupt the process at all.' He grabbed her quickly and pinned her down on a heap of linen waiting for the wash. 'This is what I have in mind and I'm sure you'll enjoy it. But if not, I love a fight.'

Guy proceeded to tear off Rachel's clothes, handling her roughly. 'Why do you wear knickers? Bad girls don't need them! You'll feel hotter without!' He pulled them off.

Rachel struggled and screamed, but he was too strong for her. Guy was surprisingly strong and used his weight to pin her down. She was helpless; so this was what rape was like, losing your honour on a wash house floor.

Her feet were free now of encumbering clothes and Rachel managed to kick the door open a little. Immediately, Ben erupted through the door, all teeth and growing fiercely. He flew at Guy, sinking those fearsome teeth in the youth's arm. Guy yelled and tried to hit the dog, but Ben was too quick for him. Barking and snapping at Guy, he jumped and circled round him.

'Good boy, Ben! Get him!' Rachel struggled to her feet, pulling on her clothes. 'Thank goodness you're here, Ben,' she gasped. Her face and shoulders were bruised, her lips were swollen, but she had avoided the worst.

Guy gave up and went out, banging the door behind him. He nearly ran into Cook, who was bustling across the yard. 'What's all the commotion?' she asked. 'What's happened, Mr Guy? You're bleeding.'

'The maid was trying to seduce me, they're all alike,' he lied, and limped away. 'Damned dog bit my arm. Should be shot, a dog like that.'

Rachel was smoothing her hair and trying to calm her nerves when Cook looked in. 'Are you much hurt, Rachel? Did he ... no? Well, that's something.' Cook looked her over critically, but then she smiled. 'I'm sure you didn't encourage him. You'd best lock the door, while you make the cheese. I'll bring you a bite to eat at dinner-time.'

Ben was licking his injured leg, but he was very pleased with himself. Guy had failed to get in a blow at him; Ben had won the contest easily

Rachel's hands trembled as she went through the ritual of making cheese, but the process soothed her a little. She had no idea what to do about Guy Potts. Ruth had said she thought he would go back to the London house soon, which would please everyone. Meanwhile, she would tell all the servants so that they could protect the female staff. She wondered what happened at other big houses and hoped that the young men in them had some consideration for others; Guy Potts considered no one but himself. Surely, the Potts would realize sooner or later that they had reared a monster.

At last the cheese was done and Rachel went back to the safety of the farmhouse kitchen. She shuddered to think how close she had come to being raped. What would happen to a young woman like herself, if she fell pregnant? She would be a fallen woman, with all the blame that would accrue. Her parents would know the truth, but the rest of the world would label her immoral.

Wondering what to say to her mother, Rachel smoothed her dark hair as she crossed the misty yard. But Ruth had much on her own mind and, surprisingly, she didn't notice the girl's bruises.

'A good morning for the job,' Kit said as he and Jim travelled the familiar road to the village. The sky was grey, with mist hanging in the treetops and there was only a light breeze.

'Aye, I was hoping wind would drop,' Jim agreed. A strong wind could be dangerous; it might change the angle at which a tree would fall. Warm weather would make such hard exertion a trial, with sweat blinding their eyes.

As they clopped down the village street a few children followed them, but they were sternly told to keep away.

'This is no job for bairns,' Jim told them.

At the school, instead of Mr Jackson, they found Miss Ward. Violet was just as beautiful as Jim remembered from the village meeting, small and fragile. She was just like a violet in fact, her huge eyes lifted shyly to his face.

'Good morning, Jim, it is so good of you to come to help us.' She glanced at Kit. 'And you too, Mr – sorry, I've forgotten your name.'

Since the night of the meeting, he'd been thinking of her more than he should, as a man who was practically engaged to be married. Jim swallowed and looked at Kit, but the older man was busy unloading the big cross-cut saw.

'Good day, miss,' he croaked. How could a lass have such an effect on him? It had never happened before. He pulled himself together. 'This is Mr Garnett.'

'Mr and Mrs Jackson's had to go to see his mother, she's ill,' the young teacher told them in her high, girlish voice. 'So they asked me to be here, to see if there's anything you need.'

'There's no call for you to give up your Saturday, miss,' Kit said. 'We certainly don't expect a little lass to help with cutting down a tree. I think we can manage, thank you.'

'Of course,' said Violet seriously, 'but I board just over the street, it's no trouble. And I have to give you a cup of tea and a slice of teacake. Mrs Jackson said it was only right if you're helping the school.' She smiled at Jim. 'I did volunteer to do it.'

'How – how long have you been in Firby?' Jim asked the girl, wondering how he could have missed seeing her before. He was hungry to know everything about her.

'Only this term. I'm from Skipton, but I love Firby,' Violet said a little breathlessly. 'My papa's a sheep farmer. I expect you're a farmer too, Jim?'

By the time Jim had found out what breed of sheep her family kept and what her brothers and sisters did, Kit was impatient to start work.

'Well, thank you, Miss Violet, we'd like a cup of tea later on, but you needn't stay out here in the cold. Now Jim, let's make a start or we'll be here all day!'

His future father-in-law had spoken. Jim blushed and took his end of the saw, but Violet stayed, sitting on a stump close to them. Usually so handy with tools, he felt awkward and clumsy, unable to forget he was being watched by those big blue eyes. After he had made two or three mistakes, Kit looked at him and then said to the girl, 'Look, miss, you'll be in danger here soon, you want to be nowhere near a falling tree. Why don't you go home for an hour or so?'

'But it's so interesting!' Violet breathed. Rather than saw through the base of the tree at its thickest, it was usual to cut slices out of the trunk higher up, where it narrowed. They then put a plank of wood across the trunk at that level, a platform from which to operate the saw. It was tricky work, fascinating to watch.

'You are so brave, Jim!' Violet called up to them. She was not taking Kit's advice.

Jim looked over from his side of the tree. 'We don't want to have to tell Mr Jackson there's been an accident ... Go now, lass, and if you want, come back when we've got it on the ground.'

'Do take care, Jim, won't you?' Violet departed, with many backward looks, after which Jim's work went a little more smoothly. He wished he hadn't asked Kit to help – he was too observant, he'd guessed how Jim was feeling. Would an old man like Kit remember how it felt to be young? At that moment, Jim was feeling younger, much younger than normal. He had discovered excitement, fascination, and wondered why he had not felt it before. Rachel was ... everyday, familiar.

When Violet came back he would have to pretend to be

indifferent.... It was dangerous to lose concentration. Everything she said seemed to Jim wonderful, original. Her golden hair and blue eyes made her look like an angel. How could any man be indifferent?

Jim's heart sank. It was probable that every young man in the parish would be impressed with Miss Ward and they'd be falling over each other to see her. They'd find out where she went to church and develop an interest in religion. They would ask their mothers to invite the young teacher to Sunday tea, or better still, get their sisters to befriend her. Jim wished he had a sister. Violet Ward would not be lonely for long ... better concentrate on the job.

When the saw had bitten deep into the trunk, the tree began to sway slightly at the top. Now Jim was thankful that Kit was with him, steady in the face of a possible calamity.

'Saw this side,' Kit instructed him. 'And get ready to jump.' The saw was moved.

They had planned the way the tree would fall, up the slope and away from the wall round the school grounds. What if they got it wrong, what would Violet think if they smashed the wall? The tree leaned and groaned, a human sound that made Jim shiver. In revenge, it might fall on them and crush the life out of them. There was only a hinge of wood left, for the tree itself to break as it fell.

Kit pulled out the saw and threw it well clear. Jim hesitated.

'Jump!' Kit yelled, and they both jumped into soft ground. Jim shut his eyes and prayed.

There was a crack as the hinge wood broke, then an ominous whistling sound, a moment when it seemed anything might happen. Looking up, Jim saw mist swirling round the doomed tree as it sank. Then a resounding thud shook the school yard. He started to breathe again. It was down.

Kit's experience had ensured that there was no accident that day; the tree had hit the ground fairly close to where it should be. He worked for a while, cutting off limbs and then he looked across at Jim.

'I've a fair bit of work at home, lad,' he said. 'Do you think you can manage the rest?'

Perhaps the day would be easier without Kit looking over his shoulder. 'Aye, Mr Garnett, I'm right enough now. I've just got to make it safe, so the little school lads can't hurt themselves scrambling about and falling off the logs.' Jim paused, easing his back. 'I'll cut it up smaller next weekend, for school fires. Shall I drive you home?'

Kit said he would walk and as soon as he had gone, Violet appeared with a basket.

'Where's the labourer?" she asked Jim.

'Mr Garnett has gone home, he's the farm manager for Major Potts,' Jim told her.

'Oh ... I'm sorry, I thought he was one of your workers.' Violet unpacked the basket. 'Please have a drink of tea and something to eat. You have worked so hard. I'm glad I wasn't here when the tree fell, I would have been frightened, I think.'

Jim sat on a log, glad of the rest. Kit had kept working steadily and so Jim had had to do the same. Violet perched beside him, looking very pretty in a blue cloak with a hood.

'Are you warm enough?' he asked her. The mist had lingered in the village, drifting in and out of the gardens, wrapping itself round the school bell. He felt an urge to protect this little lass from the cold.

Violet shed a few tears for the tree. 'It was old, I know, but the shade in summer was good for the children. Such a pity it had to die, Jim.'

'Mr Jackson will likely plant another in its place.' Jim had an idea. 'I'll go into our wood at home and maybe I can find a tree seedling, bring it in for Mr Jackson to plant.' He looked at her. 'They might let you plant it, Violet, since you were here today.'

The girl's face lit up like a child's. 'I would like that, Jim, if you were here to dig the ground for it.'

They talked about Violet's life in Skipton, her teacher training and her friends. She hoped to marry and have children in the future, she said, but not yet and there was no particular man in mind. Jim was more and more fascinated. This girl was clever enough to be a teacher, but she was prettier than any teacher he'd ever seen.

Violet asked him about his family and his plans for the future. Yes, he admitted, he was talking to a girl briefly at the village meeting, Mr Garnett's daughter.

'I've known Rachel a long time,' he said.

'And are you betrothed to her?' Violet persisted, using an old-fashioned term.

Feeling guilty, Jim shook his head. It was true, there was no formal arrangement, but he'd told Rachel they would marry one day. 'Not really.'

'I suppose we shouldn't be sitting here like this,' Violet said after a horse and cart had lumbered by, the driver casting glances in their direction. 'People will talk.'

Jim wanted her to stay, desperately wanted to keep her there as long as possible. He had never felt like this with Rachel ... and yet he hardly knew Violet.

'I don't think so, people are more interested in their own affairs, lass. It was kind of you to bring me the tea. What's wrong with that?'

'Well, nothing....' Violet glanced at him under her long lashes. 'To tell you the truth, Jim, the days when I'm not teaching are very long for me. I can only go home in the school holidays, but I don't know many people in Firby yet.'

'Poor little Violet! I bet it won't take long for you to settle down here. Stay with me while I tidy up the timber, make it safe for the little ones.'

Kit walked home from the school thinking about Jim. He would never have believed that the lad was susceptible to young women; he'd always been quite casual with Rachel. In fact, it seemed to be mutual. Would Rachel care very much if Jim deserted her? He was quite a hard worker and likely to be prosperous, but Kit knew he had no interest in books and had a narrow mind.

He reached home and soon forgot about Jim; he walked into a storm.

'Sorry, Father, we've got trouble, I'm afraid.' Rachel felt sorry for her father, covered in sawdust and looking rather tired. Cross-cut sawing was heavy work.

'What's wrong, lass?' He noticed that Rachel was looking harassed and she had several bruises. 'What's happened to you?'

Her own frightening experience would wait until later. 'Lady Agnes wants to see all the staff, every one of us. In the old dining room, at once.' Out in the yard, she brushed down his clothes. 'Mother's there already. They're waiting for us.'

'What's upset her?' Kit thought of the work waiting for him. 'Will it take long?'

'I don't know, nobody knows. The Major's away, of course.'

All the Hall staff, indoor and outdoor, stood shivering in the cold dining room, where the mist from the valley seemed to have cast its chill. Kit went to stand with Ruth, and Rachel followed him.

Lady Agnes looked at her sternest. She stood in front of the empty fireplace, looking down her aristocratic nose.

'Have any of you seen strangers skulking about the grounds?'

Bewildered, the servants shook their heads. 'No, m'lady.' The kitchen staff looked even more nervous.

'In the last few days, a robbery has occurred. Valuable goods have been stolen and I intend to get them back. It is likely that one or more of you are implicated in this. If you know anything at all, have seen anything suspicious, it is your duty to tell me. Even if it involves another servant.'

Kit, as the senior member of staff, was the only one who dared to speak. 'Please, Lady Agnes, would you tell us what is missing? It will help me to ask the right questions.'

Rachel could tell that her father was seriously annoyed. The Major would have told the Garnetts of the problem before he called the staff together. They were entitled to know first, unless – Rachel went cold – they themselves were under suspicion.

115

Perhaps it was the jewellery, Rachel thought. Lady Agnes possessed many rings, bracelets, necklaces and earrings, the envy of Cook, who loved such things. They were kept in a safe, under lock and key ... but unfortunately, Rachel knew where the keys to the safe were kept. The Garnetts knew all the secrets of the old house between them. They had the security of the whole place in their hands.

'It is clear to me that one or more of you knows exactly what is missing. I will give you all a few minutes to decide what you will tell me.' Lady Agnes moved and a necklace caught the light. Maybe it wasn't the jewellery that had gone, after all.

ELEVEN

ROGER TOOK TO the moor road on that misty Saturday morning, thankful his horse was moving well and was keen to be off. Leeds Corporation managers were taking an alternative dam site more seriously, following some intervention during the week by the people of influence. Leeds wanted more information, more measurements and estimates from him regarding a moorland valley, Woodley Crags, higher up the dale.

It might be a case of starting all over again. This sort of thing had happened before. When Roger talked to the Chief Engineer, Mr Bromley's boss, he had accepted the idea of looking elsewhere.

'Better get it right, son,' he had said. 'Once we start demolition it'll be too late.'

One of the office workers told him that they'd underestimated the cost of moving all those villagers and small farmers out of the way. The moorland site was more expensive in terms of piping water to Leeds, but it would be cheaper to build and the rainfall would be higher.

Roger thought that there was another advantage; a proper survey would probably find that a Woodley Crags reservoir would store more water.

He smiled to himself when he thought of Rachel's letter to the press, the letter that had sparked off a chain reaction. If she'd been a man, she would have been a very good journalist. His sister had educated Roger; he understood that women were often undervalued.

The engineer's own attitude had changed since the day he first went to the Garnetts when he was planning the reservoir at Firby. He now firmly believed that the Firby plan had too high a cost in terms of people's lives.

Industry was eating into the countryside at an alarming rate. A countryman at heart, Roger hated the onward sprawl of Leeds. Perhaps he should give up engineering and become a gamekeeper.

Thoughts of Rachel's dark eyes rose before him, but he tried to push them away. Rachel belonged to Jim, although he didn't seem to realize how lucky he was. Jim was very casual. Some farmer's sons were not willing to wait to inherit; they rented a cottage, got married and settled down as best they could until the farmhouse was available. How could Jim keep a girl like Rachel waiting for years?

To take his mind away from Rachel, he decided to estimate the distance from Firby to Woodley Crags, the extra miles that materials and men would have to travel to build a reservoir on the moor.

'Good day, Roger, are you riding my way?' A friendly voice broke into his thoughts as he passed Nathan Brown's farm gate. The man himself was riding out, warmly wrapped in a heavy riding cape for the cold morning. When he heard Roger's destination, he smiled. 'I'm heading up dale myself, to see an old friend – I keep an eye on the farm for her. I suppose you've met Alice Bolton, if you've been up that way?'

Roger remembered a white-haired woman with keen eyes, a woman who asked many questions on his previous visit. 'Yes. I remember Mrs Bolton. If ... if Leeds Corporation were to plan a reservoir at Woodley Crags, how do you think she would feel about it?' Perhaps he would have another fight on his hands.

'Let's ask her.'

They rode in silence for a while until Nathan said, 'Poor Roger ... you've negotiated and measured all up and down Firby for weeks and now it sounds as if you're going to have to face it all over again. I suppose you'll be disappointed?'

Smiling, Roger shook his head. 'I should be, Leeds has spent money on my salary and if the site changes, the time was wasted. But to tell you the truth, I will be glad if Firby is saved. From what I've seen of it, Woodley Crags is wild country, with only a handful of people. I'm hoping they'll be glad to sell up and move down dale to a warmer spot.' As though to illustrate the point, a chill wind blew round them, whirling the last of the autumn leaves.

This area was on a tributary of the river Nidd, which wound its way down to Pateley Bridge from its source on Great Whernside. One day, Roger thought, they will build dams on the Nidd itself … and change the dale forever.

As they went, the countryside changed; hawthorn hedges gave way to dry-stone walls and the green pastures of Firby were left behind. Moorland sheep grazed the short upland grass and grouse lurked in patches of heather. The far hills were shrouded in mist; this would be a lonely place in winter.

Woodley Crags was a deep ravine with boulder outcrops lining the sides.

'Good stone for building a dam wall,' said Roger. 'And the rain-fall, Mr Brown – it must be higher than at Firby.'

'It's wet, right enough,' the older man told him. 'It often falls as snow in winter, though. Woodley can be cut off for weeks at a time.' He pointed across the slope to where a small house stood in ruins, gradually dissolving back into the earth. 'Folks have been leaving, moving down dale for a long time now. Only the stones are left, to show where families used to live. It's a hard life up here.'

'A perfect place for a reservoir,' Roger said quietly. 'Bromley – you remember my colleague? He disagrees. He worked out the extra cost of carting all the materials to the site, housing and feeding the construction gangs in the cold and wet. Work could be held up by deep snow. And then, the extra distance the water would have to travel, to get to Leeds.' He laughed. 'Bromley doesn't like the idea of working at Woodley Crags.'

'That's understandable, for a city man. You're different, Roger.

A Pateley lad will feel right at home, up here.' Nathan reined in. 'Here's the gate, let's call on Alice Bolton.'

The farm track led down from the road into the shelter of the valley. The horses were tied up in the stable before they knocked; Roger guessed Nathan Brown must be a frequent visitor.

Mrs Bolton, resident farmer of Woodley Crags, had decided opinions of her own, Roger found when they called at her house. She was pleased to see Nathan, it was clear and she was very grateful for the couple of rabbits he'd brought her.

'That's grand, Nathan, I'm ready for a bit of fresh meat.'

She invited them into the kitchen and almost before they had sat at the well-scrubbed table, the kettle was boiling over a bright fire on the hearth. It was wonderful to find this oasis of comfort in such a wild landscape.

After toasted teacake and two cups of tea, Roger was ready to face another inquisition, but Mrs Bolton was ready to deliver her verdict.

'Well, Alice, tell us what you think about the dam,' Nathan encouraged her. 'I know you've given this a lot of thought.' An old sheepdog crept up to Roger and licked his hand.

'If you want my opinion,' she said, fixing Roger with her clear grey eyes, 'this is the best place to build a dam, I have come to realize. I suppose it would cost more than Firby, but once it was built, there would be more water. And only a few of us live here.' She smiled.

This was going to be easier than he'd expected; Roger waited for more.

'I've decided that it's time to go, to live down dale. Since Ernest died, it's been hard to keep going. Nathan here helps me with the sheep from time to time, but he has his own farm to run. And I have neighbours over the other side of the crags, but the days are long in winter. I hated the idea of the dam at first, but now I can see it would be a good thing. Not just for me, but for all of us here in Woodley. And for the poor Leeds folk, short of clean water.'

Roger leaned back in his chair. He had expected opposition, but here was a woman who took a wide view. For most farming people, there must come a time in life when they have to make the hard decision to leave the life they love, to let younger folk shoulder the responsibility and hard work of a farm. He wondered whether Nathan had faced the prospect. He was looking over at his friend now with kindly eyes.

'Of course, we'd all be sorry to leave.' Mrs Bolton cleared the cups from the table. 'It's been our way of life, a good life for the most part. In the old days we had a little community here and a Methodist chapel, we all helped each other. But the young folks have gone, they have to earn a living. And we old ones have to realize that Woodley Crags is finished.' There were tears in her eyes.

Nathan said gently, 'Ernest Bolton was a friend of mine, a very good sheep man. He would want you to have an easier life, Alice, and so will your bairns.' He stood up. 'Well, I'd better check the sheep and maybe move them to fresh ground.'

'Will you lads stay for a bite to eat, later? I've plenty of ham and some eggs.' Alice Bolton looked hopeful and the old dog wagged his tail, looking up from his place on the thick rag rug.

This was Yorkshire hospitality and they risked offending her by refusing it. 'Thanks, Alice, but it's going to be a foggy night, we'll need to get home in the daylight,' Nathan apologized. 'The tea and toast was champion, just what we needed.'

Roger added his thanks. 'I'll ride home with you, Mr Brown, but first I must look at the valley,' he said.

Before they left, he would ask Alice Bolton for the names of the other residents of Woodley Crags. Once Leeds was satisfied, he would need to negotiate with them. He could suggest that Mrs Bolton might have a talk to them, too. She seemed likely to have influence with her neighbours.

Walking down from the house, Roger peered up at the towering crags. The farmhouse stood on the upper slope of the valley, a ravine carved out by glaciers in ages past. A beck ran musically over stones on its way to join the river. There were trees here in the more fertile soil of the valley floor, bright with autumn colours and here and there, the scarlet berries of rowan. Perhaps these were the trees that gave the place its name.

A flock of hens scattered at his approach, squawking and then came back, looking for grain. A few geese splashed into the stream. Woodley Crags was more attractive than Roger had realized on his first visit; he could see why the area had been settled long ago, by self-sufficient people who had little need of the town. He could see, too, why it could break their hearts to leave such a beautiful place.

Then the mist swirled down from the moor above and brought with it a sense of utter loneliness. With her husband and her children gone, Alice Bolton had probably stayed too long in this place. It needed human life, strong men and the voices of children.

As he walked, Roger found that the valley widened, but it was still narrower and deeper than the Firby site. He paced out the length that would be needed for a wall to contain the stream and hold the floods of winter rain. From above, he heard a dog bark and saw sheep pouring down the fell side in a woolly tide, as Nathan moved them into a lower pasture.

Bromley would disagree with his proposal, but Roger could now see that a Woodley reservoir would be cheaper to build than the Firby dam. He would argue that the road from Pateley would carry the materials if the surface was improved and a few culverts strengthened. After the dam filled, the present road would still be above the water level since it kept to the ridge, whereas Firby would need a completely new road.

They had roughly calculated the cost of compensating people for losing their land and homes at Firby; the cost here would be much less. There remained the long journey the water would take from here down to Leeds. However, that cost would be offset over the years by the greater volume of water he believed would be available from Woodley.

As he walked along the bottom of the valley, looking at the rock formations and assessing the site, Roger heard a bleat and soon he came upon a tethered goat, with a horse grazing close by.

Tucked into a curve of the valley side was a gypsy caravan. It was not noticeable at first, being painted green, but the large yellow wheels gave it away. Through the open door he could see a richly decorated interior, with scrolls of colour on the walls.

'Good day, kind sir!' A woman was watching Roger from her seat by a small fire.

'Er – good day, I wasn't expecting to meet anyone here,' he said.

'We come down from Appleby Horse Fair to Pateley for the show every year, and then up here.' The woman's dark good looks were enhanced by large gold earrings, which flashed when she moved her head. 'The Mistress here lets us stay for some of the winter, we try to help her.' She paused.

'An interesting life, I've read about it,' Roger told her. 'George Borrow, as I remember … *The Romany Rye*.'

The gypsy laughed. 'You've read a book about us? A lot of folk are against us, o' course, hate all travellers. But even worse are the ones with notebooks that want to know all about how we live, and our language, and come round asking questions like we was animals in a zoo. But you look like a man with book learning, yourself! Maybe you'll be one o' them coves.'

Roger grinned. 'Not I! There's a lot of interest just now in the Romany way of life, I know,' he said. 'You used to be called Egyptians – did you really come from Egypt?'

'There you go, asking questions! Nay, we're from Darlington,' the woman said flatly. 'We dunno where our folk came from way back, but we're not exactly English, are we?' She looked down the valley and then back at Roger. 'My man and the two boys are out after rabbits, they'll be back soon.' She lifted an iron pot onto a tripod and suspended it over the fire.

'Mrs Bolton will be glad of some help in winter,' Roger said, to show that he didn't hate travellers.

'Aye, my man kills a sheep for her and she gives us some meat. And we make baskets and that, give one or two to her.'

'You earn a living from making baskets?' The Gypsy Lore Society would love all this; Roger had met a member once, full of admiration for the exotic race.

'That and pegs – you've no call for clothes pegs, kind sir? I thought not. But then my man mends pots and pans, we get by.' She looked at him closely. 'And sometimes, I tell fortunes. But only if I can see the way. I don't make them up, like some folks.' She laughed again, a pleasant carefree laugh. 'Some old women in the towns, they get dressed up as a Romany and take money off folks and spin a yarn, but it means nowt.'

Roger prepared to move off. 'Very interesting….'

'I can tell your fortune if you like,' the woman said in a low voice. 'I think I can see a little, just a little … come and sit here by the fire, bonny lad.'

Rather unwillingly, Roger sat down on a stool beside her and felt in his pocket for a coin. The woman took it swiftly and then retained his hand, gazing at it. He decided to give her no clues and to see what she came up with.

'My name is Vadoma,' she said after a silence. 'And yours…?'

'Roger.'

'Well, Roger, I can see a long life for you. A … farm with a good woman, I can see her smiling, and children … three, I think. Hardship at times, but also happiness. Yes, a farm, with fat cattle and sheep.'

Roger laughed and withdrew his hand. 'I'm an engineer, Vadoma, not a farmer. Unfortunately I have to work in cities for a living. I'm afraid you've got it wrong.' He stood up. 'I hope you have a good winter.'

'I am sure about the farm,' she assured him seriously. 'You'll see!'

As he walked on, Roger decided that she would have taken anyone she met up here for a farmer of some sort, or a man hoping to farm. Engineers would be unusual in Woodley Crags. But shouldn't she have known from his hand that he didn't do regular manual work? Fortune tellers were supposed to be observant.

Back at the farm house, Roger found Nathan ready to go home. He mentioned the gypsy and Alice Bolton nodded. 'They've been coming here for years and they never cause trouble.'

'Don't they steal eggs? I thought all gypsies stole eggs,' Nathan said tolerantly.

'Vadoma helps me, so I give her eggs. That solves the problem.' Alice smiled at him. 'You'll know, Nathan, that eggs are right useful, especially up here – better than money. You can trade them for whatever you need.'

As they rode out of the yard, Alice stood at the door with her dog watching them go, a small, frail figure in that immense land-scape. There was a lingering sadness about Woodley Crags, or was it just the weather?

With the fog descending, Roger's hair was soon dripping with moisture. Nathan smiled and handed him a cap. 'Put that on lad, you'll need it before we get home.' He drew another from a pocket for himself.

They rode side by side along the track, talking about the build-ing of a dam. Roger found that it helped to clear his thoughts and Nathan seemed interested, putting in a question now and then. The time seemed to go quickly and when they got back to Nathan's gate, he invited Roger in. 'Come and have something to eat before you go home.'

'I don't want to be a nuisance,' Roger said, thinking the older man would probably feel obliged to give him a meal. Part of him wanted to go back to the Garnetts and see Rachel again, although he should try to see her as little as possible. But the fog was thick-ening and the cold seemed to be seeping into his bones.

'Nay, lad, it's no trouble. There's a stew that mustn't go to waste, and I'm glad of the company.'

Once in the house, Nathan quickly blew the fire into life and set a pot on the stove. It contained beef, onions, potatoes and carrots, a hearty meal in one dish.

The stew was excellent, but Nathan would take no praise. 'Young Rachel made it,' he admitted. 'They look after me very well. I think they try to fatten me, Ruth and Rachel, but they haven't a hope.'

Nathan seemed to be interested in Roger's career, and then they talked about their families. He remembered Dr Beckwith, Roger's father and knew most of his relatives in Pateley. Roger's older brother had been training to be a doctor, before he died of cholera picked up in a hospital.

'We only had the one child, Ruth,' Nathan said. 'And a grand lass she is, as you know. A son would have been welcome. It was not to be … your father used to bring you to stay up here in the school holidays every summer, so I did have a little lad to teach to fish. We had grand times – do you remember?'

Roger was surprised. He had happy memories of staying at the Browns' farm, but hadn't realized that they liked to have him there. His father had wanted him to have a taste of country life.

'Of course I remember, I looked forward to those holidays so much! You made a countryman of me, I'm afraid. I hate working in the town.' He paused. 'How long would it take to learn to be a gamekeeper, Nathan?'

'Nay, you've had a good education, lad. Stick to your engineering … young Rachel was only a babe then,' Nathan reminisced. 'You might remember her, toddling about in a sunbonnet?'

'That was Rachel?' Roger laughed. 'Of course it must have been, but I didn't recognize her!'

'She doesn't remember, either. Now, lad, let's have a wee nip of whisky, to keep out the cold. You do drink whisky, I hope?'

'Not very often, but thank you, I will tonight.'

TWELVE

Rachel stood beside her mother, waiting to hear what had been stolen from the Hall, but Lady Agnes was not prepared to tell them yet. Was she enjoying the moment, seeing them all squirm?

In the dining room the frigid silence was broken by Donald, the coachman and groom.

'Please, my Lady,' he said, 'I did notice summat queer, other morning. One of the horses was in a lather, as if it had been ridden all night. Thursday morn, it was.'

'Did anyone hear anything?' the lady wanted to know, looking at Kit. 'The farmhouse is just across from the stables ... you must have heard it, if a horse went out.'

The farmhouse bedrooms were at the other side of the house, looking over the garden, not the yard, so the Garnetts were unlikely to hear anything.

Kit had not been told about the horse and he said nothing. If a stranger had come into the yard, all the dogs would have barked. That left the people living at the Hall.

After a few minutes, the outdoor staff were told to leave the room, with the exception of Kit. They were threatened with dismissal if they withheld any information.

'We will get to the bottom of this, however long it takes,' Lady Agnes boomed. 'My husband will hear of it, as soon as he returns.'

Then the lady turned to the indoor servants. 'Whoever stole

these goods knew where to find the keys. How many of you know where the house keys are kept?' She sounded as though she had never needed to know such things before.

Everyone except Janet the kitchen maid knew where they were, in a drawer in the housekeeper's room. Ruth spoke up. 'I keep the drawer locked, my Lady. And the library keys are in a secret drawer, they open the book cupboards.'

Kit was wondering whether wine had been stolen from the cellar, when Lady Agnes fixed Rachel with her glittering eyes. 'You mentioned books, Mrs Garnett, though I did not.'

Another silence.

Lady Agnes pounced. 'And you, Rachel Garnett, dust the volumes in the library. So you know where the library keys are kept. Who persuaded you to give them up?'

Rachel started with shock. So it was books. 'No one, my Lady. I've not been into the library for several days, a week or more.'

It wouldn't help to say that she had tried to keep out of any part of the house where she might encounter Guy. The memory of her ordeal a few hours ago was still affecting her nerves.

'What volumes are missing, ma'am?' Kit asked. 'I suppose they would be sold, so I could ask the booksellers to look out for them.'

'Ask your daughter, Garnett. Do you know what I am talking about, Rachel? I am sure you do.' The woman was almost spitting with rage.

'No, my Lady, I know nothing about missing books. Please can you tell us what has gone?' Rachel shivered with cold and apprehension. It would be impossible to prove her innocence.

For once, Lady Agnes seemed uncertain. 'It is difficult to say ... but I suppose the valuable manuscripts and older books. The shelf where the oldest books were kept has been filled with new novels. Someone who knew what was there has removed many of the valuable ones ... probably including the original plans used when the house was built. Sixteenth century manuscripts and books, any university or collector would be very happy to buy them.'

'Do you have a list of the books in the Hall library?' Kit persisted.

'No, I do not.' She was angry again.

So it would be difficult to recover the books, if not impossible. They should have had a list, to check against what was there, but it was hardly a farm manager's job.

Every year, Kit went through all the farm equipment and tools, checking it off against a list and noting what was missing or broken. He was accountable to the Major for it all. As the housekeeper, Ruth did an annual check of linen, cutlery, crockery, glassware and stores.

No one, it seemed, was accountable for the library.

Lady Agnes tried once more to get one of the servants to admit to something, without success. She ordered them to go about their business, but warned Rachel that Constable Bradley would be coming to interview her.

'Meanwhile, do not leave the grounds,' she said coldly.

'Who would steal books?' Rachel wondered as they made their way back to the farmhouse to give Kit a belated meal. 'It's not an obvious thing to do, like stealing cash.'

'Someone who wanted cash, but couldn't get hold of jewellery,' Ruth suggested. 'I believe some collectors will pay well for very old books. Years ago when you were small, Rachel, the Major sold some books for a good price. I knew about it because we had to take them down to Ripon and put them on the train to go to London.'

'It is obvious really when I think about it, but they won't believe me. I think Guy will have taken them.' Rachel looked at Kit, who nodded. 'He heard Mr Bromley say they were valuable, the day when Roger brought him to see the Hall. Guy asked how much they were worth, but Bromley couldn't tell him.'

'He's already tried to sell guns. He is capable of trying any-thing, but will his parents believe it? They would rather blame Rachel, because she knows where to find the keys.' Kit sat with his head in his hands. 'I really don't know what to do next. Guy is making this place a nightmare to live in.'

'He jumped on me today, while I was making cheese,' Rachel told them quietly. 'Good old Ben saved me, he attacked Guy and bit him. I still feel the shock of it. We'd better keep Ben out of Guy's way. He'd probably like to kill him. Father, we could be in trouble about that bite. I heard him telling Cook that I had ... enticed him.'

Ruth went pale. 'We'll have to find Rachel work somewhere else. This can't go on, Kit.' She put an arm round her daughter, a rare gesture. 'You poor lass!'

After a sleepless night, Rachel was quite glad to see Jim come to visit on Sunday afternoon and to tell him of their troubles. But Jim seemed strangely quiet. He had no comfort and no suggestions to offer of what might be done.

'That's a shame, lass,' was all he said, before changing the subject.

Rachel explained that she was not able to go for a walk, being confined to the grounds. Jim was not put out.

'That's just as well, I'm tired. We've been threshing,' he said.

He told Kit that he would have to go back to the school the next Saturday, to cut the fallen tree into firewood. Then he went home early, with a casual wave of the hand.

Roger had come in late on Saturday night and gone to Pateley on Sunday, starting out early. He knew nothing about the theft. When he arrived on Sunday evening, he found the Garnetts very subdued. They made an effort to talk to him and gave him some supper, but the usual happy atmosphere was missing. Had they guessed how he felt about Rachel? Perhaps Kit would ask him to leave....

Eventually, Roger decided that he had nothing to lose. 'Would you like to tell me what's wrong, Kit? You're all much more quiet than usual.' He stood up and poured himself a cup of tea.

Rachel couldn't trust herself to speak, but Kit told him what had happened. They had never seen Roger angry, but now he was furious. 'Guy Potts should be hanged! And he attacked you, Rachel? I will go up there and punch him right away!'

'Please, Roger,' Rachel pleaded. 'Don't make things worse. Nobody can touch him, he's Family.' Her sad face made him want to weep.

He strode over to where Rachel was sitting at the other side of the table and put both arms round her in a comforting hug. 'My poor girl!' He felt her relax against him for a moment, then it was over and he went back to his chair. 'I'm sorry, Rachel, but I can't bear to think of it....'

Rachel smiled across at him, a tremulous smile that let him know he was forgiven.

'It's a comfort to see you angry with him, lad.'

Roger was still simmering. 'Rachel blamed for the theft and Guy telling people that she ... it's dreadful.' He looked at Kit. 'Just let me know if he does anything to upset you again and I will thrash him. I'm not working for the Potts, thank goodness. He can't dismiss me.'

'I've never seen you so upset, Roger,' Ruth said.

'What's Jim going to do about it? He'll want to kill Guy Potts, when he hears!'

Nobody answered him. What did that mean?

PC Bradley rolled up on his bicycle on Monday morning as Rachel, with heavy eyes and an aching head, was preparing to make butter. He at least could offer some reassurance.

'I'm off to see Lady Agnes and then Mr Guy,' he told Rachel. 'Then I'm supposed to interview you, but I'm sure you didn't do it.' His cheerful grin made her smile for the first time since Saturday. 'We haven't forgot about those guns, down at the station. We don't need Sherlock Holmes to work out what happened.'

Lady Agnes, the policeman was told, was 'not at home'. That probably meant that she considered it too early in the morning to receive visitors. PC Bradley was shown into the library, the scene of the crime, as he said to himself. There were no evident clues, no damage to the book cases.

The Major sat at the big desk, writing letters. The desk was strewn with papers, pens and ink. Facing the Major was better any time than undergoing examination by Lady Agnes.

'Good morning, sir, PC Bradley. To see about yon books.'

'Constable, what do you make of this theft?' the Major asked him as the policeman stood before the desk like an overgrown pupil before the head-teacher.

'My wife believes that the Garnett girl sold the books for money. Garnett denies it, and I must say that as far as we know, she is of good character. However,' he looked sternly at the constable, 'as you will be aware, we have been away for four years, leaving the Garnetts to look after the estate. I am disappointed to find that our confidence may have been misplaced. If this thing is proved, the whole family must go.'

'Yes, sir.' Bradley was still trying to work out how to approach this tricky situation when Guy Potts burst into the room.

'I say, Pa...' he stopped when he saw PC Bradley, massively immobile by the desk. 'What's all this?' He looked furtively round the library.

'If I may take the liberty, Major, I would like to ask Mr Potts here what he knows about the books,' said Bradley, trying to sound very firm.

'Me? Don't be stupid, man. That Garnett girl took them, I saw her walking down the stairs with a large bag the day before.' Guy had flushed an ugly colour.

PC Bradley took out his note book and licked his pencil. 'Would you mind telling me, sir, what time of day that was? How big was the bag and where did she go?'

'She went to the wash house,' Guy blustered. 'Probably hid them, to sell later on.'

'Are you sure, Guy?' the Major asked.

'With respect, Major, I expect that Miss Garnett was taking a bag of linen to the wash house, it's what housekeepers and maids do ... we can ask when the sheets were changed,' Bradley suggested, thinking on his feet. 'I reckon you know something about the books, Mr Potts.'

'Now if you think you can accuse me...' Guy began, walking up to the policeman and glaring at him.

This was a time for very fast thinking, but the policeman had worked out a face-saving strategy before he came up to the Hall, just in case it was needed.

PC Bradley said calmly, 'Not at all, Mr Potts. I believe there's been a misunderstanding, like before. You remember? You as the heir feel entitled to use property at the Hall, it'll all be yours one day. You said as much, last time. Well, if you decide to take some of the property, such as guns, or these here books, it would help us all if you would mention the fact to the Major. I'm sure he would rather you did that, than have to call in the police. Now, Mr Guy, have I got it right?' He held his breath and glared back at Guy with all the weight of the law.

The Major jumped to his feet and for a moment, Bradley thought he was going to be thrown out. Then he looked at his son. 'Is this true? Did you take the books?'

There was a silence. Bradley looked steadily at Guy and chanced a guess. 'I'm sure the bookseller will know, when we go to see him,' he said casually. 'But it would save a lot of trouble, Mr Potts, if you ...'

'All right,' Guy said sulkily. 'I sold a few mouldy books because nobody reads them, nobody. I needed the money. I'd sell the whole lot if it was up to me, smelly old things they are.'

The youth sounded childish and Bradley wondered whether he was quite normal. There was something missing, some human decency.

'It was not fair to throw the blame onto a servant, Mr Potts.'

'Thank you, Constable, that will be all,' the Major said, dismissing him.

As he left as quietly as possible, Bradley heard the Major shouting. 'You have let us down! How could you behave so badly? It's the army for you, boy, and as soon as possible! Blaming a servant was despicable.'

It would have been good to mention Guy's loutish behaviour at the Fox and Hounds as another example of his little ways, but that could be used in future, if necessary. He felt rather sorry for the Major, oddly enough, with a son like that on his hands. The army was a splendid idea, as the Major himself said.

In the dairy, Rachel was working the butter with her wooden paddles when PC Bradley looked in.

'I'll see your father in a minute,' he told her. 'You'll be glad to know that Guy admitted it.'

Rachel looked at him with shining eyes. 'Thank you, Mr Bradley! How did you do it?'

The constable smirked. 'We police have our ways of dealing with criminals.'

In fact, as he well knew, it was a matter of luck. 'You cannot trust that lad, as I suppose you know, Rachel. Keep well clear of him.'

Lady Agnes was, if possible, even more furious than before when the Major told her what had happened that morning.

'Guy has caused us to lose face again before the servants,' she fumed. 'And now that fat policeman has been here, the whole village will hear about it. I can't forgive him.'

'I think you have spoiled Guy, that's the problem,' her husband said. 'No discipline. He never seems to consider anyone else's point of view.'

'Don't be ridiculous, Charles. Neither of us brought him up. Guy was in boarding schools for the whole of his childhood and if they couldn't teach him good behaviour, nobody can.' She nodded. 'The army's the thing, you are right about that ... now, have you written to the regiment?'

The Major sighed. 'Yes, I have. After the pheasant shoot, Sutton advised me to send Guy into the army. He seemed quite concerned about something, but someone else came up to us and he said no more. I should have asked him what had happened, but when I visited the Chase, it slipped my mind.'

'What have you said to Guy? He drank too much on the day of

the shoot, I noticed. That in itself was unacceptable, when we were entertaining guests. Did you ask him about going into the army, Charles?'

'I haven't given him a choice of regiment. Guy is not in the least interested in the army, but that doesn't matter. He needs discipline and I hope he doesn't get in with a set of gamblers.... I will make it clear that he gets no more help from me.' He looked at his wife. 'This is all very sad for both of us.'

'Can we afford a commission for him, given the state of our finances?' Lady Agnes twisted her rings. She did not want to sell her jewellery.

'We will sell one of the farms in the village, Elm Tree probably, to pay for it. Elm Tree won't be missed and I think the tenant will buy it, so there should be no fuss. I will send Garnett to see him.'

'I suppose we will have to apologize to Garnett?'

'Nonsense, Agnes. Say nothing and it will all be forgotten. The servants will be relieved that they are to keep their places, that's enough.' He patted her shoulder. 'Try not to worry about Guy; one day, he will grow up, I hope. The best thing we can do now is to plan the management of the farm for the future. It seems possible now that there will be no reservoir built here and if so, I am determined to live here for the rest of my life. We must make enough profit to live on, that's all.'

'I've had Rachel make a batch of cheese, but it will be weeks before we can try it,' his wife told him. 'Improving the farm seems to be a very slow job to me. Now, if I work on the dairy produce and the geese by organizing Rachel, what do you intend to do?'

'Ah,' said Major Potts. 'Next spring will be the time to begin your projects, Agnes. Forget the Dexter-Kerry cows. They are, after all, nothing but rich men's playthings – a fad of women like Sybil. We will get Garnett to buy some more Shorthorns and Rachel can milk them. Sutton tells me that local cattle will milk better, and that Wensleydale cheese sells well. The girl can make cheese.'

He paused while Agnes digested this information and then

went on, 'I intend to develop a managed pheasant shoot. I've been talking to Sutton about that, too. Those few days at Cranby Chase have opened my eyes to many possibilities.'

'How can pheasants make money for us?' Lady Agnes wanted to know.

'Syndicates of men, professionals from the city most often, are willing to pay to have the exclusive right to shoot over estates such as ours. We will rear pheasants under hens next spring, and release them in the woods. Eventually we'll employ a gamekeeper, to kill the vermin and guard the birds from poachers. Garnett can rear the birds for the first few years and keep away poachers, assisted by Daniel Wood.' He sat back in his chair, pleased with his plans.

'And the old Hall? That was on your list, I believe.'

'Next summer we will advertise discreetly that the Hall is open to visitors. The Garnetts can organize a tea room, in the way that other historic houses do, to offer afternoon tea to visitors. Mrs Garnett can bake the cakes and the girl can wait on the tables.'

'The geese ... I believe that Rachel could keep many more geese, Charles. They live mostly on grass and there is a demand for them, especially at Michaelmas and Christmas.'

The Potts considered their plans for some time. As they went down to lunch, Lady Agnes was struck by a thought. 'Charles, do you think we will be expecting too much from the Garnetts? All this extra work, and they seem to be quite busy already.'

'The Garnetts have had an easy time for years, while we were in India. It's time they earned their wages, my dear.' The Major held open the dining room door.

'And another thing,' he said as they drank their soup, 'I intend to ask Garnett to estimate what timber we might have to sell and what the current prices are. Then when we take out mature trees, Garnett can plant replacements, of species that will grow quickly. Some estates make a fortune that way. Timber is in demand, they tell me.'

'But,' said Lady Agnes, 'does Garnett know anything about timber?'

'I expect so,' the Major said carelessly. 'If not, he can learn. I tell you, Agnes, we should be able to live comfortably on an estate of this size. It's all a matter of getting people to work efficiently.'

'Well,' said Lady Agnes, laying down her spoon, 'We must introduce these ideas very carefully, one at a time. I have begun with cheese. It will only confuse the servants if we tell them all our plans at once.'

'Very true, my dear,' said the Major as the maid came in with the next course.

THIRTEEN

THE *HERALD* NEWSPAPER owners were pleased with the increase in circulation following the reservoir story.

'We're going to provide you with a horse, to get around the country,' said Mr Barton, the chairman. 'It must pay to get out and meet the people face to face, especially when you're new to the district.'

'Thank you, sir,' said Alex, feeling pleased. The hacks he hired from the Unicorn stables were not very spirited beasts.

'And a slightly higher budget, it's time to launch the new women's page. We've talked about it long enough,' Mr Barton continued. 'The details I will leave up to you.'

Alex was given a stylish bay gelding, with the promise of a gig or other vehicle in the future. The horse was bred locally and his name was Ripley, apparently after a famous Ripon Hornblower in the late sixteenth century, an association that pleased Alex, once he worked it out.

On nights when the paper was printed, Alex worked late and from his window he could see the Hornblower sound the curfew on the market square at nine o'clock, an old Ripon ritual that had survived for hundreds of years. The clatter of the printing press drowned the mournful sound of the horn, just as the pace of life was overwhelming the medieval city.

Alex wrote an editorial about the symbolic Hornblower and the need to keep links with the past. At the same time, he was trying to attract younger readers with stories that reflected the current life of the area. A country paper had to be all things to all men – and women.

Ripley was stabled at the Unicorn, where he would be fed, groomed and exercised just across the square from the *Herald* office. Alex was pleased to think that he could ride out any day when he got a chance to leave his desk. It was important to get to know the local people in all walks of life, so as to understand local affairs. He was due for another visit to the Suttons and he thought Susan would be impressed with the noble-looking Ripley; she loved horses and had made disparaging comments about his hired mounts.

Rodney Dacre, the chief reporter, was given the task of finding a knitter with reliable patterns for the new feature. He was not enthusiastic, but promised to ask his mother. People said that Rodney had inherited his nose for news from his mother, who seemed to know everything there was to know about her neighbours, none of it good.

Rachel, the special correspondent, was the next to be consulted. Alex rode up to Firby to see the Garnetts on a blustery November day, tied Ripley to a rail and found Rachel in the dairy. She was startled to see him looming in the doorway; there was fear in her eyes.

'Did I surprise you?' he asked gently, wondering why she would be nervous.

'I – thought it was someone else,' she admitted. 'Let's go into the kitchen, you must be cold after your ride.'

'Thank you, but first you must admire my horse. This is Ripley, a great improvement on the hacks from the livery stable.' Alex led her over the yard to where the horse stood. 'I came here today in much less time.'

'He's beautiful,' Rachel said sincerely. 'He must be seventeen hands ... but he's rather warm from coming up the hill from Masham. Let's put him in the stable, out of the wind.'

The editor's visit was welcome. Since the affair of the stolen books, Rachel had felt unusually low in spirits. The books had not been mentioned again and she noticed that some of them had reappeared on their shelf. But she felt that the cloud still hung over her. The Potts were even more distant than usual – was it possible that they felt embarrassed? Of course, they couldn't bring themselves to apologize, not to the lower ranks.

Guy was vindictive whenever he saw her, spitting out insults, but she managed to keep him at a distance. The sooner he went into the army, the better for everyone at Firby.

Jim seemed preoccupied and his visits were short; she wondered what was worrying him. A frown seemed to have replaced his usual sunny smile. Surely he wasn't jealous of Roger? He'd warned her once in a light-hearted way about spending time with the engineer. Rachel was beginning to understand Jim a little better; he tended to consider what was to his own advantage and he had little sympathy for others.

Roger was away a great deal, going out early and coming in late because he was working at Woodley Crags. He went to Leeds, coming back with the news that Bromley opposed the new dam site, but that some of the corporation managers believed it was a better option. The dam was still in the balance.

Rachel dreaded the day when Roger would go back to Leeds to live. She tried to suppress her feelings for him – what would an engineer want with a farm girl? They lived in different worlds, and she would have to forget him as soon as possible.

Kit was away at Masham market on the morning that Alex rode into the Garnetts' yard. Rachel's mother was crossing the yard as they came out of the stable.

'Good to see you, Mr Finlay. We're very proud of Rachel's reports in the paper! I have to go over to the Hall for half an hour. Rachel will give you a cup of tea.'

Rachel made the tea and sat with Alex at the big table.

'Thank you for the latest piece on the reservoir,' he said. 'It sounds as though Firby could be spared – that's good news. And now, I would like some ideas for the women's page. Have you had time to think about it?'

Rachel brought out her notebook and leafed through the pages. 'Just a suggestion…' she said diffidently. 'Why not start with a section on basic recipes, for young women? How to make Yorkshire pudding, and parkin, and Fat Rascals – all the traditional recipes, even apple pie. We serve apple pie with cheese in Yorkshire!' She paused. 'My mother taught me to cook, she learned from her mother.'

Alex laughed. 'I'm going to learn a lot from this! Yorkshire food is new to me. What is parkin?'

Rachel pushed a plate of cake towards him. 'This is our famous Yorkshire parkin, we bake it during the colder weather. We always have parkin on Bonfire Night. I made it myself a few days ago, we don't eat it the same day as it's made. Try a piece, Mr Finlay.'

Hungry after his ride, Alex was not dismayed by the size of the slice of parkin. It was a solid cake, made with oatmeal and treacle.

'It's like gingerbread, but heavier. Delicious! Good food for outdoor workers,' he commented, brushing away crumbs. 'This proves that you will be writing from practical experience.'

'You will know that pork pies are very important in Ripon. There's a great art in "raising a pie", as it's called.' Rachel made a note in her book for another recipe. 'And,' she continued, visualizing the page, 'I imagined a separate section, sort of square instead of a long column, with a border, for a different recipe each week. It would stand out on the page, and people could cut them out and paste them in a scrap book. Some people would find that useful, I think. When I was at school we girls all had scrap books.'

'Excellent, we'll do it, lay it out as you suggest.' Mr Finlay seemed to be looking at her with respect.

Rachel had thought of a problem and she decided to mention it. 'But … I'm afraid that some older women might disagree with my recipes, they could be annoyed to see a young woman telling them how it should be done. I can imagine our groom's wife saying, "*I've been making parkin for forty years, nobody can tell me how to do it!*"' She imitated Mrs Metcalfe's rather aggressive tones.

Alex laughed. 'Some people enjoy getting cross and they love criticizing, you know. I don't see it as a problem.' He took a sip of tea.

'It might start an argument. Some women are very ... er, certain that theirs is the best way, the only way. And of course, there are many different ways of making the same thing. I will have to make that clear!'

'All the better! Controversy sells newspapers, Rachel. You shouldn't be upset if people disagree. Imagine the Great Yorkshire Pudding Debate! We'll get sackfuls of letters. We could even run a competition for the best one.'

'There's not much room for variation in a batter pudding recipe,' Rachel said thoughtfully. 'But I suppose Yorkshire puddings do vary, from soggy ones to light and crisp ones.'

'I haven't been here very long, but I've noticed that my landlady makes soggy ones! Perhaps it depends on the oven temperature,' Alex suggested.

'Are you interested in cooking, Mr Finlay?' Rachel looked at him curiously.

'Of course. I'm interested in food, and journalists are interested in everything. In my job, you get to know just a little about a wide range of subjects. Yes, I'd thought of recipes, but your idea for regional dishes is better. There will be more passion generated!'

Rachel laughed; his enthusiasm made her feel much more cheerful. 'We won't run out of Yorkshire recipes, not for a long time.'

'Another idea was to find a children's nurse who could write about bringing up children, there's a lot to be said on that subject and once more, people will disagree. I think we'll be able to find someone in Ripon to supply the information.' Alex looked at Rachel for confirmation and smiled when she nodded. 'I thought you would like that one, of course we're not expecting you to supply all the material yourself.'

'Thank goodness! And then,' Rachel turned another page, 'I could write out some home remedies that you can make for yourself, just as Mother and I do here. We use garden plants and weeds to make tonics and salves ... some say that every plant on earth has a use, if we only can find out what it is. We sell packets of dried herbs, and salves too.' She moved the parkin out of the way and waited for his reaction.

'We could call it "Country Cures,"' Alex suggested. They looked at each other, pleased with the shape that the project was forming.

Alex scribbled some notes. 'What about local news of interest to women? We could have a small news column from time to time. I imagine you could visit a local show, for example, and report on who wins prizes for produce. People like to see their names in print—' he broke off as they heard a rap on the door and Jim walked into the kitchen.

'Good day, Rachel, I want to borrow your father's big saw...' He broke off and the frown deepened when he saw Alex. 'Who is this? What is going on?'

Alex rose to his feet. 'Alex Finlay, editor of the *Herald*,' he said pleasantly, holding out his hand.

Jim ignored the outstretched hand as Rachel introduced him: 'This is Jim Angram, a neighbour.'

'And what is the editor of the *Herald* doing here, alone with you in the kitchen?" he demanded, his blue eyes angry. 'Where's your mother? She should be here!'

'I'm old enough not to need constant supervision, Jim,' Rachel told him with a touch of acid in her tone. 'Mother's gone over to the Hall, she'll be back soon,' she said, more patiently. She was rarely impatient with Jim Angram, but his views on a woman's place had always irked her.

'And you're sitting side by side, almost holding hands!' Jim was getting angrier. 'You should be ashamed of yourself, Rachel. Why did you let him in?'

Alex was looking embarrassed, as well he might.

'We are discussing a women's page for the Ripon *Herald* and I am making a few suggestions.' Rachel realized that she should have told Jim before now of her work with the *Herald*.

'You? You're just a farm girl! What would a dairymaid know about newspapers? I don't believe you. I'm going to tell your father about this.' He went to the door and then turned to face them. 'I can see that you've deceived me, Rachel. You can't be trusted, you obviously know this man well. I never thought that my girl, a shy country lass, would turn out to be a loose woman. First it was the boarder, and now this. I don't want to see you again and I will tell the whole village!'

'Go away, Jim. I will not forget that you called me a loose woman.' Rachel was aware that she was breathing quickly. She almost threw the plate of parkin at Jim, but managed to restrain herself. What would Mr Finlay think of this exhibition?

There was silence for a while after Jim had gone out, banging the door.

'I am so sorry, if I've made things difficult for you.' Alex looked worried as he sat down.

Curiously, Rachel felt no emotion. 'I should have told him about the reporting, but somehow it never came up,' she admitted. 'Jim and I are supposed to be … courting, but we've never been very close.' She smiled. 'He wants to marry a good worker, you see, the person doesn't matter much, I've come to realize. Clearly he doesn't know me at all.'

The editor took off his glasses and polished them, and then looked again at Rachel's notebook.

'You'd be wasted on a man like that,' he said with a smile. 'The poor man must be very limited.… I suppose it's not conventional for us to sit together without a chaperone, but things are changing, I believe. Women are taking a more active role in society, which means that men and women have to work together.'

'I never thought about it,' Rachel confessed. 'You are just doing your job and I'm trying to help. It was just coincidence that Mother wasn't here.'

'I'm very glad of your help. I like your ideas for the women's page, we'll get on with it as soon as we can.'

Before he left, Alex suggested that Rachel's name should appear on the women's articles.

'We'll keep the reservoir reports anonymous, but you should take credit for other work,' he said firmly. 'Let them know that you're not "just a farm girl".'

'But they'll know that I'm young, some of them. They might prefer to believe an older woman with more experience, don't you think?'

Alex shook his head. 'Mrs Beeton was very young when she wrote her monumental cookery book – did you know that? Everybody quotes Mrs Beeton.'

Ruth came back then and she agreed with the editor that it wouldn't hurt for people to know that Rachel wrote for the *Herald*. 'Plenty of us know how to cook, but not many folks could write about it,' she said. 'It's good to share what you know.'

'That is exactly my point of view,' said Alex. 'A good writer can gather facts from other people as well, remember. Not to steal them, but to quote them. Now, Rachel, can you send me a recipe in the next few days?'

When the visitor had gone, Ruth asked to know what had been decided. About Jim's visit, she sympathized. 'It was bad luck that I wasn't here, love, but you weren't to blame. He's been a bit quiet lately, hasn't he? Jim seems to have a jealous streak, you know,' she said. 'He asked me the other day whether I thought you were too friendly with Roger. I told him that Mr Beckwith is a friend of the whole family.'

'I really wonder whether he's angry because he wants to be,' Rachel suggested. 'He will have to apologize, it was a dreadful scene. He called me a loose woman, Mother.'

'Jim is not turning out as well as I'd hoped,' was Ruth's comment.

When Kit came in that afternoon he was surprised to hear of Jim's outburst.

'Mind you, I can see how it looked to him,' he conceded, 'especially as he had no idea you were sending off reports to the paper.

145

You need to talk to him more, Rachel, tell him what you're doing.'

'I'm not going to get the chance, Father. He said he won't see me again and I must admit, I don't really care.'

Kit looked at his daughter. 'I wasn't going to mention it, but Jim seemed very taken with the new teacher, when we went to fell the tree,' he said. 'But it'll be a pity if you disagree, you two. You'll make good farmers, one day.'

'That's it, then. He's fallen in love,' Rachel laughed. 'I thought at the meeting that he seemed to talk to her for a long time.' It was strange to think that her future was not as certain as she had thought, but to her surprise there was no misery.

'He'll get over it,' Kit decided. 'Miss Ward seemed to be rather – childlike, I suppose you could say.'

'Too much time spent with children, maybe,' Ruth suggested. 'She's a very pretty girl.'

Six months ago I would have been heartbroken, but not now. Jim and I have been growing apart. Rachel remembered, too, what Mr Finlay had said. He'd only met him for a few minutes, but that was enough to decide that Rachel and Jim were not suited. Sometimes an outsider could see things more clearly, perhaps?

Then there was Roger, a warm and courteous lad … a very dear man. Without meaning to, Roger had shown up Jim's limitations. But Roger was out of reach, she must remember that.

Over the next few evenings, Rachel worked on her recipe for Yorkshire pudding and how to make the lightest, crispest puddings, adding what little she knew of pudding history. By Saturday, it was ready and she walked down to the post office to send it off to the *Herald*, together with a short article on making various kinds of herb tea for the 'Country Cures' section.

The wind was cold, blowing grey clouds across the pale sun. As she passed the school, Rachel saw that Jim was working on the fallen tree, chopping it up for firewood. Beside him was a small figure wrapped in a long cloak, watching with great interest. Her anger with him had evaporated; she felt indifferent, but perhaps she should go up to him, try to patch up the quarrel. They were neighbours, the families would have to work together to a certain extent in this small community. She hesitated, then went through the school gate.

The person beside Jim was Violet Ward, the young teacher, who saw Rachel first.

'I was just going,' she twittered nervously. 'I brought Jim a cup of cocoa to keep him warm.'

Jim looked up from his work in surprise when he saw Rachel. 'What are you doing here?' It was not a friendly greeting.

Rachel noticed he was wearing a knitted scarf that she'd never seen before. He usually rejected scarves and gloves, as being for old men. She forgot her good intentions; here he was, alone with a young woman, who was gazing at him with a rapt expression.

'Nice scarf you're wearing, Jim. Did Miss Ward knit it for you?'

The girl blushed bright red and moved from one foot to the other. Rachel continued, 'I wonder, shouldn't you have a chaperone, out here alone together like this?'

For a moment he looked guilty, and then he turned back to the wood. 'Too busy to talk to you, Rachel,' he muttered. 'Got to get home for milking.' Then he glanced at Violet and his expression softened. 'Stay here, Violet, there's no call to leave.'

At that moment, Rachel knew with finality that her future would not be with Jim, after all. His quarrel with her the other day had been deliberate. He'd used Alex Finlay's presence as an excuse to distance himself from her.

The cold wind blew round her and Rachel shivered. The feeling of rejection was not pleasant ... but was some of it her fault? She'd never explained to Jim how she loved to write. If he had known about her work for the *Herald*, he would have understood her much better, but would he have approved? He wanted a farm girl, after all.

Well, Violet Ward was a teacher, but since she came from a farm, she might suit Jim's plans quite well. She was very pretty, but too small for rugged farm work.

'Good luck, lad,' she said as she turned to go home. At the gate, she looked back at the pair; Jim was saying something to Violet and he was holding both her hands.

If Jim had been honest, he would have told Rachel that he'd changed his mind.

FOURTEEN

The sound of raucous singing made its way into the Major's bedroom, waking him from a deep sleep.

'What the …' he struggled out of bed. It sounded like peasants from the village, disturbing his peace.

In dressing gown and slippers, the Major went out to the top of the staircase. Moonlight filtered through a window above the stairs, revealing bodies down below. Were they being invaded?

'What is going on?' he shouted above the din.

On the staircase, a dishevelled figure was crawling up, one step at a time. He was the source of most of the noise. Two village louts, evidently having delivered the body, were backing away. 'Goodnight, General, here's your lad. He's caused enough trouble in village. Don't let him out again.'

Beer must have made them brave; villagers would not normally speak to him like that. It could not be allowed to go on. Guy was still singing and it was no use trying to talk to him. Major Potts kicked him into his bedroom, hurting his slippered foot, and closed the door.

Lady Agnes came out from her room, anxiously peering into the gloom with the aid of a candle. 'Charles! Is it a robbery?'

'Go back to bed, Agnes. I will deal with Guy in the morning.'

For the rest of the night, Major Potts tried to devise strategies to deal with his son. The dignity of the family name was being compromised and the sooner they could send him away, the better.

If only Guy had an interest, something to occupy him … there was evidently nothing for him to do on a country estate except get into trouble.

That morning's post held out a solution, at last. A military contact of the Major's wrote after some delay to offer to look after Guy, with a place in his regiment assured.

He will not receive special treatment, of course, but I will make sure he is treated fairly, his colleague wrote from India. *Send him out on the next boat. We are about to move in about three months, he needs to be here before then if possible.*

The letter ended with the hope that Guy had been given a good education and an appreciation of military discipline, *otherwise it will be hard for him to fit in. But since he is your son, I am confident that he will do very well.*

In his present mood, the Major didn't care whether Guy was treated fairly or not. He had no confidence that Guy would do well, but it was essential for him to begin some sort of career.

'We should have packed him off years ago,' he muttered. It was shameful that he, an army major, could not control his son.

The Major read the letter to his wife at breakfast and saw the relief on her face. 'We will send him off to London straightaway and ask Smithers to make his travel arrangements.'

Smithers was in charge of their London house, a born organizer and a reliable servant.

When Guy emerged from his room at about eleven o'clock, pale and bleary-eyed, the Major told him to report to the library in an hour's time and meanwhile to make himself respectable. He got out the railway timetables and rang for the groom.

'Metcalfe, I want to you to take Mr Guy to the train early tomorrow morning, to travel to Ripon and then to London.'

He noticed a faint smile cross the man's face. The servants would all be glad to see the back of Guy.

'Yes, sir. I believe the train leaves at eight thirty.'

Waiting in the library at the appointed time, the Major copied out the address of his contact in India and wrote down a suggested travel route. Guy would need the right clothes, but he could get them in London. Smithers had access to funds, which was just as well; he did not want to trust Guy with cash. He wrote a long and detailed letter to Smithers.

Guy still did not appear, but there were sounds from the gun room next door. The Major strode in and glared at his son, who appeared to be cleaning a gun.

'Is it that time already? Sorry, Pa. Well, we might as well talk here.'

'You must apologize for your disgraceful behaviour last night. I suppose you can remember what happened? I really cannot allow this sort of thing to continue.'

Instead of looking contrite, Guy continued to fiddle with the gun. 'I'm sure you must have got drunk when you were young, Pa. Don't make such a fuss over nothing.'

It was a waste of time to reason with Guy, to appeal to his better nature. Speaking calmly and slowly, the Major delivered his sentence.

'Last night you disgraced us once again, but it will be the last time you do it in Firby. I have arranged for you to join the regiment immediately. You will take the train to London tomorrow morning, and Smithers will make arrangements for you to sail to India.'

The effect on Guy was immediate. Still holding the gun, he turned bright red, his temper flaring. 'No! I will not go to India. I never thought you would send me to that hellhole! You hated it yourself, I know you did. I am your heir, I should be here. It's my rightful place. I will not join the damned army!'

In all his army career, Major Potts had never come across insubordination such as this. He looked at the young man, flabby and unfit, the opposite of how he had been as a young man. He had a cold feeling that it might be too late to redeem Guy.

'Put that gun down, you fool! You have no sense at all, you are not fit to be my heir. I will disinherit you—' the Major walked towards him.

151

'No, you won't do that,' Guy said quietly.

He raised the gun he was holding and pulled the trigger. In the small room, the explosion was deafening and he dropped the gun with a clatter.

The Major fell, shot at close range, a terrible groan escaping him. As the echoes of the shot died, Guy set up a wail.

'What happened? I never meant to do it …'

Lady Agnes had been waiting for the outcome of this meeting in the library next door and now she rushed into the room.

'Guy, what happened? My God! Charles! Can we help you?' But it was too late. The body on the floor was lifeless, a mass of blood. 'My poor Charles!'

She knelt by his side, weeping. The Major had died instantly, his life ended by a second's decision.

'Pa was cleaning that gun, it went off, it was an accident,' Guy babbled. He had dropped it so that it was close to his father. 'Mother, you've got to believe me, they've all got to believe it was an accident. Pa and me were the best of friends, we were just having a friendly talk …'

For a few minutes his mother knelt, frozen with horror, gazing at the body of her husband on the floor. It had come to this – after all the dangers of army life, to die in his own house. She must act quickly, it was up to her to preserve what she could of their shattered lives.

This was no time for tears. An army wife, Lady Agnes had always been prepared for the worst and now she took charge.

'Be quiet, Guy. Of course it was an accident. Pull yourself together.'

Cold and calm, Lady Agnes rang the bell and when Ruth answered it, she asked her to send for the doctor. 'There has been a dreadful accident,' she said, with just a slight tremor in her voice. 'The Major has been shot.'

Ruth made herself take a look at the body on the floor, before running to find Donald. The groom set off for the doctor without delay, shocked at what Ruth told him. It was his duty to hurry, just in case the Major could be saved. Strange for a military man to make a mistake with a firearm, though.

The next few days were full of comings and goings, organized by Lady Agnes. PC Bradley took statements and sympathized with the bereaved.

'Dreadful accident,' he echoed. Guy Potts kept to his room for most of the time, seemingly devastated by shock and grief after witnessing his father's death. Bradley felt sorry for him. The lad had a lot to learn, but this tragedy might make him grow up a little, take some responsibility.

It was established beyond doubt that the Major himself had pulled the trigger of the gun in a freak accident. The gun had been faulty, Guy said and they were discussing what to do with it. Major Potts had been talking to his son and turning the weapon in his hands. There had been nothing that the horrified son could do.

The undertaker was called in and the funeral arranged, with a grave in the special plot in Firby churchyard reserved for the Family. Lady Agnes engaged a dressmaker to make mourning clothes and summoned her brother, Lord Danby to support her.

The servants were assembled once more in the big dining room. Lady Agnes looked round the subdued faces and realized that they were truly sorry that this had happened; she felt their sympathy, which was unusual. The Major had been calmer of late and not so likely to shout; Kit Garnett had had several good conversations with him. He had even treated his wife with more consideration.

'The Major would want us to carry on with the work of the estate,' she said, 'and that is what we must do. He had decided to stay here, not to sell and to extend the farming business. I will continue with this work and I expect you all to support me. Your place here is secure, for the present at any rate, unless they take the land for a reservoir.'

Guy was standing to one side and she looked at him. 'Mr Guy has given up a career in the army to stay at Firby and work with me,' she continued.

He looked grim, but said nothing. The servants' expressions changed to those of resignation. Mr Guy was not going away, after all. He'd been no trouble since the tragedy, but …

The funeral was a large one, presided over by the vicar at his gloomiest. People were shocked by the accident, realizing that it could have happened to any one of them.

'It's easily done,' they said to each other. They recalled that the year before, a gamekeeper had been badly injured when his gun went off while he was climbing over a stile.

One man had his doubts about the official story. Mr Sutton said to Kit in passing him outside the church, 'I wonder. That young man will bear watching. I haven't forgotten the pheasant shoot.'

Kit himself had grave suspicions that Guy was responsible, but kept them to himself. 'Er … yes, sir.'

The large man put a hand on Kit's shoulder. 'If you find yourself and your family without a job, let me know. I won't steal you from Lady Agnes, she will need your support at the moment. But if you leave, I would be glad to give you a farm to run. I can't imagine how you could work with Guy.'

'Thank you, sir. I would be pleased to work for you, if we have to leave.'

'Well, I like what I've seen of your work, the Major's estate is in good order. It has none of the neglect that you see so often, where the owners are abroad.' He paused and looked round, but there was nobody within hearing. 'Watch your back, Garnett. That youth is dangerous.' Mr Sutton winked at Kit and moved on, a cheerful figure on a gloomy day.

That conversation removed a burden from Kit; at least the Garnetts had an alternative, if they were forced out of their home. Mr Sutton seemed to be a man of good sense and a kindly one. He treated servants as though they were human beings.

After the burial the mourners moved back to the Hall, where Ruth and Rachel had laid out food and drink in the old dining room. There were a few military uniforms among the crowd, but most were the local gentry and the Major's tenants.

Lady Agnes, dignified in black, presided. 'I apologize for my son's absence, he has gone to his room,' Rachel heard her tell one guest. 'He is overcome with grief.'

In fact, he had taken a bottle of whisky with him, saying to his mother, 'I've had enough of these boring people. I can't stand soldiers and the farmers only talk about sheep.'

It was only a few days after the funeral that trouble started again at Firby Hall. Guy Potts knocked on the farmhouse door one evening while the Garnetts were at supper, walking straight in and standing with his back to the fire. They all looked at him with astonishment.

'As the owner of this estate I am going to make changes,' he announced with a smirk. His eyes travelled over Rachel as he spoke. 'You Garnetts have had an easy life for far too long. You are dismissed, the lot of you. I will give you a month to leave Firby Hall for good.' He folded his arms and watched their faces.

Kit Garnett stood up so that he was level with the youth. 'I will talk to Lady Agnes. She assured us that she wishes to keep the farm going, with me as the manager. Mr Guy, I advise you to go carefully. The estate needs careful management and you can't do that without staff.' He paused. 'Your father trusted us for many years.'

'The more fool he. I don't need you to tell me what to do, Garnett. The whole estate will be sold as soon as it can be arranged. It won't need your interference.'

Guy strode to the door and banged it on his way out.

'Poor Lady Agnes!' was Ruth's first thought. 'To have a son like that!'

Kit shook his head. 'I was wondering how on earth we could work with a man like Guy. Now it seems that we won't have to.'

Soon after Guy had gone, Roger came in for supper. He was horrified at the news, but said he wasn't surprised. 'Bromley told me that he's had a letter from Guy saying he wants to sell and that puts the Firby reservoir site back on the map, so to speak. Sutton was always in two minds, you know, and Judge Rupert would probably agree with Sutton.' He sat at the table and looked round. 'After all the ups and downs of the past few months, this is hard for you.'

Mr Richards the solicitor brought the Major's Will to present to the widow and the heir.

'Apart from a few small bequests,' the man told them, 'the estate is left to Mr Guy.'

'Of course, we didn't need you to tell us that.' Guy glared at him.

The solicitor pursed his lips and continued. 'There is the matter of debt, of course. Some of that is yours, Mr Guy, I believe. It will probably be necessary to sell some land, in order to clear the debt. After that, the estate will need careful management, in order to avoid debt in the future.'

'That is what we have in mind,' said Lady Agnes. 'My husband suggested we sell one of the outlying farms to the tenant. I miss his guidance, at the moment.'

Guy Potts stood up and lounged against the mantelpiece. 'Excuse me, Ma, but remember I am now the owner of Firby Hall Estate.'

'Of course, but the plans we have in mind will ensure your future, Guy,' his mother said. 'We can—'

Guy interrupted impatiently. 'And I intend to sell the whole place as soon as possible, and go to live in London. I have an appointment with Bromley from Leeds Corporation tomorrow, there is still a chance that the reservoir will be built here and I intend to pursue it.' He turned to the solicitor. 'I instruct you to offer the estate for sale on the open market, in case the dam project falls through. Either way, you will have no need to worry about piffling debts. Most of them were caused by Pa buying bad shares, anyway.'

Lady Agnes said, her voice shaking, 'You can't do this, Guy!'

'I can and I will. You can go where you like, Ma, and as soon as you like. I'm dismissing the Garnetts, for a start. I've already given them a month to get out. And I'll sell off the antique furniture. Probably arrange an auction sale and advertise, get rid of the shabby old stuff! I hate it here, the whole place smells of hundreds of years of boredom.'

The solicitor was alarmed. 'Mr Guy, I beg you to consider – do nothing rashly. No doubt your sad loss has affected your spirits, this is quite usual after a bereavement and the Major's passing was entirely unexpected. Let Lady Agnes direct you.'

'No!' Guy strode up and down the hearthrug. 'I've had enough of direction, and now I'm in charge. You have the Will, Richards, you know very well you can't stop me!'

Gone was the grieving son; Guy was enjoying himself. Richards was amazed and Lady Agnes realized that the lawyer had never met Guy before and had thought that he was genuinely feeling his bereavement. She knew by now that Guy had no feelings at all.

The lawyer rustled his papers. 'There is one proviso, Mr Guy, which I am pleased to say your late father added to his will for your protection.' He rustled again, adjusting his spectacles. 'Ah, here it is. How old are you? Barely twenty? ' He nodded. 'Well, until you come of age, Mr Guy, that is, you attain to twenty-one years of age, the Lady Agnes is in sole charge of the estate.'

'That's not fair!' Guy was livid. 'A whole year to wait before I can lay my hands on the money?'

His mother sighed in relief. 'One day, I hope you will thank your father for his foresight,' she said quietly.

'Right. Now I know that everyone is against me … I know where I stand. I will make things as difficult as possible for you all, for the next year.' Guy stood over the solicitor. 'You will have to give me an allowance and pay all the debts, since you've been in charge of the money for some reason. I don't care how you do it.'

'Sit down, Guy.' Lady Agnes was angry now. 'Mr Richards has looked after our finances in England because it was impossible for us to do so from India. While I am in charge he will continue to do so.'

'Thank you, Lady Agnes.' Richards put the papers in his brief-case and mopped his brow. 'I will do my best.'

'For now, I suggest you speak to Mr Garnett, our estate manager about the procedure for selling Elm Tree farm. And will you please tell Mr Garnett that I hope he and his family will remain in our service.' His mother looked at Guy.

'Get rid of them!' Guy growled. 'Parasites!'

Lady Agnes stood up and walked to the door. 'We are in a difficult situation and as you can see, Mr Guy is not himself. I hope you will come back in a few weeks to report on progress, Mr Richards, and that by then Guy has seen the wisdom of this course. Perhaps, Guy ... you would like to consider joining the regiment after all, to see something of the world before you come of age?'

It was a forlorn hope. 'Like hell I will!' Guy flung out of the room.

Mr Richards walked across the yard to the so-called farm office, which was small and full of tools. At a battered desk, Kit Garnett was deep in columns of figures. He stood up when he saw the lawyer and passed a hand over his eyes.

'Good day, Mr Richards. I'm doing my best to sort out the accounts and give you a final report on the farm and the estate. I suppose you know we've been dismissed?'

'I did hear so, but I bring you better news. May I sit down?"

Kit cleared a saddle from the only other chair and then sat down at his desk.

'It's a bad job, you know. The Major was just getting to know the farms again ... what is your news, then?'

'Lady Agnes is in charge until Mr Guy turns twenty-one. He is not impressed.'

Kit whistled. 'So she wants us to stay?'

'She does indeed, she specifically asked me to tell you so. Of course, Mr Guy is bound to cause difficulties, but legally he can't do anything.' He sighed. 'I just hope the young man does not run up any more debts.'

'Can't you restrain him at all, Mr Richards?'

'I don't think anyone can … I was astonished this afternoon to meet such a – a headstrong youth. At first I thought he was grieving, but he's not, Mr Garnett, he's just for himself. Nothing else.'

'We have noticed,' Kit said grimly.

'By the way, Her Ladyship referred to you as the Estate Manager,' Richards continued, giving the title capital letters. 'I shall speak to her about a rise in salary for you. She wants you to negotiate the sale of land and that is estate management.'

'A year isn't very long in estate management,' Kit said thoughtfully.

FIFTEEN

'I'VE PLENTY OF orders for Christmas geese,' the butcher told Kit one December market day in Masham. 'Geese from Firby Hall are favourites, think on. I can do with forty or more.'

'Well, we can't manage that many,' Kit said. 'Her Ladyship wants to keep some for breeding this time. We'll maybe have more next year, that is, if we don't get flooded after all.'

'Wouldn't fancy your chance of keeping your head above water – ha, ha!' The butcher looked over a pen of fat pigs. 'Thank goodness we're safe in Masham. They'd never dare to make a dam here on the Ure and if they did, the town's above the river valley.'

'Don't be too sure,' Kit said darkly. 'Leeds doesn't care what happens in the country.'

People were beginning to realize that it would be Firby for the flood water, after all. The Major's death had changed everything and his son was known as a city man who hated the estate.

Rachel plucked the Christmas geese in the big stone barn, watching out all the time for Guy. The barn couldn't be locked, but she had the dog Ben beside her, which should keep Guy away. She was on edge all the time and so was Ben, peering into corners and pouncing on mice.

At last all the geese were ready to go to Masham; she had managed the job without attracting attention from Guy. It felt strange to think of Christmas without Jim, but she would get used to it. No doubt Roger would go to his sister's house in York ... she tried not to think about Roger.

Alex Finlay had asked for a Christmas recipe and Rachel decided on Yule bread, a rich, spicy fruit bread that was only made at Christmas. This year, she and Ruth made the bread together and Rachel made a note of each step. She wanted to add her own comments to the recipe.

Writing was enjoyable and it was good to earn a little money, but it was more than that. This was the first time that Rachel had undertaken anything on her own. She'd worked as a part of the Garnett team since she was small. If she'd married Jim, the rest of her life would have been dictated by him and his family. By accident, she had come across something else that she could do.

'Well, this year's Yule bread is champion, best we've ever made,' was Ruth's verdict. 'You'd better take a loaf to Grandfather, we haven't seen him for a while.'

The December days were short, so Rachel set out as soon as the Yule bread was cool, promising to be back for the evening milking.

Nathan Brown was not about the yard or buildings. Rachel knocked on the door and instead of coming to greet her, Nathan called out, 'Come in.' He was sitting by a low fire with a blanket round his shoulders.

'What's wrong, Grandfather?' This was so unlike him that Rachel was alarmed.

Moving stiffly, Nathan stood up. 'Nothing much, lass,' he said. 'I fell off old Brownie the other day. That horse should know better than to start when a pheasant gets up, but he threw me off and I fell onto a big stone. Ribs cracked, but there's nothing you can do about that. Just don't make me laugh, that's all.'

'That's nothing to laugh about. Shall we go for the doctor?' Rachel tried to keep the alarm out of her voice. 'Is there anything we can do?' She looked round and saw something to do immediately; the fire needed more wood.

'Nay, I've cracked a rib before and I know there's nowt but time will heal it. Doctors can't help. Don't worry, I'll be there for

Christmas dinner!'

'Of course you will, Father will fetch you in the trap.' Rachel made him sit down again and found some wood for the fire. 'Shall I make a cup of tea?'

'You'll have to get back for milking, Rachel. Don't worry about tea, I can do that. But I wonder if you've time to feed the ewes? The old girls are due to lamb early and I'm giving them a bit extra, a bite of hay and a few oats ... but they haven't had any for a few days. I can't carry the fodder, you see.'

'Of course I can. I just yoke up the trap and take the feed from the barn?' Rachel had often helped Nathan with his work and she knew just what to do.

'Aye. Ewes are handy enough, I brought them down from top pasture. That's what I was doing when this happened.' He smiled, but it was a tired smile. 'You're a grand lass, young Rachel. You'll make a farmer!'

On her way out to the yard, Rachel noted the signs; dishes unwashed in the sink and dirt on the floor, most unusual in Nathan's house. Grandfather was finding it hard to keep going and they would have to do something to help him.

'It's hard to be getting old,' Nathan said as she left. 'You don't heal up as fast, that's for sure and a fall hits you harder.'

'I'll be back as soon as I can, Grandfather,' Rachel assured him. 'Keep warm and don't try to lift anything.'

Lady Agnes was quieter than the Garnetts had ever seen her. Dressed in stark black, she spent her days in the library, going through papers. Rachel felt that she genuinely mourned her husband, but what would she do about Guy?

The lady told Kit that everything on the Firby Hall Estate was to continue exactly as it was. No changes were to be made, in spite of the fact that the heir was swaggering about and dismissing staff regularly. Kit advised the servants not to confront him, but to carry on with their work as usual. Guy wasn't likely to know what their duties were and he certainly wasn't up early in the morning, the busiest time of day in the farmyard.

Guy had sulked for days after the solicitor's visit, riding moodily round the estate as though he was trying to work out how much it was worth. All the Garnetts stayed out of his way as much as they could. On Kit's orders, agreed by Lady Agnes, the gun room and the wine cellar were kept permanently locked and only Kit knew where the keys were hidden.

The day after Rachel visited Nathan, her mother decided to drive over in the trap to see him in the afternoon. 'I can bring his washing home, and take him a dinner,' she said.

Rachel went to the kitchen garden for vegetables for their evening meal. At this time of year, John the gardener grew Brussels sprouts and hard winter cabbages. There were bags of potatoes and turnips stored in a dry shed.

Ben was not allowed in the gardens, since he was likely to water any plant that took his fancy. He was excellent with sheep, but with gardens he resisted training; it made no sense to him.

John was nowhere to be seen, but sometimes on a cold day he found work in the glasshouses, so Rachel went into the steamy jungle of exotic plants to look for him.

It was pleasant to wander through the heated houses, warm and fragrant with the scent of growing things. Here there were flowers for the house, a succession of blooms all the year round. Palms and twisting vines cast a green shade; it was peaceful and Rachel began to relax. It would be pleasant to work in gardens, she thought. Although very few women were professional gardeners, there were some who were brave enough – or maybe privileged enough – to go against convention. Someone like Lady Agnes could take an interest in gardens and she would have labourers to do the hard work.

Rachel had read in a magazine at the Hall about a woman called Gertrude Jekyll who designed landscapes for large houses. That would be a wonderful thing to do, using your imagination to work with nature. Miss Jekyll's gardens were quite famous; the magazine had listed several mansions where her gardens could be seen, including Newby Hall near Ripon.

Seeing a figure in the distance, she called out to him.

'John! I've been looking for you …'

The man came closer and she realized her mistake. Rachel had been daydreaming about gardens and had forgotten to watch out for the serpent that lurked in this one. Guy was coming towards her.

'Young Garnett! I followed you here. Come down here for a bit of fun with the gardener, have you? You can play with me instead. I've been looking for you for days.' He backed her up against a bench.

This youth's mind seemed to run on one thing.

'Mr Guy, please leave me alone. The gardener is here … John!' Her voice was deadened by the foliage.

Guy laughed; he must know where John was. 'Now, I'm not going to fight you today. Just have a little chat, to get you to see sense.' Fumes of alcohol surrounded him, in spite of the locked cellar door.

'I don't want to chat with you. Let me go.' Rachel looked round desperately. 'Where are you, John? John!' There was no answer from among the greenery.

Suddenly she felt pity for this miserable human being. 'Guy, what's wrong with you? You're a lost soul. Can't you feel some sympathy with other people? Have you no friends?'

Guy lurched a little, but for a moment he looked stricken. 'I am a lost soul … but nobody cares about me, do you see? If only … no, it's too late. I take what I want.' The expression in his eyes hardened again. 'You can make life easier for yourself, you know. And for your family. Just be a good girl and give me what I want.' Guy licked his lips. 'Now, I have a plan. There's a cottage over at the far side of the estate, an old codger called Daniel has had it rent free for too long. He does no work, he's no use to the estate. I'm going to tip him out and you and I can meet there. Have a little love nest at the other side of the wood. You'll enjoy it and nobody else need know, and I might turn human again.'

'You can't! You can't turn Daniel Wood out of his home, he'd have to go to the workhouse. And I'm not going to meet you any- where. I can't think of anything worse!'

Guy looked at her and she saw the coldness in his eyes.

'Still wearing your knickers, Rachel? I warned you not to. You don't realize the situation. I am the owner here now, I make the decisions and I have decided to take you as often as I can, with or without your underwear. Once you get used to the idea, you'll like it.'

'No! John, are you there?' Rachel struggled, but his grip tight- ened. Guy was a powerful man.

'Come on, Garnett, face the facts. Treat me right and you and the family are safe. But if you won't play, young woman, I'll turn you off without a character reference and make sure that you never work again. All of you will be homeless.' He gave her a shake.

The man was deluded. Guy did not have such power over them; the Garnetts could leave at any time and take a farm on Mr Sutton's estate.

'Who's going to take a scrap of notice of what you say, Guy? A character reference from you would be worse than useless!' Anger replaced fear as Rachel stared him down. She was not going to lie to him, to save herself. Somebody had to stand up to this bully. 'You have no feelings at all, have you? You're a monster.'

The man looked murderous. The red furious look came into Guy's face and as he moved in closer, Rachel remembered some- thing she'd been told long ago. Nice girls carried a hat pin for protection against men like this, but if you had no hat pin, you used your knee. And this time, she was in the right position. He was pressing against her.

Rachel brought her knee up sharply and Guy let out a howl of pain. His hold on her slackened and she stamped on his foot with her heel, then managed to wriggle free. She picked up her skirt and ran like the wind down the length of the greenhouse. At the far end she collided with John the gardener, who was coming through the door.

'Rachel, lass, what's wrong?' John looked down the row of plants. 'I see ... well, you'd best be off as fast as you can. I'll bring vegetables over later.'

A sensible middle-aged man, John thought quickly. He managed to slow Guy down by overturning a barrow to block the greenhouse doorway. It earned him a cursing and a threat of dismissal, but it gave Rachel enough time to get out of the garden. All the staff knew by now how dangerous Guy could be.

When milking was over, Ruth returned and the family assembled for supper. The soothing routine of milking the cows had calmed Rachel's jangled nerves. They talked about Nathan's accident.

'Father's not managing,' was Ruth's verdict. 'If you agree, Kit, I think maybe Rachel should stay with him for a few days. She could help him with the stock and make him some proper meals. What do you say, Rachel?'

Grandfather's farm would be a refuge, a place where Guy could never find her.

'I would love to ... he needs help and I would really like to get away for a while. When I went for the vegetables today, Guy was in the gardens and came after me again.' She choked with emotion, but not for herself. 'He – he's threatening to throw Daniel Wood out of his cottage, Father. Can he really do it?'

'I'd better warn Lady Agnes. The Major would have been horrified, he did try to look after his people,' Kit said quietly. 'Yes, go to Nathan's, lass, it will be good for both of you.' He grinned. 'But don't forget to write your piece for the *Herald*!'

Ruth had a piece of good news. 'Lady Agnes said that she and Guy would go to London soon and stay for Christmas with her brother. With a bit of luck, Guy might not come back. He seems to hate the country. But his mother will be back, she wants to see us make more cheese.'

'That's good, you'll have less work in the house while they're away, Mother.'

Rachel spent her first few days at Nathan's putting the house

166

and yard to rights. She did some washing and baked scones and cakes. Nathan seemed much more cheerful, more like his old, serene self, once order had been restored.

Several neighbours called in to see him. His absence from church on Sunday had been noticed as soon as the relief organist began to play the first hymn.

'Get yourself back to church as soon as you can, lad,' one farmer told him. 'That there organ sounds like a cat being tortured when Phoebe Watson plays!'

'Poor Phoebe never gets much practice,' Nathan reminded him. 'Since she retired from teaching, she doesn't play music right often. This is a good chance for her.'

One bright morning as Rachel was shaking the mats in the yard, she heard the clopping of hooves; they had another visitor. A trap rolled up to the door, driven by a woman in a warm cloak and with a scarf round her head.

'You must be Rachel?' she asked cheerfully. 'I haven't seen you since you were a bairn. Good day, lass, I've come to see your grandpa.'

Rachel offered to help her to unyoke the pony and stable it, but she said she would not stay long. She drove a sturdy Dales pony, shaggy in its black winter coat but in very good condition.

'I'm Alice Bolton,' the woman said. 'From Woodley Crags, I'm off down to Pateley for supplies. My daughter and the family's coming to stay for Christmas, weather permitting of course.'

Alice had heard about Nathan's accident, much to his surprise. 'Can't keep anything quiet round here,' he told her.

'Well, and I'm surprised too. I never thought you would fall off a horse, Nathan. I came to see if there's anything you need, but Rachel here's evidently doing a good job.' Alice Bolton stood by his chair. 'Can you sleep at night? That's the main problem with cracked ribs.'

'Ruth's given me a tea with willow bark in it, very bitter. But it does help me to sleep.' He turned to Rachel. 'Mrs Bolton was a nurse, and a good one, before she married a farmer and went to live up dale.'

'Willow bark's the thing,' the nurse agreed. 'Apart from that, all you need is time and plenty of sympathy, of course. Men always need sympathy.'

They had a cup of tea and a piece of Yule bread.

'Now there's a thing,' Alice said. '*Herald*'s got a Yule bread recipe this week, but it has more spice in it than ever I use. I fear it would be too strong.'

'This is the same recipe,' Rachel told her. 'Do you like it?' She passed over the plate.

'It's grand,' the older woman said, taking another slice. 'I suppose you followed the recipe from the paper. I thought it would be too spicy, but it's not.'

Rachel smiled and said nothing, but Nathan gave her away. 'Did you notice who wrote that recipe for Yule bread, Alice?' He handed the paper over to her.

'Well, I never thought to look – "by Rachel Garnett", that's you! Writing for the paper! You'll be famous, lass,' Alice beamed.

'I just hope I don't ruffle too many feathers,' Rachel admitted. 'People can be very attached to their own recipes. If people don't look to see who writes them, it will be just as well. I won't get the blame.'

'That's as may be, but it doesn't hurt to try something different. Are you going to write a different recipe every week? My, I'll be watching that page every week, after this! Rachel Garnett, on the Women's page!' Alice's eyes twinkled in her brown face. 'Don't you worry about a bit of criticism, Rachel. If we worried too much about what other folks think, nowt would get done.'

About the reservoir little was said; Rachel got the feeling that everyone was tired of the subject. Sometimes it seemed that they would save Firby but at others, it looked like a lost cause. It seemed best to keep busy, which was not difficult, and wait for events to unfold.

'Keep him warm, lass,' Alice said as she climbed back into the vehicle. 'You're doing a grand job, he'll miss you when you go home.' She took the reins and the pony moved off with a shake of the mane, pleased to be moving again.

The house was fairly warm but the fire had burned low, so Rachel went into the woodshed with a basket for logs. It was nearly full of neatly stacked dry wood.

As she made up the fire again, Rachel remarked on the wood. 'You must have chopped all that wood before the accident, and a good thing, too! That's one job I can't manage, I'm afraid.'

Nathan smiled. 'That was young Roger,' he said. 'Weeks ago he came here and spent most of Sunday chopping wood, he could see it was a help at this time of the year, with short days and cold nights. He's a grand lad. He said it was good for him, the exercise.'

Rachel busied herself with sweeping the hearth. Since she'd been at Grandfather's, she had tried very hard not to think of Roger. This was an example of the sort of man he was; how many lads would spend their one day off chopping wood? She missed him more than she had imagined possible. Perhaps the pain would subside, once he had left for good. It was almost a physical pain, knowing that he would soon be gone.

It was while they were eating supper that night that Rachel said, 'I remember sitting at this table when I was very small, with you and Grandmother....'

Memories were coming back to her; it was a long time since she had stayed at Grandfather's farm. She was always too busy at the Hall.

Nathan looked across at her. 'Can you remember a little lad sitting here too, a lad with bright red hair? You couldn't say his name, so you called him—'

'Wodge! I remember Wodge, he made me a skipping rope!' Rachel was amazed that it had taken her so long to remember Wodge. She had loved him, but then he didn't come to the farm any more. 'That ... was my version of Roger, I suppose?'

'It was, lass. He was taken to York when his mother moved there, so we lost touch with him.' Nathan told her what he knew of

Roger's life; he had known his parents well.

'I wonder where that skipping rope is now,' Rachel said.

SIXTEEN

Roger was in Leeds when the blow fell. Grey, grimy Leeds, where the wealth of the nation was being produced – how could he escape from living in the city? He was working on the calculations for the Woodley Crags dam site, hoping that he could convince the managers to leave Firby alone.

Bromley strode into his office and stood with folded arms, glaring at him. 'I've just found out what you're doing, Mr Foster told me. You're wasting your time. What's more, you're wasting the Corporation's time.'

Roger stood up and looked out of the window at the drab city streets.

'I hope not,' he said quietly. 'Most people agree that a reservoir at Firby has too many disadvantages. The more I look at Woodley, the more I can see it's the best site.'

'You're stupid! Use your brain, man!'

Roger knew that there was no point in arguing. Bromley had the last word.

'Your problem is, you've become too friendly with the locals, Beckwith. That's always a mistake. In future, remember to keep your distance and remember who pays your wages. I'm afraid I shall have to take you off this job.'

'No ...' Even if it went to Firby, Roger still had a job to do.

Bromley smiled; he was enjoying himself. 'Getting too emotional about a shabby old house – a waste of time. Nobody will really care if Firby Hall is knocked down, especially the heir. He wants to knock it down himself!'

It was hard to know what to say. 'You've been talking to Mr Guy Potts, I gather.'

'There's a man with no false sentiment,' Bromley sneered. 'He came to Leeds, he wants to push the project as hard as he can.'

'So what next?' Roger looked down at his work. The Woodley project was coming along well and he was proud of it. 'Would you like to see the Woodley figures?'

'Who authorized you to work on this? Just because you talked to the Chief, it didn't mean that I agreed to it. No, I don't want to see the work you've done on Woodley. I am opposed to it.' Bromley pushed his flushed face close to Roger.

'Mr Foster suggested some preliminary work, which is what I'm doing,' Roger explained, taking a step backwards. The Chief Engineer was much more open-minded than Walter Bromley. 'I was hoping to show it to you very soon, so you can have all the facts. I've written a report.' He had been working hard on a rational, scientific approach, with a list of the benefits of the new site to Leeds Corporation.

'Well, you can forget about it. You are to go and investigate a bridge over the Aire that's about to fall into the river. We've closed the bridge, you will work out what needs to be done and estimate the cost of repairs. Start tomorrow.' Bromley's thin lips shut like a trap.

'But … I've left equipment at Firby, and a horse….' This was terrible, he couldn't just walk away from Firby.

'And you've probably fallen in love with one of the village maidens, I know your type.' Bromley walked to the door. 'Oh, very well, go and claim your possessions. You won't be going back, I shall put another man on the job once the project has been approved.'

'Thank you, Mr Bromley.'

At least he could go back and explain to the Garnetts what had happened and pay what he owed. The horse Charlie would have to be sold; he had no room for a horse in Leeds. On the other hand, how long would he be stuck there, before he could get out into the countryside again? Perhaps he could ask the Garnetts to stable the horse for a few weeks, until he found out where the next big job would be.

Even if Bromley was not taking him off the Firby project, Roger knew that nothing could happen there until official approval had been given.

'And be ready to work on the bridge next week,' Bromley added. 'The citizens are restive, they have a long detour now that the bridge is closed. We need to be seen to be doing something.'

Roger looked at his boss. 'Then maybe you should go down there, to show them that a senior manager is working on the problem.'

Bromley smirked; reference to his position always pleased him. 'Perhaps I will.'

Roger caught the Harrogate train the next day, after a few hours in the office. On the journey through the Pennines, he thought about Firby and the blow that was to come. It was hard to believe that he had ridden into Firby with a light-hearted laugh some months ago, planning to flood their valley. He hadn't considered the human cost.

As so often these days, Roger thought about Rachel and how wonderful it would be to spend the rest of his life with that bright, honest, beautiful girl. But he'd given his word to Jim that he wouldn't suggest anything of the sort.

Should he have told Jim that it was every man for himself? But although Rachel was far from being 'just a farm girl', she was a country lass, through and through. It was one of the things he loved about her. She would hate Leeds; he could not take her away into the city, it would be too selfish.

There were few jobs in country areas for a civil engineer. He was attracted to the idea of farming and had read about the new scientific methods of livestock breeding. The obstacle there was his lack of capital to buy and stock a farm. Even if he were lucky enough to find one to rent, he wouldn't be able to afford to run it. Landowners would look for a tenant with experience as well as capital; it would be impossible to get a start.

Sometimes recently, Roger had thought that Rachel felt the same way about him, but it was probably just her friendly nature. She was pleasant to everybody, valued everybody. It would be better to keep to his word; after this visit, that would be easier. He wouldn't be living at the Garnetts again.

His train arrived in Masham in the afternoon. Roger eventually found a ride up to Firby with the carrier and walked up the village with a heavy heart. Rooks were cawing their way homeward and Pearson's cows plodded along their home pasture in single file, on their way to milking.

Mr Jackson was seeing the last students off the premises as Roger walked by, so he was the first person to be told the news from Leeds. The city seemed to be infinitely far away as Roger explained that the balance had shifted and that he would not be sent to Firby again. It was a relief to talk to someone who understood how he was feeling.

'My boss thinks I'm biased,' he told Jackson. 'He won't look at my report about Woodley Crags. He told me that Guy Potts has been to Leeds, to talk to the managers. Things have changed a great deal since the Major died.'

Jackson agreed. 'We probably didn't appreciate the Major enough. If he'd been with us a little longer, I think he would have been a good influence in the area.'

Roger lingered at the school, talking to Jackson about whether anything could still be done.

'I really don't know whether Mr Sutton and Judge Walton will be able to do anything now,' Jackson said and sighed. 'But I'd better go to see them, since you can't do it.'

Roger gave him a summary of the report on Woodley Crags. 'To my mind, the best way to argue the case is to stress the advantages to Leeds of the Woodley site. They are only interested in their own advantage – their own rate payers.'

He knocked at the Garnetts' door just as night fell on the short December day. Ruth answered his knock and her face lit up in a heart-warming smile.

'Roger, it is so good to see you! Come in. We were wondering when you would be back again.'

The evening chores were done and it was time for supper. The Garnetts made room for him at the table, gave him a plate of soup and made him feel welcome, just as they always did. This time, though, it could be the last.

Roger tried to hide his disappointment as he looked round the kitchen; Rachel was not there.

'Nathan had an accident, Rachel's up there helping him,' Ruth explained.

'That's bad news ...' They told him the details.

It was hard to have to tell them that due to the actions of Guy Potts, aided by Bromley, it was likely that their valley was doomed.

'After all we've been through ... I thought we had won.' Kit was dismayed. 'But at least we'll have you here, Roger, when the project starts. It needs to be somebody who knows how people feel.'

'Well,' Roger began, 'that has changed, too. Mr Bromley will send another man here when the time comes. He ... he told me to stay in Leeds.'

'What about your work at Woodley Crags?' Kit wanted to know. 'Surely they can see that it would be the better site, once they see your calculations?'

'He wouldn't look at the figures, Mr Garnett. So ... I have to start work in Leeds on Monday. I should probably sell Charlie.'

There was a shocked silence round the table as the news sank in.

'Well,' Ruth Garnett said as she got up to clear the plates, 'we won't give you up, Roger. Please come here for Christmas – unless you have other plans?'

'Thank you,' Roger said, feeling their sympathy. The news was bad for them, but they were thinking of him. His sister was to spend Christmas in the south with her husband's family. 'I haven't any plans.' He had no plans for the rest of his life, come to that.

'If you'd like to leave the horse here for a while, that may be best,' Kit suggested. 'I can use him occasionally, keep him active. If you really can't manage to come back here, we can sell him for you. But you never know, the tide may turn!'

They began to make plans for Christmas, only a week away. A few days' leave could be added to the holiday, Roger thought. Kit said that if Roger could be there on Christmas Eve, he could help with getting in the logs and decorating the house with holly and ivy.

'And then we'll go carol singing in the village,' Ruth told him. 'Can you sing, Roger?'

'I used to sing in the school choir, when I went to school in York,' Roger admitted. 'That's a long time ago!'

The next morning, before setting off to go back to Leeds, Roger saddled up Charlie.

'I'd better go to see Mr Brown, tell him the bad news myself,' he said at breakfast.

'Aye, he likes visitors, he can't get about much,' Kit said. 'Rachel will be pleased to hear you'll be with us for Christmas, remember to tell her.'

She was crossing the farmyard with a basket of eggs when Roger arrived at Nathan's farm, in a blue dress with her dark hair blowing in the wind. He knew he would never forget the sight of her that day; she put down the basket and crossed quickly to where his horse stood. He swung from the saddle and she ran into his arms.

'Rachel!' His face was buried in her hair and he caught the scent of rosemary. There were tears on Rachel's face as she looked up at him.

'I'm sorry, Roger. I forgot myself....'

He kissed the tears away and tasted the salt, then Roger kissed her on the lips, a long, satisfying kiss, a mutual kiss.

Roger felt delirious. 'Too late, lass, you've given yourself away!

I've missed you so much, then last night you weren't at home ... I love you, Rachel.' He hadn't meant this to happen, but he couldn't help himself. For a magical moment they held each other close.

Rachel stood back and looked at him. She was serious, sad as she said, 'But there's no future for us, Roger. No hope.'

She must mean that she was going to marry Jim. That, and the fact that he had no real prospects....

'Rachel ...' Roger said, happiness draining away. 'I wish I could argue with you, but it wouldn't be fair.'

Taking the bridle from him, Rachel led his horse into the stable. 'Go and see Grandfather, I will be there in a few minutes.'

Nathan Brown looked a little thinner and older, but his grey eyes were still alight with a kindly welcome as Roger walked in. 'It's good to see you, lad, you've been missed.'

What could a country lass offer a clever man like Roger? Rachel sobbed as she put Charlie into the stable and slid off the saddle. He knew it himself, he wouldn't argue. He said he loved her, but did he really know her?

From her own point of view there were more problems. He had his profession to think of, he had to earn a living, but it was something she couldn't help him with. Rachel knew that there was a great gulf between the city and the country. She didn't want to live in a city, patronized by city folk – they often thought that those living in the country were simple. Roger would tire of his simple country lass in time; she would have to remember that and be strong.

Roger's horse nuzzled her shoulder and she gave him a carrot. Charlie made her feel calmer; she patted him gratefully. The company of animals had always been important to her. At Grandfather's there were plenty of animals, but she missed her dog Ben's easy company. She was a farm girl.

It was time to go in. Drying her eyes and smoothing her hair, Rachel went into the kitchen and found the two men at the table, deep in talk. Roger was sketching a plan on a scrap of paper. They both turned to her and Nathan said, his face serious, 'You won't have heard Roger's news, lass. The city bosses are going to build the dam at Firby, after all.'

Roger looked up without his usual smile, but he too seemed to have recovered his calm manner. 'Unless we can twist a few arms, that is. Mr Jackson has promised to try.' He sighed. 'How many times has the site shifted up onto the moors and back again, in our minds at least? You've met my manager, Mr Bromley. He's always been very much in favour of the Firby site.'

'People are tired of it all by now, they just want to know one way or the other,' Rachel said bitterly. 'When the Major died, I really thought this might happen. Guy Potts is out to upset as many people as he can. He told my father he's going to sell the estate and he wants Leeds to build the dam here.'

Roger looked at her carefully. 'Has Guy Potts given you more trouble, Rachel?'

She paused before answering. Roger had promised to thrash Guy if he molested her again, but she didn't want that. 'Next year he will come into his inheritance. Until then Lady Agnes is trying to keep things as they are, but the poor woman has no control over him.'

Roger shook his head. 'There's nothing we can do, although Leeds want the matter to be decided quickly, the Chief Engineer told me. The site should be decided before Guy turns twenty-one … which means nothing of course, if the other landowners are pushed by Bromley into agreeing with him.'

'Why is Mr Bromley so much against the Woodley site?' Nathan wondered. 'He could at least have looked at your work.'

Roger laughed. 'He's a city gent, I really think he hates the idea of working up there, among all those fells and that wide expanse of sky. He would be one of the site superintendants and would have to go there in all weathers and listen to the labourers' complaints! Firby's more civilized, he can imagine building a workmen's village here with no trouble at all.'

Rachel remembered meeting Mr Bromley on his tour of the

Hall and his rude remark about her ancestry. 'I don't think he cares about people. The fact that hundreds of people will have to leave won't worry him at all. He probably thinks he's doing them a favour, sending them to live in a town.'

'I suppose he might be thinking of the climate in winter,' Nathan suggested. 'There's more rain and snow up there and it's a coat colder than Firby.' The older folk often compared climates in this way.

'More rain means more water for Leeds, as I have pointed out ...' Roger leaned back in his chair and Rachel thought he looked suddenly tired. 'I'm afraid I have to leave now, to go back to the office. Mrs Garnett invited me to join your family for Christmas, and I will take a few days' extra leave. I'll chop some more wood for you then, Mr Brown.' Roger would not stay for a meal. 'I have to catch a train.'

After he had gone, there was silence in the kitchen except for the ticking of the old clock. Nathan walked about the kitchen for a while.

'I'm improving every day,' he told his granddaughter. 'It's time you went back to help out at home, much as I like having you here. Kit can come and fetch me for Christmas, if he will.'

Rachel sat at the table and pulled a sheet of paper towards her. 'If I post a note to the *Herald* today on my way home, it should be in time for this week's edition,' she said. 'I will go home, Grandfather, but I will be back tomorrow.'

Walking down the village street to post her report, Rachel wondered whether she should tell the *Herald* what Roger had said. But Guy Potts was apparently telling everyone the same story, so why not? These thoughts were occupying her mind when she saw a cart coming towards her: Jim Angram with bags of grain.

Jim pulled up the cart beside her and jumped down, then stood awkwardly at the horse's head. 'Good day, Rachel. I ... er ... was coming to see you.'

'We haven't seen much of you lately, Jim,' Rachel said quietly. 'How is Violet?'

Jim jumped as though he'd been stung.

'It's all right, lad,' she said gently. 'I know about Violet.'

'Violet's going home to Skipton for the holidays after Christmas, she's staying for the school nativity play,' Jim said miserably. 'But ... how did you know? I've been feeling that bad, you and me are practically engaged and all that ...' He stood fiddling with the horse's bridle, not looking at her.

Rachel said lightly, 'Good job we're not married, isn't it? We can forget about you and me, Jim. I've seen you with Violet ... whether it lasts or not, there's something between you. And there's not much between you and me. We're friends, I suppose, but that's all.'

'I don't want to hurt your feelings, lass ...' Jim was looking more cheerful.

'You're not. I am ending our so-called engagement, so you, my lad, are being jilted. How do you like that?' Rachel laughed; she was happy that it was out in the open.

'I'm that glad you're not angry,' Jim said fervently. 'I – told my Ma about Violet and she was upset, she's worried about you and says she wants you for a daughter in law.'

'Because I make good sausages?' Rachel laughed again. 'You don't marry a girl just because she suits your mother, not in Yorkshire these days! Happy Christmas, Jim, and don't worry!'

SEVENTEEN

JUST BEFORE CHRISTMAS, Alex Finlay decided to try out a daring idea. He wanted to start a book publishing business in Ripon, but the owners of the *Herald* were not keen to invest in books. They preferred newspapers.

'Everybody reads newspapers,' the Chairman told Alex, 'but how many read books? Not so many, I think.'

However, the Board had no objection if he wanted to invest in the venture at his own expense, provided it did not take up too much of his time.

His plan was to use the printers who had a business in Ripon just across the square from his office, rather than set up his own press. The owner of the business, Edward Darley, was an experienced man who would guide him through details such as the choice of paper and binding, things that would affect the cost and also the appearance of a book.

'You're a professional when it comes to editing and layout ... I suppose you're thinking of local history books, like Edmund Bogg's?' Darley chuckled. 'They are very popular. Unless you've written a novel, of course!'

'Local history would be a good idea,' Alex agreed. 'No novels, Mr Darley.'

A legacy from an uncle was sufficient to see the venture off the ground; Alex was prepared to forget about buying a house in Ripon for the present.

Susan Sutton was also on Alex's mind. He was fascinated by her bright, confident personality. The publishing venture would, he hoped, interest her and she might even want to be involved in it. Although few women would venture into a man's world, Susan helped her father with the running of the Cranby estate.

'I like to have plenty to do,' she had told him.

Alex had begun to visit Cranby Chase quite often; his mother's family were similar people to the Suttons and he felt at home there. Mr Sutton owned a brewery at Tadcaster, the profits from which were invested in improvements to his estate. He was often away on business, but Susan was always pleased to see Alex. An aunt of hers lived with them and acted as chaperone, so that the conventions were observed. But sometimes Alex and Susan went riding and the aunt stayed at home.

One fine afternoon they had arranged to ride through the park surrounding the Sutton's house.

'Did you know that Father has gone to London, about this reservoir affair?' Susan greeted him when he reached the stables. 'That little toad Guy Potts has organized the Leeds people to build the dam at Firby, after all! He's a traitor to his class and to his tenants as well!' Her eyes flashed; Susan looked magnificent when she was angry. 'If tenants lose their farms, there is no recompense. I wonder how many of them, or their workers would find a living somewhere else. I've talked to our tenants, the ones that could be affected and they are very worried.'

Alex smiled. 'The next edition of the *Herald* will carry similar information, without the – um – epithets. My correspondent says that the decision is likely to be Firby.' He paused. 'Do you really think Potts could influence the decision, on his own? One of the engineers is very much in favour of Firby, although the correspondent doesn't name him.'

'Excuse me, Alex, but have you met Potts? I don't know how poor Lady Agnes puts up with him! I was there for the pheasant shoot and that day, he was obnoxious! Father and the other two were discussing the dam and Guy was obviously in disagreement.

He wants the estate to be sold immediately. I am sure that it will be his fault if Firby is flooded.'

Alex had met Potts; he had a vivid memory of his encounter with Guy's fist, in the farmyard at Firby Hall. He privately thought the 'little toad' was mad, but decided to forget about that experience.

'Yes, unfortunately. Obnoxious is the word.'

A groom had saddled her horse and he held the bridle while Susan mounted, spreading her riding skirt gracefully around her. Miss Sutton looked well on a horse. She had the fresh complexion of a countrywoman and had obviously spent a great deal of time outdoors. Alex had often wondered how women managed to ride side saddle, but Susan did it with ease and grace. She could jump fences as well as he could.

When they were out of earshot of the stables, Alex asked, 'What does Mr Sutton hope to do in London, Susan?'

'He knows a few politicians and he's quite friendly with people who pull the strings in government. He had no strong feelings about the dam at first, of course the Chase here won't be flooded. But our tenants bordering Firby will lose their land and there's not much we can do about it. Papa's concerned, he says he will talk to everybody in the area, to find out where there might be other farms to let. He does try to help our people where he can ... unlike Guy Potts.' Susan was obviously proud of her father.

'He's a considerate landlord,' Alex agreed.

Susan nodded. 'As time has gone on, he's become a champion of the Firby cause and he really wants to beat Guy Potts. He has grave suspicions about the youth.' She laughed. 'Father is very ... determined when he wants to beat somebody.'

'I must ask whether Mr Sutton will give us an interview for the *Herald*,' Alex suggested, but Susan thought not.

'With respect, he probably won't, he's talking to the *Yorkshire Post*. That's a really influential paper,' she said robustly. Alex winced, but he knew she was right. 'It's published in Leeds, so the men who make decisions there will read it. They need to know the truth about the human cost of flooding Firby.'

Susan was a bold young woman with decided opinions. She would tell him what she thought about the publishing idea; it would be useful to consult a woman, since the booksellers reported that many books were bought by women.

'A splendid idea!' was Susan's verdict, when he mentioned publishing as they were on the homeward ride. 'Some sort of Yorkshire content would be very popular – look at Edmund Bogg's walking tours! Is that the sort of thing you have in mind, Alex? May I be involved?'

Alex was surprised at her enthusiasm. 'What would you like to do – have you written a book yourself?'

They were cantering up a rise and Susan urged her horse forward, to beat Alex to the top. When he caught up, she was laughing and breathless. 'That gave Ripley a stretch! But we were talking about book publishing. I'm interested because I would love to be involved in a business, calculating costs and returns, that sort of planning. I think I might be good at business, I've learned a little from helping Father here.'

Alex's cautious Scottish brain, inherited from his father, thought that Susan might want to enjoy speculating with his money, but he put that aside. 'You're welcome to help me with the planning, if you like,' he said. 'I believe you would be good at letting people know about the books – discreetly advertising them and making sure that booksellers want to stock them.'

'Very good – what's our first book going to be?' Susan looked as though she was ready to start immediately.

'I'm not sure yet. Of course, Susan, this will be a very small publishing house compared with large, well-established publishers in London and Edinburgh. It won't have prestige at first and it probably won't attract established writers. We wouldn't get people like Scott or Dickens or the Brontës! That's one reason why I don't want to publish novels.' They reined in at the stables and Alex jumped down, then helped Susan to dismount.

Susan was persistent. 'The big publishers must have started

somewhere!' She was quiet for a few minutes. 'A local book, pub-lished here in Yorkshire, could appeal to the people who read the *Herald*. People who don't read novels.'

As they walked up to the house, Susan clapped her hands. 'I know what you should do! A recipe book, Alex, of Yorkshire or even North Country recipes. You've told me your new Women's page is popular.'

Susan, unlike most women Alex knew, never chattered. She glanced at him with her bright eyes and left a silence for him to think about her idea as they went indoors.

Beside a log fire in the sitting room, Susan's aunt was busy with needlework. She looked up with a smile for Alex, who was a favourite with her.

'Enjoy your ride? Of course you did! There is fresh tea over there.'

Susan led Alex over to the tea table by the window.

'That is a good idea, if we can find a second Mrs Beeton,' he said cautiously. It was a brilliant idea, but he needed time to think about it.

'What enthusiasm!' laughed Susan. 'You obviously don't rush into things.' She poured tea for them both and carried a cup over to her aunt. 'I can visualize it ... one recipe to each page, with a drawing and a note on the history or folklore that relates to it.'

'I think Rachel Garnett would be able to come up with some useful material,' Alex said thoughtfully. 'In fact ... it could be Rachel's book. She could try out recipes from other sources as well.'

'Rachel would be a good choice.' Susan passed him a plate of biscuits. 'Cook made these, she would be pleased to give us some of her recipes, I think.' She turned to her aunt and explained what they were talking about. 'Yorkshire recipes, Aunt, for a book.'

'The recipes in the *Herald* are sensible,' Aunt Jane said brightly. 'Cook and I have talked about them. Are you planning something?'

'I'm hoping that Miss Garnett who sends in the recipes will

help with the book,' Susan told her. 'I will try to research the history of some of these foods ... someone told me that Yule bread came originally from Norway.'

They talked about illustrations. 'A good drawing of the finished cake or whatever it is ... to make people want to try it,' Alex decided. He looked round the room and saw an easel in the far corner. 'Are you an artist, Susan? Perhaps you could be the illustrator?'

An hour was spent looking through Susan's portfolio of drawings, which were impressive.

'I had a good art teacher,' she said. 'I love drawing, but not painting – too messy!' As in everything, Susan was not coy about her art. She said in her straightforward way, 'I will try a few drawings to see whether they would be suitable for book illustrations. But if they're not, I won't be offended. I only have a mediocre talent.'

The afternoon had gone very well. Alex was pleased that Susan was so interested in his project and that she wanted to work with him. Fleetingly, he wondered whether Mr Sutton would approve. He might have made plans for a brilliant marriage for his only daughter and not want her to spend more time with a lowly newspaper editor.

In fact, he reflected as he looked through the drawings, his friendship with Susan was on fragile ground. Well born and well educated, Alex Finlay was not wealthy. He could never offer Susan a home like Cranby Chase. They were drawn to each other from their first meeting, but what of the future?

A maid came in with lamps and Alex realized that outside the big windows, night was falling.

'I'd better be off,' he said.

They agreed to meet soon after Christmas, to start work on plans for the book. Where they could do this was not yet clear; he could hardly use the newspaper office for a private venture.

Riding back to Ripon under a rising moon, Alex decided not to worry about the future but to concentrate on the present. He had two days off at Christmas, not long enough for him to visit his parents in the south. The weather was cold and snow was talked about, so he was glad enough not to be travelling. He would spend the holiday planning his new venture. On Christmas Eve, it would be good to go to the service in the cathedral and for Christmas Day, he was invited to the home of a friend of his father, a Ripon solicitor, Robert Denham.

The only drawback with dinner at the Denhams was Mr Denham's twittering daughters. Mrs Denham was a well-built lady who was looking for suitable husbands for her two girls, a fact which made them self-conscious. The girls competed with each other for Alex's attention and he found them tiring.

The next day at his office, Alex had a visit from the *Herald* Chairman, who was in a good humour. He seemed to be interested in the publishing project and Alex told him what they had planned.

'Miss Sutton wants to be involved,' he said, knowing that the Chairman was Miss Sutton's uncle.

'Young women want to be involved in everything, these days. Heaven knows what they'll get up to in the future!' He looked over his half-moon glasses at his editor.

Alex had talked to Susan long enough to know some of the arguments.

'Well,' he said mildly, 'women are half the human race and they do possess brains, they tell us. Some of them would like to do more than look after a home.' He thought of Rachel, who loved to write.

The Chairman chuckled. 'I can see that my niece has been influencing you. She's a charming girl, but a mite too forceful! She knows a lot of people and won't be afraid to promote your book … I can imagine that she'll be a great help.'

The Chairman went off to a meeting of the Board and came back with a suggestion. 'The room we meet in – it's used very little. Would you like to borrow it for your publishing project? If Susan's involved you need to meet somewhere respectable, you can't just sit about in public houses as you journalists often do.

ANN CLIFF

Just keep a record of the hours you take off from the *Herald*, I'm sure they will be made up in overtime. You've worked long hours recently.'

Alex beamed. 'Thank you, sir, that will be excellent!' He had wondered how to overcome that particular obstacle. It was a perfect solution; he needed somewhere to sort out the material as it came in, as well as somewhere to talk over the book with Susan and Rachel.

'You have Susan to thank for your horse, you know,' the older man said as he turned to go. 'She told me that the *Yorkshire Post* were after you, so we decided to give you Ripley ... to make you more comfortable here. But you wouldn't want to work for the *Post*, you know. Ripon is much more pleasant than Leeds.'

Alex suppressed a grin. 'I agree, sir. Did Miss Sutton find Ripley for you?'

'Of course she did, Susan knows horses. Happy Christmas, my boy.'

Susan Sutton was obviously a girl who used guile to get her own way. Alex wondered whether the idea was to make it possible for him to visit her more often; it was an exciting thought.

He wasn't aware of ever having had a job offer from the *Yorkshire Post* ... but then, Susan knew a lot of people, as her uncle had said. She had told people lately about the increase in circulation of the *Herald*, since Alex took over as editor.

He thought it was possible that Susan would attend the carol service in St Wilfrid's ancient cathedral, but Alex was disappointed. On the morning of Christmas Eve, snow began to fall, delicate flakes fluttering from a leaden sky. People from the nearby villages prudently stayed at home, so the congregation was reduced to Ripon's citizens. Even so, the nave was at least half-full; the Methodists forgot their differences and the atheists joined good-naturedly with the Church of England stalwarts for the carol service.

The choir was a good one and the music soared as only cathedral music can, up into the shadows of the roof. Candlelight

188

flickered warmly across the famous fifteenth-century carvings of the choir stalls, lighting the choristers' earnest faces. The scarlet berries of holly shone in the light. Ripon was a little city with a small cathedral, but with centuries of history.

Alex exchanged greetings with several citizens he knew. If Susan were there, the evening would be perfect. He wondered how many days would pass before he saw her again. The snow was beautiful, but it would keep them apart.

Christmas dinner with the Denham household was a traditional affair of roast goose and plum pudding. Alex took with him a bottle of port and some chocolates. The day passed pleasantly, with food, drink, jokes and music provided by the young ladies, who sang and played the piano.

'Watch out tomorrow morning for the Sword Dance,' one of the girls told him – he always forgot which was Isabel and which was Marjorie. They were very much alike.

'It's Mr Finlay's first Christmas in Ripon,' their mother said. 'He won't know what you mean.'

'Well,' began Isabel – or was it Marjorie? Alex felt guilty for not learning their names. 'You will have heard of the medieval mummers' plays, Mr Finlay? The Ripon version is the Sword Dance. Local lads dress up in strange costumes and act out a play, with a dragon and ...'

'They have wooden swords.' The other sister took up the story. 'They have music, a fiddle and pipes and they dance round until the swords are all locked together in a pattern ...'

'Very interesting,' said Alex politely.

'If you're on the square about ten in the morning, you'll see them,' they told him.

Their father agreed. 'They go round the town to various locations, including some of the public houses. It's best to see them perform at ten, before they start the rounds.' Mr Denham grinned. 'They must be incoherent by the end of the day.'

EIGHTEEN

SNOW WAS FALLING as Roger's train reached Masham on the morning of Christmas Eve, but he was in luck. Kit's trap was lined up outside the station and the tall man was waiting on the platform to greet him.

'Real Christmas weather,' said Kit cheerfully, 'and there's more snow to come. It does make farm work harder, but it's seasonal. It snowed a couple of days ago, up here.'

As they jogged up the hills to Firby, Kit explained that Lady Agnes had decided to stay at Firby after all because of the weather, so he'd had to make a trip to Masham for extra supplies and had timed it to fit in with Roger's train.

'She's invited the Waltons to the Hall, she wanted a ham and a big Wensleydale cheese ... oh, a lot of other things. We can now go home. She sent me because Donald the coachman's got the influenza.'

Roger, his collar turned up against the snow, looked over at Kit beside him, an independent man and a clever one. Years of working as the Firby Hall manager had conditioned him into being a servant. Perhaps that would happen to him, if he became a gamekeeper.

'Where is Guy at the moment?'

'He was going to London ... but he's afraid of the snow,' Kit said grimly. 'I don't think his friends will miss him. But he won't be much trouble for a few days. The Dale brothers gave him a hiding he won't forget. It was well overdue.' Kit handed over a rug. 'Wrap this round you, lad.'

'It certainly was about time someone taught him a lesson ... but won't they suffer for it?' Roger took the rug gratefully; it was soft and carried the scent of lavender. The air was bitterly cold, much colder than Leeds.

'They know they've nothing to lose, everyone knows that now. Guy is going to sell us all up no matter what, he's boasting about it. So now,' Kit said with satisfaction, 'he's got nothing to protect him. He must realize that by now.'

Roger helped Kit to deliver the supplies to the Hall kitchen, where Cook was frantically trying to make Christmas fare at the last minute.

'I thought they was off to London,' she said crossly to Roger. 'And now, all of a sudden we're entertaining, guests invited for dinner. Some folks have no consideration. Mr Guy's in bed, so we have to carry meals up ... a lot more work, o' course.'

'Mr Guy has the influenza, has he?' Roger said innocently. 'There's a lot of influenza in Leeds.'

'Nay, that's what Her Ladyship says, but he's black and blue after a beating,' Cook said happily. 'He won't be let out till the bruises have faded.'

'The carol singers might come here,' Kit reminded her as they left.

'Aye, I've made four dozen mince pies and we have some ginger wine. We're ready for 'em.'

Rachel was in the dairy and greeted him shyly as Roger crossed the yard. He too felt the constraint; they had lost the easy friendship of the past few months. *Jim's girl, and don't you forget it.* He couldn't help feeling a leap of happiness at the sight of her.

'It's good to be here,' he said and Rachel nodded with an answering smile.

'I was afraid the trains would stop running and you'd be staying in Leeds.'

The snow continued to fall, piling up in corners and covering the yard with a blanket of dazzling white.

'The snow is beautiful here,' Roger said. 'In Leeds, it's dirty slush.'

Before they went into the farmhouse kitchen, Kit looked at the sky. 'There's more to come. I doubt we'll have to make it a short trip round the village with our Christmas carols this year.'

Roger and Rachel decorated the rooms with holly and ivy, dark evergreens with the fresh smell of winter woods about them. The day went quickly with preparations for Christmas; Kit went out in the trap again and brought Nathan back with him, to spend the night with them.

'I love singing carols in the village, but it's ower cold for me this year,' he told Roger. 'I'll stay here with Ben and stoke the fire up.' Nathan had aged since his accident, but he seemed to be improving slowly and he never complained.

Roger realized that they were all concerned about the animals. If the snow was too deep, sheep could die in the drifts. Most of the cattle were housed in sheds at this time of year and fed on hay, but they had to be able to feed and water them. Nathan said his sheep were on a lower pasture where they could get shelter under bushes, but he daren't leave his farm for very long. A young neighbour had been helping him.

As soon as darkness fell and the farm chores were done, the carol singing party met at the school. Mr Jackson was to play the accordion, to try to keep the singers in tune.

'We did have one practice, but it wasn't enough,' he told Roger. 'I'm glad you're here, we need more baritones.'

'I haven't sung for years except in the bath, but I'll do my best.'

What the two dozen singers lacked in training, they made up for with enthusiasm.

'Methodists always like a good sing, and we've got a few here tonight,' Ruth whispered.

Roger stood with the Garnetts in the circle of light from Kit's lantern, as the snow fell lightly on them. There was no wind and no moon, only the invisible snow clouds above them.

Moving up the village, the choir stood in a semi-circle outside various houses. Some of the villagers gave a donation for the church, others handed round food and drink. When they got to the Hall, a fire was burning and lamps were lit in the old dining room, where a subdued Lady Agnes greeted them with warm ginger wine.

'The old customs must be observed,' she said, but sadly.

It was a subdued group that gathered round the fire, thinking of the Major, whom few people had known. The poor man had only been home for a few months when he died...

For the first time, Roger was able to look round and see who the singers were. Most of them he had met earlier in the year, when he visited the village to talk about the dam project. He saw Jim Angram – why was he not with Rachel? Jim was standing next to a pretty girl.

After a few minutes, he remembered that she was Mr Jackson's assistant schoolteacher.

As he drank the ginger wine, Roger watched Jim. He was talking earnestly to the girl and then he put an arm round her waist. She looked up at him with an adoring expression ... something was happening between these two.

A movement at his side made him turn and here was Rachel, also looking at Jim. The lad blushed and the couple moved to the other side of the fire, away from Rachel. Roger looked at her, eyebrows raised.

'Yes, that's Jim's new love,' she whispered.

Roger felt a weight roll away from him, he felt light and young. 'Really? And do you mind?' Rachel was not Jim's girl after all....

'I don't mind.... Now we have to sing another carol.'

Rachel's smile told him that she was quite happy about Jim, her heart was not broken. Roger Beckwith had a chance, after all. But why, then, was she still keeping him at arm's length?

Roger and Rachel stood side by side, singing: 'Rejoice! Rejoice!'

This was the last call and the singers dispersed.

'I'm going to give a carrot to Charlie,' Roger said. 'A stable's a good place to be on Christmas Eve.'

He took Rachel by the hand and she went in with him. She lit a lamp and Charlie's head appeared over the half door of his box, his coat shining in the lamplight. He crunched the carrot loudly and then looked for more; they both laughed.

Roger leaned on the door. 'So ... Jim is not your, er, suitor anymore? That is a big obstacle removed.' Charlie stuck his head between them. 'You're not going to be an obstacle, Charlie! I've been reminding myself about Jim, ever since he warned me off. He told me you were his girl and I promised not to stand in his way. But apparently things have changed.'

'Did you? Well, this has happened since then. I saw them together ... so I told him, let him off. That made him feel better. His only problem is his mother, she wants a good sausage-maker in the family! We were friends, but ...' Rachel hesitated. 'It was more of a convenient arrangement than real love. We were at school together. He will need a wife who can help him with farm work and I expected that I would marry a famer. When he met Violet, he must have realized what was missing.'

Roger felt the weight of problems descending again and he sighed, stroking Charlie's soft nose.

'What you and I have is far from a convenient arrangement, but it's a bit more exciting! I want to spend the rest of my life with you, lass. I want to marry you, but I don't see how. You would hate Leeds, as I do, but at least I have work there. I'm trying to be practical ...' He moved round Charlie, took Rachel in his arms and kissed her.

After a while, she moved away. 'I am practical too, Roger. A farm girl would not make the right wife for an engineer. I've thought about it, believe me. You'll be leaving us after this and we won't meet again. I'll ... have lovely memories of the last few months.' Her voice shook a little. 'This has been an episode in our lives, Roger. It's over. We live in different worlds.'

'That sounds as though you've given up.'

Sighing, Rachel faced him. 'You're making it hard for me, but

I believe I'm right. Wherever we are, you will still be an engineer and I'll be a farm girl. Better to suffer now and get over it in time, than to regret it for the rest of our lives.'

'Your folks will be wondering where we are ... I'll talk to you tomorrow, lass.' She looked so lovely in the lamplight that Roger smiled at her.

'That looks more like the Roger I used to know!' Rachel said. 'When you first came here you were always laughing, but now ... so serious!'

That night, Roger kept turning over alternatives in his mind.

It was clear that farming families were closer than others.... Could he find a job with a private company somewhere more rural? But rural areas were in depression and there were few new projects on the books. He'd been told how lucky he was to have a job with Leeds Corporation.

Roger made up his mind. He would try his very best to find some solution and eventually, he would marry Rachel. This was the most important thing in their lives, their chance of happiness. Once that was decided, he fell into a deep sleep.

Snow fell all night, but by Christmas morning the sky was clear. In pale sunshine, Roger helped to dig pathways across the yard so that they could get to the cowshed, dairy and other buildings. Rachel milked the cows and fed the calves. Ruth fed the poultry and collected the eggs, while in the kitchen Nathan prepared breakfast.

'I make good porridge,' he told Roger.

They all met for breakfast and Roger gave small presents he had brought from Leeds: a book each for Rachel and Kit, and fine woollen scarves for Ruth and Nathan.

'I will always remember your kindness to me,' he said. He'd meant to make a speech, but suddenly his eyes misted over and he couldn't trust his voice.

'Well, lad, you're part of our family now, you know,' Kit told him.

There was laughter and friendship round the table that

morning; Roger fervently hoped that it was not his last visit. The family gave him a diary and a necktie especially chosen by Kit.

The next job was to check the sheep. Armed with shovels Kit, Roger and John the gardener went to look for the ewes and found several that had to be dug out of the snow.

By the time they and the cattle were fed and the cowshed cleaned, it was time for Christmas dinner. They assembled in the sitting room round an enormous fire and drank a glass of sherry. Ruth was spared the task of working at the Hall; Cook said she could manage, as the expected visitors had stayed at home.

The previous week, Kit had shot a deer, one of a few that wandered the estate. He had dressed the meat with care and they sat down to a feast of roast venison, with braised red cabbage, roast potatoes and all the trimmings.

Roger produced a bottle of red wine and they toasted each other, bright faces round the table.

'And here's to a happy year ahead,' Kit said bravely, looking at the firelight through his wineglass. 'Though we don't know what the year may bring.'

'How you enjoy a meal when you've worked hard to earn it!' Roger exclaimed, and the others laughed. They always worked hard before a meal.

Kit went down to the village after dinner to visit an old couple who had once worked at the Hall, taking with him some Christmas cheer. He came back tired with the effort of wading through snow.

'Nothing's come through from Masham all day,' he reported. 'Trains will have stopped running, sure enough. But by the time Roger has to leave, roads should be clear.'

Nathan was unruffled when he realized he could not go home. 'Jacob next door promised to keep an eye on the place for me, the dogs are with him and he'll feed the stock. I've paid the lad to work for me, last few days.'

The cowshed was the warmest place, when Rachel was tucked in beside a large, placid cow. Normally Kit milked some of the

herd, but the snow made the work of the farm much harder, so
Rachel took over. She was sitting beside Bessie, singing quietly
to encourage her to let down the milk, when the big horns slowly
moved round and Bessie stared at the door. Roger came in with a
milking stool and pail and wearing an old cap.

'Your father sent me to help you,' he said happily. 'It's a very
long time since I milked a cow, but Mr Brown taught me when
I was a little lad.' Rachel took him to the quietest cow of all, the
serene Honey, who was next to Bessie. They sat on their stools side
by side, so she could keep an eye on his progress.

To her surprise, Roger made a good job of milking. He soon got
into the rhythm and Honey, after inspecting him carefully, decided
that he was acceptable and turned back to munching her hay.

They talked about the work of the farm as they milked.

'In my job, if the weather is really bad we just stop work.
Teachers and lawyers can keep going, as long as they can travel to
work. But if you farm livestock, you have to face the weather every
day. City folk don't appreciate that.'

'So you wouldn't like to be a farmer, Roger?' Rachel was being
mischievous; she knew he would.

As the milk spurted into the pails, Roger explained that civil
engineering had attracted him in the first place because it was
mainly outdoor work. He loved the changing seasons and the
phases of the moon. He knew the names of stars, but in Leeds the
moon and stars were hidden by smoke and city lights.

They moved to another two cows and Rachel had a question for
him.

'Why did you stop coming to Grandfather's farm, lad?' If he
had kept up his visits, they would have grown up together. 'He
loved having you there, he says so.' Rachel stole a glance at him
and saw a look of sadness pass over his face.

'My father died and my mother took me to live in York. I went
to school there. It was just too far to be able to visit Firby. When
I came here with the reservoir project, it was the first chance I'd
had.'

The milking was finished in good time.

'Is there as much milk as usual?" Roger asked anxiously and Rachel assured him that there was.

Gangs of men opened up the roads, after which Nathan Brown went home to his farm. Roger was in no hurry to leave. He and Rachel had a week of quiet companionship, working together and talking as they had before the shadow of Jim Angram had come between them.

One evening as they were washing the milking pails, Roger said, 'I'll be going back to Leeds soon. More than ever, I want to keep in touch, to come to see you often, my love. Please don't give up! Someday we may be able to see a way through.' He smiled. 'I don't want to be like Jim and keep you waiting for years, but we belong together. '

Rachel felt relief steal over her in spite of her misgivings. This was not to be Roger's last visit, after all. 'If you leave Charlie here, you'll have a horse to ride when you come back.'

His face lit up. 'So you won't insist on goodbye forever?'

Soon after this, Roger went to look for Kit and found him chopping kindling for the fires.

'I'll do that,' he said and took the job over. Kit stood watching him and Roger said as he deftly split the wood, 'Mr Garnett, I want to marry Rachel. Now I've found out that she's not engaged to Jim after all … and I hope that you will approve.'

Kit looked serious. 'And she, of course, feels the same about you. I had guessed as much. You're a grand lad and part of our family already, Roger. But how do you mean to go on?'

'That's what we haven't yet worked out. I can't expect Rachel to live in Leeds, especially in the sort of cottage that I could afford. But how could I get a job in the country? I have wondered about learning to be a gamekeeper … what do you think?'

'You'd have a tied house like we have, long hours and a small pay packet,' Kit said promptly. 'I suppose it's a possibility … but things are changing, you know. Now that Firby is to be flooded, the estates in the valley will be broken up. Our family will be looking for another place …' he dropped his voice. 'Even without the dam, when Guy takes over, there will be no room for us. He has said so, and I fully agree. I won't work for him.'

'So it would be a good time to plan Rachel's future. It might be easier to find a new place for two of you, rather than three.'

Kit put the pile of kindling into a wooden box and Roger straightened his back. 'Mr Sutton told me once that he'd give me a farm to rent or manage if we left here and that's always at the back of my mind.'

That night, the thaw set in. Water dripped from roofs and down spouts and made puddles in the yard. The warm breeze brought out the scent of the earth, making them think of spring.

'If I can get to Masham tomorrow, I should be able to catch a train to Leeds,' Roger said without much enthusiasm. 'They will expect to see me back, I've no excuse now to stay longer.'

NINETEEN

Guy Potts emerged from hiding as the snow melted in the New Year, pleasing his mother if not the peasants. Rachel had better look out.... The bruises had faded and he had money again, having sold his father's pocket watch in Ripon.

A thirst for drink was coming on and in spite of the danger from local louts, he decided to pay another visit to the Fox and Hounds. Trust Ma to hide the key of the wine cellar. He would try to keep quiet and not mention his plans for the estate, since the peasants objected so violently, although it was hard when they were so stupid. Once he inherited, he would drown the lot of them in Leeds water. Thanks to Guy Potts, the dam would go through. It should be called the Guy Potts Reservoir.

As Guy walked through the door of the inn he looked round warily, but the brutal Dale brothers were not there. On weekday evenings the drinkers were few. Two shepherds with dogs at their feet sat by the fire, discussing remedies for liver fluke, not the sort of topic Guy could stomach. It was enough to put you off your beer.

In one corner, a group of men looked up from their cards. 'Let's take the fat little squire's cash,' an apprentice blacksmith called Sam suggested. 'Bound to be rolling in it, stands to reason. Big estate, he's inherited it all.'

His friend Jake agreed. 'Squire'll have even more brass when he's drowned the valley....' He raised his voice. 'Come over here,

Mr Guy. There's a place for you at table. Put your brass down.'

Guy had heard it all and smiled to himself. 'Do you really think you can beat me at cards?' He put on more of an upper-class drawl than usual, to fool them. He saw them look at each other and smirk. 'Hardly likely, old chap. But you can try.'

The blacksmith was all muscles and hair, it would not be wise to fall out with him.

At the bar, Richard Sayers the landlord stood guard with a truncheon in full view, evidently ready for trouble. Guy bought a tankard of beer, had a drink and pulled a face.

'You've put water in it,' he complained.

For some reason this seemed to annoy Sayers. 'This beer was brewed in our cellar, it's best in county,' he said loudly. 'If you don't like it you needn't bother.'

The card players laughed loudly.

'Give me a bottle of whisky,' Guy growled, gulped down the beer and went over to the card players with his bottle. They made room for him at the table. They were playing brag, a game similar to poker. Easy.

Taking a swig of whisky, Guy looked round the table. These peasants were no match for a man who had played frequently in the last few years, in London and during his tour of Europe. He had learned to play poker on ships travelling to India when he went to visit his parents, long before he left school.

The peasants did their best, but as card players they were no match for Guy Potts. Even as the level in his bottle went down, he could still hold his own. He was careful not to say anything that might annoy them; these were yokels, toughened by manual work, wiry and strong. Strength was the only thing he respected.

'By gum, you're a better card player than you are a fighter,' Jake said after a while. 'We never expected you to take brass off hard-working folks like us ... Mister Guy.'

'Do you want to play, or don't you?' Guy sneered. 'You should stay at home if you can't afford it.'

'Go on then, we'll try again.' Try they did, but Guy beat them every time. When they started to whisper to each other, he threw down his cards.

'That's enough, I'm going home.'

The blacksmith stood up to his full height and Guy felt his bruises beginning to ache again. He pulled on his overcoat and left quickly, taking the whisky with him. He had cheated for some of the time, just for fun and he thought they knew it.

'Let him go, don't go after him,' he heard Sayers tell the men. 'We don't want any more fights, this is a respectable house.'

They started to argue and Guy decided to move quickly, while Sayers still held them up. His muscles were still painful from the previous beating and another would not be welcome.

He stopped and took a deep drink of whisky, then lurched off up the road.

'I'll drown the lot of you, just wait!' Guy muttered to himself. He should have told them before he left, about the Leeds water coming up to their ankles, then their knees...

Firby Hall was not far from the village, but they could catch him easily on the road; he was never a good walker and he hadn't run since he left school. Guy heard the door of the bar open. Looking back, he saw light spilling out; they were coming for him. Three of them, wanting their money back. They would enjoy beating him. His only hope was to take a short cut to the farm track that led round the back of the Hall.

Kit Garnett had warned him not to take the short cut. 'It's not safe on dark nights, especially when you've been drinking. I am telling you for your own good.'

Guy could imitate the Yorkshire accent and the earnest expression. What was the man talking about – did he believe in ghosts? There were no ghosts. There were no leopards in Yorkshire either, like the ones he'd been warned about in India. These peasants were afraid of their own shadow. They would learn to be afraid of Guy Potts.

Garnett was full of good advice, but he wouldn't be in charge much longer. Even before the place was sold, Guy intended to get rid of all the Garnetts. If he could get them convicted of stealing, they might all end up in jail. He grinned at the thought. It would be a real taste of power and he looked forward to it. But before that, he had to catch Rachel Garnett and show her once and for all who was boss.

The card players were stumbling along the road, cursing; he could hear them plainly. The night was black as hell, no moon and the stars hidden in clouds. He was safe enough if he moved quietly; they would never find him.

Guy smothered a hiccup, walking as quietly as he could. There was a gate somewhere, he couldn't remember just where it was. He blundered into a remnant patch of snow. It was time for another drink.

In the cold air, Guy felt the alcohol affecting his balance. He would have to push on, to save himself from the peasants. Why didn't the louts know their place and treat him with respect? There seemed to be water under the snow.

Lady Agnes had made up her mind to send Guy to London. It was the only thing he would willingly do and it would get him away from Firby. That last beating had been serious, but she doubted whether he had learned his lesson. Guy was not in the dining room for breakfast on the morning after his card game, but then he seldom left his room before eleven. By lunch-time his mother began to lose patience. Once she had made up her mind, she liked to act on it straightaway. She had planned what to say to Guy and how to make him promise not to gamble or drink too much. When Cook brought in her lunch, she asked whether Mr Guy had been seen.

'No, m'lady, but if you like I'll go and look for him,' Cook said obligingly. She knew not to send a maid to find Guy; they were kept out of his way.

Cook soon came back to report that Mr Guy was not in his room and his bed had not been slept in. Had he gone off to Ripon the evening before? Guy often went out without telling his mother where he was going, or when he would be back.

Trying to conceal her irritation, Lady Agnes asked for Ruth Garnett and when the housekeeper appeared, she suggested that the Garnetts might search for Guy. Was it possible that he had stayed in the village overnight?

Kit was out on the farm, supervising a ploughing team, so Ruth went to the stables. The coachman reported that none of the horses was missing.

'He might be down there at Fox and Hounds yet,' Metcalfe suggested. 'He won't be far away, not without taking a horse. I'll take a look, when I've finished here.'

Donald Metcalfe trundled down to the public house towards the end of the afternoon, wondering what he would do with Guy. He decided not to confront the youth, who had treated him like dirt at all times. He would take a look and report back to Kit. The lad must be there, where else could he be? The farm horses would be back from ploughing soon and he liked to give a hand with them. Gentle giants, they were, much easier to do with than the skittish horse that Guy rode.

The landlord was polishing glasses when Donald appeared. 'Now, how's things up at Hall? Haven't seen you here for a while, Mr Metcalfe.'

'Nay, missus won't allow it,' the coachman said ruefully. He looked round cautiously.

'Is Mr Guy here, by any chance? He seems to be missing.'

'He's not.' Sayers leaned over the bar and said quietly, 'That lad is a damned nuisance, as I'm sure you know. He was here last night, diddled some lads playing cards and went home early. With,' he added, 'a bottle of Scotch in his hand. He's nasty enough sober, but when he's drunk ...' He shook his head.

The two men looked at each other.

'Where is he, then?' Donald wondered. 'He left here – and didn't arrive home. Do you think the lads he gambled with would know?'

'Nay,' Sayers said firmly. 'But I'll ask them what they know. I'll slip out for five minutes before we start the evening.'

Kit Garnett went to see Sayers when he heard the news. 'Any clues as to where Guy's gone? Not that I blame you, Richard. Lad's old enough to look after himself.'

'Nay, no news. I went to ask Sam, that was here last night. They went out after Guy, although I did my best to stop them. Sam and Jake, they were angry with him for taking their brass by cheating. Can't blame 'em, neither. Sam said they went up the road a piece but couldn't find him. They were back here again not long after, to get warm by the fire before going home.' Sayers poured Kit a glass of beer. 'No foul play, I'm certain of that. Although I've allus said he would meet a bad end.'

'He's taken the short cut, as I told him not to.' Kit took a drink of beer. 'A grand drop, this brew, Richard.'

'I'm right glad you said that. Guy told me it was watered.'

Kit shook his head. 'Looks as though he might have met a bad end, drinking and going on that track.'

'Aye. That's where pond is. Better tell PC Bradley, I'm thinking.'

Dusk had given way to night when Kit went home up the road, avoiding the short cut because it was too dark to see the way. The search would have to wait until daylight.

Lady Agnes decided that Guy had probably gone off to London. She had found that some of their antique silver was missing, so he would have had money for the journey.

The next day, Guy's body was found in the duck pond not far from the farmyard. He lay face down in a few inches of water; a sober man would have been able to get up again. The police grimly took down all the details and recorded a death by misadventure. They believed the lads who said they had chased him and turned back. Guy was known even to the Ripon police as a man to watch.

Another Accident at Firby Hall, ran the headlines in the *Herald*. Rodney, Alex's assistant, wrote a gloomy piece, coloured by local gossip of ghosts and curses. He linked the deaths of the Major and his son to the impending doom of the reservoir hanging over the valley.

'Her Ladyship's taking it badly,' Ruth reported to Kit. 'She blames herself for Guy's behaviour, seems to think she should have been able to control him.'

'I tried to help him, and I'm sorry I failed. But only Guy is to blame,' Kit said.

Everyone at the Hall was saddened by the thought of a wasted life. Gloom hung over the entire village and his funeral was a quiet affair. Guy was laid to rest in the churchyard, amid a general feeling of relief.

A few days afterwards, Lady Agnes went to London to stay with her brother. She told Kit that she would live quietly for a while. Since coming home from India, life had been very difficult and Guy's death was the last straw. Kit felt sorry for her.

Rachel felt guilty; she was so thankful that Guy was gone, would never accost her again. In time, she would stop looking over her shoulder and jumping at shadows.

The Garnetts were left in charge of the estate once more. The only threat to their future now was Mr Bromley and his Firby plan. Roger reported it was certain that Firby was to be the reservoir site. *Guy had told them what they wanted to hear and they're not going to change now*, he wrote gloomily, in a loving letter to Rachel.

TWENTY

In the first week of February, Alex held a meeting of his publishing committee, in the boardroom of the *Herald* offices. Susan and Rachel were there, and Alex said he had a solicitor friend, Mr Denham, who was interested in the venture and would join a meeting at some future date. The meeting was arranged for a Thursday, which was market day in Ripon.

Rachel felt shy as she took her place at the long polished table, but Susan Sutton had a remedy for that.

'We are very glad you could come, Rachel, we need your experience. I think you'll enjoy planning this book!'

It had been an effort to get to Ripon, jogging along in the carrier's cart squeezed between farmers' wives going to market with their big butter baskets. Rachel would have to leave in time to catch the carrier's homeward trip and would miss the evening milking. But it was exciting to be here, to talk about making a book; a complete change of scene. Firby Hall was quiet, brooding, waiting for the axe to fall.

Alex said sympathetically that he imagined Firby would be a sad place, after the latest news. Rachel's article with the reservoir decision had appeared in the same edition of the *Herald* as the headline about Guy's death.

'Tell me,' he asked, passing Rachel a cup of tea, 'do you think that there is a ghost? Rodney seems to think so. He saw the ghost of a monk once at Fountains Abbey, so he believes in them.'

Rachel hesitated. 'Well ... I have heard footsteps on the stairs, and in the Long Gallery ... and sometimes there's a cold feeling in certain places.' She smiled. 'Once I was terrified, it was getting dark, but the ghost turned out to be Roger Beckwith.'

Susan laughed. 'How I would love to see a ghost! Perhaps we should hunt for one, now that Lady Agnes is not there. I don't think she would mind.'

They were soon deep in plans for the recipe book. Rachel loved Susan's drawings, so crisp and clear. Alex thought that two or three drawings could be displayed on one page.

They agreed that to produce a huge book like Mrs Beeton's was not a good idea.

'People want something different these days, so several smaller books would be popular,' Susan told them.

Susan was always so definite; Rachel envied her confidence, but then her own had been eroded of late. Even Roger couldn't give Rachel confidence. She felt the gulf between them, the difference between his life and hers, and she knew that he would tire of her in time. She would stick to her plan and soon, he would be gone from Firby and she would get over it. Roger had said he would come to Firby for a visit in March and that was when they would say goodbye.

The plan Rachel had in mind was a daring one for a woman; she wanted to earn a living from writing. To do that she would stay single and live with her parents into their old age. The first part of the plan was to help make a successful book for Alex's new publishing house.

'We could keep to ... er, teatime recipes, for the first one,' Rachel suggested diffidently. 'Cakes, scones, biscuits ...'

The others agreed and the committee fell into a deep discussion about oatcakes and griddle cakes, baked on a flat sheet suspended over the fire. They agreed to include yeast cookery because everyone wanted Yorkshire teacakes.

'We will all make a list of recipes that might be suitable. They can come from a variety of sources, but I would like Rachel to try out each recipe herself. Only the ones that she approves will be used,' Alex announced.

Planning in this way was enjoyable, but the ache of loss was still there. A memory of Roger's face, or his voice would come between Rachel and her concentration on the job in hand. He wrote loving letters to her – how could she stop him? It only made the thought of parting worse. Instead of writing a reply, Rachel sent him newspaper cuttings of her *Herald* articles. She should try to forget Roger; the book was the important thing.

'Perhaps you need to decide first of all how big the book will be, so we know how many recipes will fit in,' Rachel suggested to Alex.

Choosing from the hundreds of north-country recipes and then trying them out would take a great deal of time and she didn't want to waste time by trying too many.

Susan put her hand lightly on Alex's arm. 'This is what I said – do you remember? First things first!'

Alex beamed at her and Rachel thought how well they seemed to work together. She hoped they would have a happier ending than she could ever hope for.

Her father had decided that they should stay on at the Hall until Firby was evacuated by Leeds Corporation, but all too soon they would be gone, destination as yet unknown; Kit hoped to find a job where Ruth and Rachel would also be needed.

'Don't look so sad, Rachel,' Susan said, calling her back to the matter in hand. 'This project will be successful!'

Rachel thought of her grandfather's spirit and pulled herself together. 'I'm sure it will. How long have I got to bake all these cakes and biscuits?'

With these people, her Yorkshire accent didn't matter. She was here as an equal and she would enjoy it.

Nathan Brown could feel spring stirring in the countryside as he watched his lambs dancing and kicking up their feet on a warm breezy day in March.

'I haven't got that many springs left,' he said to young Joe, his helper. 'I reckon I'll have to make the most of this one, so I'll take a ride up dale.'

He had not ridden Brownie since the accident. It was still rather painful to get up onto a horse, but his ribs were healing and with the aid of the mounting block, Nathan was aboard once more. He immediately felt much younger. In the late morning, he set out in sunshine with bread and cheese in his pocket, on the road to Woodley Crags. In a saddlebag, packed in moss, was a bunch of violets.

Nathan took the horse at a walk and when he reached the halfway mark, he pulled up and ate his bread and cheese. This was the real moorland, wide skies overarching the heather that clad the bare bones of the hills. The curlews were back on the moor with their mournful cry. They would still be here, wheeling in the sun-light, when he and all his friends were gone.

What would happen when his farm was drowned under the reservoir? Nathan wondered briefly what God had in store for the people of Firby. He loved church services and he played the organ at church every Sunday, but he couldn't imagine praying for any-thing less than world peace. Their own local problems seemed too trivial to offer up as a prayer to the Almighty. He wondered what Alice would say about that.

Alice was pleased to see him, as she always was, although she chided him gently for riding instead of driving. Nathan didn't tell her that riding made him feel younger and he was on a young man's errand. Rather diffidently he offered his violets; Alice took them with a lovely smile and inhaled their fragrance.

'The scent of spring,' she said.

'Come and sit down, lass. We have to have a serious talk.'

They sat beside the fire. 'Now what's to do, Nathan? Is there trouble of some sort?' Her clear eyes searched his face.

'Nay, Alice. I think we should discuss the future. Our future.'

Eyes wide, Alice paused for a moment and then suggested, 'You're talking about the reservoir, upsetting our last few years?'

'Forget the reservoir for a minute. Quite apart from that, you and me both are farming, at an age when maybe we shouldn't be. This accident of mine made me think, I've had to rely on Joe from next door.' Nathan took a deep breath. 'We're both on our own. Now, if you were to agree, Alice, we could get married. And,' he looked over at her, but she hadn't fainted yet, 'buy a little place near Pateley, with an acre or two – keep a few sheep. What do you say, lass?'

The clock's tick was loud in the silence. Alice smiled slowly; at least she wasn't going to reject the idea immediately. 'Do you know, I've been thinking the same thing myself. But it wasn't my place to mention it!'

Nathan moved his chair nearer to Alice and took her hand. 'That's champion, we both think alike. It's not just – for convenience, Alice. I've – well, I love you, have done for a long time.' He got out a handkerchief and mopped his brow theatrically to make her laugh and ease the tension. 'I was fair terrified in case you turned me down. I feel like a young lad again.'

Alice laughed, a laugh of pure happiness. 'You need somebody to look after you, men always do…. I thought of sitting on your knee, but I might hurt the ribs. Let's have a cup of tea, then we'll do some planning.' She leaned over and kissed him. 'Your farm will be under the water, but maybe I can let this place, give us money to live on,' she added as she handed Nathan a scone. 'If I can find a tenant, that is. Woodley hasn't many folks left. It's too hard for young folks with bairns, up here away from everything.'

'Aye, things have changed since we were young. But then, Alice, men who lose their farms to the water might be looking for a farm up dale. Kit Garnett knows all the farmers in Firby, you could talk to him about it.'

Nathan and Alice went for a walk, hand in hand across the fields, where the first tinge of green was appearing.

'Spring's a few weeks later up here.' Nathan's mind was working on what was to be done with Alice's farm. 'At Firby, grass is growing well and all my ewes have lambed.'

They came to a gate and Nathan took Alice very gently in his arms. Her head fitted into his shoulder naturally as she said, 'We will be happy, Nathan, I'm sure of it. We'll look after each other for as long as we're spared.'

Riding home, Nathan decided to keep his news to himself for a while, until he got used to the idea of marriage to Alice. They were well suited and he didn't know a better woman. But they had both spent long years living alone. They were independent spirits and would have to go gently to forge a new bond and a new way of living.

It was time to give up farming, but Nathan knew that both he and Alice would feel the loss of their farms. The remedy might be to look for a little holding straightaway, so they could start planning. Surely they could manage twenty or thirty acres and a few sheep? Somewhere handy for the little town of Pateley, in the sheltered valley beside the Nidd. There would be a bit of spare money to pay a labourer for the heavy work. They could keep Brownie and Alice's Dales pony ... and the best ewes from his flock.

As he turned in at his gate, Nathan grinned to himself. Alice might want to keep her favourite sheep, too.

'We're off to Pateley tomorrow, lad,' Nathan told Joe, his helper. 'But this time I'll drive, not ride.' It wouldn't be wise to tempt fate.

TWENTY-ONE

IN THE MIDDLE of spring, Roger came back to Firby, having obtained a few days' leave. Daffodils nodded in village gardens, blackthorn flowered in the hedges and birds were beginning to build their nests. Surely this time Rachel would listen to him. He was determined to marry her and he knew that she was just as stubborn as he was; she had decided that they could never be together.

Roger had a plan that he would reveal when the time was right, to help Rachel to change her mind. He had seen an affordable cottage in a green area near Leeds and he thought that if they could rent it, Rachel could grow herbs in the garden and he could take the train to work every day. In time, it might be possible to find an engineering job in a more rural part of Yorkshire. With Rachel beside him, anything would be possible.

Charlie, Roger's horse, was in excellent condition. He had been trained by Kit to pull the trap and had been taken on several trips to Masham and Ripon. Full of optimism, Roger suggested an outing in the trap to Woodley Crags, to see Alice Bolton. Rachel could go with him and they would pick up Nathan Brown on the way.

'I'm too busy,' Rachel told him when the idea was proposed. Part of her longed to go on the trip, but time spent with Roger would make the parting even harder. 'Two cows have just calved and I have to teach the calves to drink.'

Roger felt desolate. He had planned this for weeks; he needed time with Rachel to get her to see his point of view. When they got to Woodley, he was hoping to take her for a walk away from the others, up on the moors high above the valley of the Nidd. There, she might see things in better perspective. It was important to make her see how small the objections she was raising were, in the scheme of things. He had always loved the high moors and he thought Rachel would feel calmer there, more ready to listen to him.

Ruth Garnett urged her to go. 'You've been looking pale lately, lass, a change of air will do you good!' she said firmly. 'Mrs Bolton will be right pleased to see you, living up there on her own as she is. It must have been a long winter at Woodley. She might give you a recipe or two, for the book.'

That seemed a good idea, so Rachel agreed to go to Woodley, against her better judgement. Recipes might take her mind off Roger for a while. She and Ruth packed a picnic basket with cheese, ham, crusty bread and fruit cake that they would share with Alice Bolton.

The day chosen for the trip was sunny and Roger whistled as he yoked up Charlie. Rachel wished she could feel as cheerful as he was, but it was impossible. She decided to take a few packets of herbs that she thought Mrs Bolton might find useful: dried sage, rosemary and mint. Perhaps they might be exchanged for some of her lifetime of experience, hints that would make their book stand out from the rest. Susan Sutton had suggested that Rachel should talk to experienced women and ask them for detailed recipes.

Nathan too seemed very cheerful, standing nearly as straight as he used to do as he waited for them at his gate. He shook Roger's hand and said how grand it was to see him.

'You're in good fettle, lad, I'm pleased to see,' he said with a smile.

'Springtime's always a good time,' Roger said as he helped the older man into the trap. 'And this year it seems to be the best for years, Kit says.'

'Plenty of blossom on fruit trees, let's hope we don't get a late frost,' Nathan said in the timeworn formula, as Charlie trotted up the road.

Wrapped in a warm rug, Rachel sat beside Roger and pointed out various landmarks to him as they went along. Many of them would be lost when the water came, but she pushed the thought aside.

Alice came into the yard with a flock of hens following her as they clattered in. The hens scattered and her face lit up when she saw who the visitors were.

'My, this is a nice surprise!'

Nathan climbed stiffly down from the vehicle and kissed Alice on the cheek. There and then in the yard, he turned to the others and said, 'We have news for you and I'll tell you right away! Alice and I are going to be married.'

Rachel felt a moment of shock, then joy. Grandfather was going to have a few more years of happiness, and neither he nor Alice would be lonely any more. They stood there hand in hand, looking happy.

Alice laughed at his enthusiasm. 'Nathan, let's go inside before we talk anymore.' In the kitchen, Rachel said how happy she was and Roger smilingly told them he was envious.

They spread their picnic on the scrubbed table and Alice made a pot of tea. When she sat down, Nathan explained that they planned to move to a little holding near Pateley; he had one in mind.

'Of course,' Alice said, 'Nathan will lose his farm to the reservoir quite soon, so we plan to move afore winter. And I am hoping to find a tenant for Woodley.'

Roger sat up and put down his bread and cheese. 'Now I had better tell you my news. I have waited until today to be quite sure, but I collected a letter at the post office this morning and now I have the decision in black and white. The reservoir is going to be built here at Woodley, Alice. Not at Firby. So you will lose your land, but Nathan will keep his. Firby Hall will be spared, Rachel,

215

so Kit and Ruth will be able to keep their home.'

There was silence in the kitchen for a minute or two, then the other three all spoke at once. 'Are you sure? Why? What's happened?'

Two shocks in one day! Rachel put her hand to her head. 'I can't believe it, Roger. Mr Bromley was so certain, he came to see us only the other week! Leeds had made the choice when Guy went to see them and that was it, he said.'

'So I thought,' Roger grinned. He turned to Nathan and Alice. 'I hope you'll be happy with the decision. Mrs Bolton ... if you plan to move, it won't be such a blow.'

'Aye, I'm right enough,' Alice said calmly. 'Folks down at Firby stood to lose much more than I will, over this. Rachel here will be easier in her mind, won't you, lass?'

Nathan smiled in his serene way. 'I'm very glad for Firby, Roger. For myself, well, we're off to Pateley and that won't change. I'm a mite too old to be farming, I fear.'

Roger waited a few minutes for the shock to subside a little and then said, 'You may not realize it, but we have Rachel to thank for this decision. She wrote the letters and articles in the *Herald*, that was what turned the tide in our favour.'

'How could that be?' Rachel was mystified. 'I brought it to people's notice, but how could the *Herald* change anything at Leeds?'

'In a couple of ways. Number one, when Lady Agnes went to stay with her brother, she took *Herald* copies with her, to show to Lord Danby. Apparently he's the sort of man who likes a crusade, so he started asking questions. Even went to Leeds, although I didn't see him.'

Rachel thought for a minute. 'Lady Agnes was trying to get over Guy's death ... maybe she was hoping to put right the damage he was doing to Firby.'

'Number two, Mr Sutton of Cranby Park had joined the fight and he got together with Lord Danby. Mr Sutton is very much influenced by his daughter, who is of course influenced by ... Rachel Garnett! Susan Sutton admires you, Rachel. So it happened in London and then Leeds was given to understand that they'd never get the scheme through Parliament, unless they took it up to the moors.' Roger sat back, his eyes bright. 'I spoke to the Suttons on my way to Firby, but it wasn't certain then.'

'And Mr Bromley?' Rachel couldn't quite believe that he had lost the fight.

'Mr Bromley has gone to work for a company in the south – much more civilized than Yorkshire, he told me. So I've been given the Woodley project.' Roger lifted his cup. 'May I have another cup of tea? Thirsty work, talking.'

After the meal, Roger suggested that as the happy couple may have things to discuss, he and Rachel would take a walk.

The breeze blew Rachel's dark hair away from her face as they walked and she relaxed a little, thinking over what he had just told them. Roger led her to the upland track, climbing all the way until they reached a ridge. From where they stood, they could see the river snaking across the valley floor on its way to the sea. Small white clouds drifted above them, looking rather like the fluffy white sheep dotted about the heather slopes below.

'I hadn't realized just how worried we have been – about Firby, and our future, and Grandfather too,' Rachel confessed. She breathed out slowly and felt the weight of worry roll away. 'He seems so happy! We have a lot to tell Mother and Father tonight.'

Roger put an arm round her waist. 'So … now let's think about your future and mine, my darling.' He was looking at her with love in his eyes, his hair shining in the sun. 'Can you take a leap of faith and agree that we should, we can be together? The details will work themselves out, you'll see. We will be so happy!'

'I'm trying to be sensible, Roger,' Rachel said, sticking to the old argument. 'I just can't see that it would last. We come from different worlds.' Even to herself, it sounded lame, the excuse of a girl who was too scared to embark on marriage.

'We'll make our own world, together.' Roger paused and looked out across the landscape. 'We both love the same things, the countryside, the animals…. I have a plan to rent a cottage, somewhere not far from here. The Woodley dam will take some time to complete. I'd have to go to Leeds at times, of course.'

They could live together in the country, in her own world! Rachel could hardly believe it.

'You could work on your recipes and the *Herald* columns and send them in by post, just as you do now.… Please say that you'll give me a chance, Rachel. I love you very much. Please marry me.'

Rachel looked out with him across the smiling landscape, basking in the spring sunshine. Roger's argument was so persuasive … and he knew that she wanted to go on writing.

'You love me, Rachel?' It was a question, but very gentle.

With a sigh, Rachel put a hand on his shoulder. 'I love you, Roger. I've been dreading our parting. Yes, I will marry you.' She thought of Susan Sutton, who had given her the gift of a little more confidence, even today. *Susan Sutton admires you*, Roger had said.

It was lack of confidence that had held her back, the confidence to leave home and go to live with Roger, away from her family. That, and the worry at home, their uncertain future. Rachel knew it was still a big step, she would still be leaving home, but they would be in the same world.

'I promise to love and look after you, Rachel. Forever.' There on the moor, in full view of the indifferent sheep, Roger took her in his arms. She felt his warmth and strength as she responded to his kiss. Time seemed to stand still.

They perched on a huge boulder, not talking but looking at the scene, the sunlight and cloud shadows on the rolling slopes of the moor. Planning would come later. Gradually, Rachel felt the peace of the afternoon stealing into her soul. She would learn not to worry so much, to take one day at a time. The distant bleat of a ewe was the only sound.

'This is the happiest day of my life,' Rachel told him, her hand in his. 'I never thought … we could be together. I didn't feel brave enough.'

'But now you do, my love. You are a brave woman!' Roger stood up and held out his hand. 'Time we went back. We will always remember this spot, Rachel. To tell you the truth, I planned this in my wily way, to bring you here, to the peace of the moor, for a quiet talk.'

They sealed their promises with several more kisses and went back down to the farm hand in hand.

'May I tell the others straightaway?' Roger asked. 'It's been a day of surprises. Your father and mother have been left out so far, but we'll tell them tonight. I did tell Kit at Christmas, but neither of us could see how it could work out.'

It seemed, however, that when they got back to the kitchen and Roger told their news, Nathan and Alice were not surprised at all.

'I told you so!' Alice said triumphantly.

Nathan stood up and shook Roger's hand. 'Congratulations, young man. You know how lucky you are ... we are both lucky men. I couldn't have picked a better husband for Rachel, myself! In fact, it did cross my mind when you were both bairns.'

'Thank you, Mr Brown, you must have seen into the future!'

Alice looked across at Roger. 'Have you worked out where you will live? We even got as far as discussing that, while you were on the moor.'

Roger explained his plan for a little house nearby and they nodded. Then Nathan said, 'I have a better idea. Rachel is to inherit my farm, you see. And now that we are moving to Pateley, I wonder whether you, Roger, would like to farm it with Rachel? She's got the experience now, but she needs a good man with her. You could maybe complete the Woodley dam before you resigned, but in the end you'd have to give up your career.'

Alice chimed in, 'Aye, some of the work's too hard for a woman. Take it from me. I couldn't have got by without Nathan's help, bless him.'

Once again Rachel was dizzy with shock. Roger was an engineer ... could he learn to be a farmer?

'Do you think I could do it, with Rachel's help? I've always wanted to farm.' Roger looked at Rachel. 'I have learned a little from Kit, of course, and you've taught me to milk ... but my problem would be lack of capital. I'd need to buy livestock, implements, tools... I haven't much money, Mr Brown, my inheritance was spent on my training.' He was frowning. 'I doubt whether we can do it, you need a tenant with more money than I have.'

'We've thought of that.' Alice Bolton's face was alight with interest. 'You could take over the farm as it is, with the Shorthorn cattle and the sheep. Nathan will get a valuation and you could pay back their value over time, as a sort of rent.'

Roger was looking shocked now and Rachel went to his side. 'Of course we can do it, Roger! This is your leap of faith for both of us. Unless you can't bear to leave Leeds and engineering?'

It was time she challenged him. Rachel realized that if this plan worked out, she would be essential to its success. They would have an equal partnership.

'But maybe you will need more time to think about it?'

'I would never regret leaving Leeds,' Roger admitted. 'As for engineering, I think the training will probably help me, just the experience of solving problems, for a start. We'll do it, Rachel! I can't begin to thank you, Mr Brown. You're giving us the chance of a lifetime.'

'Aye, well, it's a relief to think that farm will be in good hands.'

There was a silence while they all thought about the implications of their plans.

Nathan said quietly, 'The farm will make you a living, there's no doubt. It's big enough ... been too big for me, lately. If you have a bad year, well, we all do at times, you'll get through it.'

'In a bad year, I could sell herbs and eggs. Maybe we should keep geese?' Rachel laughed.

Kit and Ruth Garnett were delighted when they heard all the news. Nathan had gone back to the Hall in the trap, so he could join in the celebrations. Ruth brought out a bottle of blackberry wine and they toasted each other.

'I did wonder,' Ruth admitted after a while, 'whether Jim was really more interested in Rachel's inheritance than the lass herself.

Folks knew that she is Grandfather's only heir and it's a tidy piece of land. Any lad would be pleased to get his hands on it.'

The next week, Lady Agnes returned to the Hall and asked to see the Garnett family after lunch the next day.

'What now?' Ruth wondered, putting spring flowers on the library table.

In the library, Lady Agnes sat in her black widow's dress and the Garnetts filed in at the allotted time. She looked down her nose at them as always, but then she smiled.

'You will be pleased to hear that the reservoir is not to be built at Firby,' she began. 'I am proud of the fact that my intervention helped to save the valley.'

'It was very well done, Your Ladyship,' Kit said quietly.

'My plan is to take a small house on my brother's estate in the south, the climate is too cold for me here. I do not wish to sell the Firby Hall estate. I would like you to take over the Hall and home farm as tenants and farm it as you wish. The Hall can be open to visitors and you can take the income.' She paused. 'I will, of course, expect an annual rent, but your duties as estate manager will require remuneration, so the rent minus your salary will not be high, the solicitor tells me. You will send to my solicitor the rents from all the Hall properties each quarter and supervise the tenants as you have always done.'

Kit was beaming from ear to ear. 'Thank you, Lady Agnes.'

'One other thing ... I have examined our books and manuscripts, returned from the bookseller. There is a document that will be of interest to your family ... their descent from the builder of the Hall is clearly traced. The family of Brown sold the estate over a hundred years ago, after a succession of bad harvests. I have left the document on the library table, for you to examine.' The lady held up an imperious hand. 'That will be all. You may go now.'

Roger went to work at Woodley Crags straight away. He spent days surveying the area and on one trip, he met the gypsies again. The caravan was back in the valley and the woman was talking to

Alice at the farm gate as he arrived.

'It's the young engineer! Have you found your farm yet, bonny lad? And the lass to share it with?' Her dark gypsy eyes looked deep into his.

'Thank you,' Roger said. 'I have found my farm and my lass, both. You were right, Vadoma. You were right.'